MAIL-ORDER REDEMPTION

EAGLE CREEK BRIDES

BOOK SIX

KARLA GRACEY

This book is dedicated to all of my faithful readers, without whom I would be nothing. I thank you for the support, reviews, love, and friendship you have shown me as we have gone through this journey together. I am truly blessed to have such a wonderful readership.

CONTENTS

CHARACTER LIST

- **Imogen Potts**
- **Bartholomew King (Greg Waters), manager and maître d' at The Eyrie Hotel, Eagle Creek**
- Ansell Potts, Imogen's father and roving bank manager
- Clarissa Potts, her mother
- Martin (Marty) Fitzgibbons, leader of the gang of robbers, Deadwood
- Hal, Matt and Abel, gang members
- Emily Winthrop, friend of Imogen's in Sheridan
- Eddie Dobley, clerk at The Eyrie
- Runs With Horses, stable manager at The Eyrie
- Fred Kipsey, stable lad at The Eyrie
- Jane Algood, seamstress

- Peter Algood, shipping company owner and philanthropist
- Mark Algood, bookkeeper, Peter's brother
- James Denny, Schoolmaster
- Marianne Denny (nee Delaney, first husband Gerry Wilson), widow
- Cook, the Denny's cook and occasional cook at The Eyrie
- Aston Merryweather, Eagle Creek postmaster
- Helen Merryweather, his wife
- Nate Hale, Sheriff of Eagle Creek
- Many Birds, Crow tracker
- Walks With The Sun, his son and Jonas' apprentice
- Chief Plenty Coups, revered Crow leader
- Strikes The Iron, his wife
- Jonas Gilpin, smith, in charge of the public stable
- Mr. Hemsley, owner of The Eyrie
- Joanna Hemsley, his daughter and Imogen's best friend
- Major Danvers, guest at The Eyrie
- Mr. and Mrs. Halbard, and Julian their son, guests at The Eyrie
- Monsieur Colbert, the chef
- Edgar Greenslade, local artist
- Mr. and Mrs. Dalton, musical guests at the hotel
- Edwin Graham, Eagle Creek's Master Carpenter

- Cable Poole, unorthodox shipping magnate and philanthropist
- Wilbur, Peter's protégé.
- Rises With Joy and Helps With Honor, Crow mountain guides
- Matthew Tindall, a man Joanna rather likes in Billings
- Byron Macomber, manager of the bank in Eagle Creek
- Marta Kelly, Mr. Potts' secretary in Deadwood, killed in the robbery
- Dr. Barnard, Mr. Potts' doctor
- Mrs. Honey, the doctor's housekeeper
- Feldman Muldoon, the magistrate
- James Longworth, head waiter
- Mrs. Tinsley, Billings neighbor
- Mr. Waters, bank manager in Billings
- Eli Goldman, Clint Carter, Hamish Mactaggart, Willie Jones, Dylan, waiters
- Mrs. Dupree, Great Falls boarding house owner
- Dr. Firmin, head doctor at the mental institution

PROLOGUE

APRIL 11TH, 1875, DEADWOOD, SOUTH DAKOTA

The town was unusually quiet. For a place so full of vice it always struck Greg Waters as a little funny that everyone donned their finest clothes to attend church on Sunday, as if their sins the rest of the week could be absolved by bowing their heads for an hour or two. There were a few folk who stayed away from services, but fewer than most might have expected. It was the perfect time to commit a crime, especially one that needed time and patience to undertake.

"Greg, I want you on the street corner," Marty Fitzgibbons said, placing a hand on his shoulder and giving him a searching look, as if he was trying to see any weakness in Greg. He demanded his men not show an ounce of fear and

Greg wanted to impress him so badly that he would have walked through fire for him. He straightened his spine and gave Marty a look he hoped conveyed his confidence.

"I'll not let you down."

"I hope not. Your whistle could be the difference between us getting away from here and finding ourselves locked in a jail." One of the men behind Marty mimicked a noose being put around his neck, and pulled a face with wild eyes as if he were being hung. Hal thought himself such a joker, but Greg flinched a little at the thought of what might wait in store but hardened himself quickly. The gang had not been caught yet, and there was no reason to think that they would be now. He had to have faith in Marty and the others, that they would follow the plan and get out unscathed, as they had in Rapid City, Custer and Minnekahta.

"I'll stay alert, I promise," Greg assured Marty.

Marty mussed his hair and grinned at him. "You're a good lad, Greg."

Buoyed with pride at Marty's compliment, he left the gang's hideout and headed into town. He took a ball with him and pretended to play with it, the way any young boy might, bouncing it hard to see how high it might go, or up against the side of a building. An old prospector sat on the porch of the saloon. "Why you not in church, boy?" he demanded, frowning at Greg.

"What's church got for a boy like me?" Greg asked with

a nonchalant shrug. "You're not there either, so you must think it's not worth your time, too."

"I'm old and sinned more than a boy like you can imagine. I doubt there's redemption for a soul like mine, but you're just a boy."

"Then I'll have time to go when I'm older." Greg gave him a cheeky grin and the prospector grinned back.

"You'd best make it sooner rather than later," he warned. "Don't live your life with the regrets I have."

"I've no regrets, Sir. I'll go as soon as I have some." The old man laughed at his impertinence and waved him on his way.

Greg walked on, still playing, then peered over his shoulder to see if the old prospector was still sitting there. He'd gone inside. Greg was glad of it. The gang did not need any spectators – even if they were hardened sinners themselves. Once he'd reached the corner he and Marty had picked out, he looked around carefully. There was nobody around. The street was as quiet as it ever would be in Deadwood. He put his fingers in his mouth and whistled. Not even a curtain twitched at the sound, but four horses rode along the street, their riders dressed all in black, the silver on their holsters and spurs glinting in the sunlight.

Greg smiled at the sight of them. These men were his friends, his brothers. He'd had nobody until Marty had found him and taken him in. No doubt Marty had seen that Greg would be useful to him, rather than taking in a boy out of the goodness of his heart, but he'd always treated Greg well. He looked out for him, and for a boy with no family, it had felt good to belong somewhere again.

They rode past his lookout point straight to the bank. Greg wondered if it would be as easy to break into as the one in Rapid City had been. Custer and Minnekahta had been harder. Word had spread after the gang's raid in Rapid City. Greg hoped that Deadwood had not had word of the spate of robberies, that they'd not changed their locks, or installed new safes. It just made everything so much harder, and slower – and Greg on the outside had no idea what was going on inside. He hated the interminable wait for his friends to emerge into the sunlight again, their saddle bags filled with gold.

Within moments, they had dismounted and gained access to the bank. As Greg watched them disappear, he felt his heart begin to speed up in his chest as the snakes in his belly began to writhe and slither, making him feel nauseous. He whistled softly to himself and threw his ball up against the wall of the general store and tried to stay calm. His eyes flicked from side to side, always watching, always alert. He could not miss a thing. But there was nobody and nothing around, not so much as a rat scurrying along the street.

But suddenly, the sound of men shouting came from the bank. Greg looked over, trying to fight the urge to run over there and see what was happening. He had to stay quiet, to get away if he could if something had gone wrong. Marty had insisted he remember that. But Greg had never had to put his words into action before. It felt wrong to stand here and do nothing. What if they'd been jumped from the rear of the bank? Marty had thought that would be unlikely, but it was possible. Perhaps there had been a guard inside?

As three of the gang were marched out into the sunlight by the sheriff and his deputies, Greg was racked with guilt that he'd not warned his friends about the danger. He felt sure that it was his fault, that he must have missed something that might have kept them safe. But Marty wasn't with them. How had Marty got away, but Hal, Matt and Abel had not? It didn't make sense. Greg hadn't heard gunfire, so he couldn't be dead, could he?

What should he do now? Marty hadn't told him what happened to him if everyone was taken. Would they rat him out? Would his face end up on one of those wanted posters they saw all over? Would he have to look over his shoulder for the rest of his life, for fear that someone would give him up for a reward? He was just a boy. He'd not done anything, other than be a lookout for his friends. But he was man enough to know that the law would treat him the exact same way it treated them, and that meant the noose. Greg fled. What else could he do?

JUNE 4ᵀᴴ, 1893, BUFFALO, WYOMING

The room was stuffy, full of stale cigar smoke and her father's bitter anger. He sat at his desk, his skin as gray and lifeless as the ill-fitting suit he wore. "I told you to pack your things," he said wearily.

"But why must we move again?" Imogen Potts asked her father. "We've barely been here three months."

"Because the bank wishes it," he said simply, as if he had no choice in the matter. Imogen was not so sure of that. Her father could never settle anywhere, not since Deadwood, more than eighteen years ago. She'd barely been more than five years old then, but she knew that everything had changed on that fateful day when her father's bank had been robbed.

The culprits had been caught and brought to justice, well, three of them had at least. One had got away, and there had always been rumors about a fifth member of the gang, perhaps somewhere keeping watch, who'd obviously cared more for self-preservation than coming to the aid of his compatriots. That they were still at large haunted her father. He'd not been able to settle anywhere since, for fear of them robbing him again, or perhaps seeking him out for retribution for their lost colleagues.

Mama had tried her best to soothe her husband's fears. She'd even suggested that he leave the bank and perhaps find a new occupation, but Papa had steadfastly refused, vowing that they'd not take his work from him as well. He'd already lost his pride and his courage, though he'd never admit to having lost them to his wife and daughter. Imogen longed for the life she'd known as a young child. Deadwood hadn't been the safest town, but she had never felt unsafe there until the robbery. Papa had used her fear, and Mama's, to explain his need to leave the town. But subsequent moves had been claimed to be because the bank wished it, though Imogen and her mother both knew better.

She shook her head. She'd barely had time to make any friends here at all. She was a young woman, and chances to find a husband were passing her by as her father dragged them from place to place before she could blink. She'd soon be an old maid and would be passed over by any eligible young men if she wasn't careful. But Papa didn't seem to notice that her life was being ruined by his actions. She doubted if he even saw that she was no longer a child.

"Imogen, I don't expect you to understand," her father said wearily. "But I am an employee of the bank and must do as they ask. They wish me to move to Sheridan, to manage the new branch of the bank there, and so I must go."

Imogen shook her head and left his office. Mama was already chivvying the servants to bring out their trunks and was ticking off items on a list as they packed them into crates once they were carefully wrapped. Imogen ignored them all and went outside into the gardens. She had liked it here. The house was impressive but comfortable, and the gardens were a delight to her. Buffalo had a number of young people, with many social events and she had hoped to make real friends and perhaps even be courted by some of the handsome young men in town. None of that would happen now. She would have to start all over again somewhere new.

At least Sheridan wasn't too far away from here. Not that it made any difference, really. Papa could have said he was taking her to the moon, and she'd have to obey him. That was her lot, to obey her father until she had a husband to obey instead. She wasn't much good at the former, and she doubted she'd be much better at the latter when the time came, but as she'd never live anywhere long enough to find a husband, perhaps that didn't matter anyway.

She sighed heavily as she sank down onto the neatly clipped lawn and began to absent-mindedly pull up some weeds from the flower bed. How could she take matters into her own hands? She did not think she could bear to be plucked from another home, lose another set of friends, and have to start again somewhere new. This had to be the last time. Somehow, she had to find a way to convince Papa that it was safe to stay in Sheridan, at least long enough for her to find a husband.

But how did one set about changing another's mind? How could she banish her father's memories of that fateful day and the emotions it had stirred within him? For everyone's sake, there had to be a way, but Imogen could not see how it might be managed. Few men ever listened to a word a woman had to say, much less a woman as young as herself. But her own future happiness depended upon it. Surely Papa would be able to see that she had to be given a chance to find a match?

Once she was free of him and his need to flee, Imogen imagined a wonderful life for herself. She saw a handsome husband and a lovely home somewhere. She was not averse to the idea of traveling for pleasure, but she had no desire to be constantly on the move, not ever again. She had seen enough of the world, if she was entirely truthful. What she longed for was a place to call home. She'd never truly known that and was envious of those she'd met over the years who had never been anywhere else. They, of course, envied her the constant novelty of her nomadic life, no matter how much she tried to disabuse them of their fantasies about it all. For her there was no romance involved in her father's constant need to move on, to move away from perceived threats and dangers.

She would give her father one last chance. If he could stay in Sheridan long enough for her to find a husband, she would find it in her heart to forgive him for his weakness. If he could not, then she would be forced to find a match for herself. She would not give up her own hopes and dreams. Not for anyone, and most certainly not for a pair of phantom robbers who may or may not even exist. They did not get to ruin her life, too.

CHAPTER 1

AUGUST 15TH, 1894, SHERIDAN, WYOMING

Papa had lasted more than a year. That was at least something, Imogen thought as she shook her head at the news her mother had just given her that her father would be moving banks again. But she had not yet found a husband. Sheridan wasn't that big, and most of the young men were already married or affianced. She had been able to make some friends, at least, but in some ways that made it harder, as she would miss them terribly.

But it would appear that this time they would have four months before the move was to occur. The bank was building a new branch in Billings, Montana, and they wanted Papa to open it up for them. His willingness to move around often had become a godsend to them as the bank had grown and expanded from a four-branch outfit to more than thirty branches throughout South Dakota, Wyoming and now into Montana. He was excellent, it seemed, at getting things up and running, and so he and Mama would have to keep on moving.

But Imogen would not. She had vowed that if they did not stay in one place long enough for her to find a husband, she would take matters into her own hands, and so the time had come to do just that. Her only true friend, Emily Winthrop, had showed her the matrimonials pages in the newspaper, laughing about the idea of men and women advertising to find a bride or a husband. But Imogen had seen her chance to escape on those pages. She would place an advertisement and would find her own husband.

But what should she write? She had scoured the pages for inspiration, but so few of the advertisements told her anything much about who was at the other end of them. She wanted to say so much, to truly introduce herself well and to say what she wanted in a husband. But when she'd enquired at the local newspaper office about the cost of such advertisements, she'd discovered why they were so often short with little to no explanation at all – the cost per word was quite extortionate.

She had been working on what she might say for days, and still felt no closer to being happy with what she had written. How did one condense everything one was into a short paragraph, and also to ask for what one wanted? She did not wish to have to explain herself over and over again or write to many men in the hope that one of them might be suitable. She did not have the patience for that, nor could she spare the time required. She had to find a husband, and fast.

But she wanted him to be the right man. She did not wish to grasp at the first man to offer her honeyed words and promises he might not keep. She wanted to be sure he was kind and decent, and so she had only one option available to her to narrow her search – to limit any replies she might send to enquirers to those who live no more than two days train ride away. She wanted letters to reach her quickly, and if they decided that they might suit, that an in-person meeting could be easily arranged. She knew that it might potentially make the possibilities more limited, but it felt a reasonable compromise in her mind. It didn't hurt that only advertising in Wyoming and Montana newspapers would keep the costs a little lower than if she wanted it posted further afield.

Finally content with her wording, she left the house and walked the three blocks to the newspaper office. The young man on the desk smiled at her as she entered. "Well, Miss, how lovely to see you again," he said as he stood up to greet her.

It was rather odd to be remembered, she'd barely been here for five minutes, almost two weeks ago now, but she supposed that it was his job to remember people, even if he looked a little too pleased to see her again. She handed over her advertisement, the newspapers she wanted it to be placed in, and the coins required to do so. He looked it over carefully. "That will be printed in next week's editions, though I'm not sure why such a pretty thing as you needs to advertise for a husband." His smile was flirtatious, almost lecherous in fact, as if he'd make her his own in a heartbeat.

It made her shudder a little inside, especially when she noted the thick gold band on his wedding finger as he placed her money in the register. Not many men wore wedding rings, but he did – and he still thought it was perfectly reasonable to flirt with her. That was one thing she certainly did not wish to encourage, men who thought that every woman was his right, even if it meant betraying the vows he'd made before God.

Imogen left the office hurriedly. She walked along the street, trying not to think about the amorous young clerk. Were all men that way? She wasn't sure anymore. Some certainly were. Others seemed to be kind and polite, at least until they were wed when they then seemed to stop all pretense at being reasonable human beings, treating their wives as chattel and expecting them to be at their beck and call at all hours of the day and night. She'd seen many of her friends wooed and won, then conquered by their husbands, until they were hardly recognizable as the bright, funny young women they'd once been.

And, of course, she'd heard of men who beat their wives. Such a thing was common enough, but it wasn't a future she wanted for herself. She wanted to be free to be herself, not to be seen as an extension of the man she had married. She certainly did not wish to be punished for being herself and could not imagine wishing to change who she was for anyone – no matter how much a man tried to beat it out of her.

Then there were the men like her father. Withdrawn from their wives and families, from human contact of any kind, and they might as well not be here at all. But Mama said that he hadn't always been that way, that he had once been a fine husband, respectful and loving. But the more she thought about it, the more she feared that she might never find the match she longed for – and that all women deserved, because she wasn't sure that any man could be that manner of husband.

But she had to hold onto the hope that there was a good man out there, one who would love her and cherish her as she would love and cherish him. Someone who would encourage her to be the best person she could be, as she would encourage and support him to achieve his goals and dreams. She longed for a partnership, where both would be equal and have the same rights and responsibilities as each other.

She shook her head at her optimism. She was not naturally given to flights of fancy, but when it came to the man that she intended to spend the rest of her life with, she wanted to aim for the stars. She did not wish to be as miserable as her mother had been, watching her father fall apart more and more with each passing year, growing more afraid of others and giving up on the joy to be found in life. Nor did she wish to be a pretty little thing, hanging on a man's arm, only doted upon in public and ignored at best in private.

A woman's lot was not an easy one. She knew that all too well, but she was not afraid of hard work, or a drop in her living standards. She would take both willingly if it offered her the kind of relationship she hoped for. She deserved happiness. She could not accept less. She would not accept less.

"Imogen, Imogen!" A hand grabbed at her arm. Imogen was surprised to see Emily standing before her. "I've been calling you from across the street. Are you quite well? You seemed utterly lost in your thoughts."

"I am terribly sorry, Emily. I must have been, for I didn't hear you. How are you? It has been too long since we saw one another."

"Two weeks exactly," Emily said nodding. She tucked her arm through Imogen's. "And I have so much to tell you. Do you have time to take some tea with me? I could use your wise counsel."

"I can make time for you," Imogen assured her as Emily steered them towards Sheridan's only tea shop. Imogen didn't much like it, but it was the only suitable place for young women to meet. The coffee shops were entirely inhabited by men, and the saloons were quite obviously not the place for a young lady to be seen.

Once they had been shown to a small table by the window, Emily beamed at her. She pulled off her glove and Imogen couldn't help noticing a rather vulgar diamond twinkling on her friend's ring finger. "So, he finally asked you?" she said with a smile, taking Emily's hand and looking at the ring. She knew that large, bold settings were fashionable, but she'd never much taken to them herself. She had always much preferred smaller, less obvious jewelry.

"He did, and it was terrible," Emily said dramatically. "Father refused to give his consent, but William stood his ground and said he hoped that Father might change his mind when he saw how much happiness it would bring me."

"I'm not sure that would have been the best argument to win your father over," Imogen said drily, as one of the young waitresses appeared with a loaded tea-tray. She quickly placed all of the items onto the table and disappeared without a word.

"No, it wasn't. If only he'd assured Father that he had sufficient income to support us, a sizable townhouse and excellent prospects."

"Does he have those things?"

"Not yet," Emily said with a grin. "But he will. His father has to die soon, and then he'll inherit everything. Who else could old man Hansen leave it to?"

"The church, his old school or university, a hospital?" Imogen said with a grin.

"Stop it, you know he won't do that. Jebediah Hansen wants his name to live on, it won't if he gives everything to some charitable foundation."

"It might not if he leaves it to William, either."

"Not you, too. He tries so hard, and nobody ever believes him to be capable. Old man Hansen puts him down at every turn, makes him feel useless. But he's not. He's far cleverer than people think. He just gets tongue-tied around his father."

"I'm sorry, I know he is a better man than most give him credit for, and my father always says that you should not judge a man by his past achievements, that you should give him the benefit of the doubt that he can make something of himself - but you have to admit, Emily, that if he can't stand up to his father, how well will he manage in difficult business negotiations? There are much tougher, harder men than Mr. Hansen out there."

"I know that, and so does he. He has no concerns about disappointing them, though," Emily said perceptively. "He is truly only ever nervous around his father. He speaks with my father as though they were old friends, at least he did until last night, and you know how hard it is to please Father."

"I do, and I am sure that William will gain your father's blessing in time, so is it wise to be wearing that ring before he does? Your father will not take kindly to the two of you going behind his back."

"I've only been wearing it under my gloves. I've not shown a soul – except you."

"And I'd suggest that you take it off while we are in here. You never know who might walk in and see it, and then your secret will be all over town before you can blink."

Emily nodded and reluctantly removed the ring and tucked it into a small green velvet box inside her reticule. "I am just so happy that he wants me to be his wife."

"Just keep that to yourself," Imogen warned her. "He has a lot to do to convince your father, don't make it any harder for him."

Emily picked up the teapot and poured some of the hot amber liquid into their cups. "How are you?" she asked.

"Papa wants us to move again," Imogen said.

"Oh, but you can't," Emily said aghast. "I've barely gotten to know you, and you are too dear to me. I cannot lose you so soon."

"I don't wish to go, but unlike you I don't even have an ineligible suitor knocking at my door."

"What will you do?"

"I've placed an advertisement for a husband."

Emily's eyes widened and her mouth formed a perfect oval. "Oh my," she gasped. "You're so terribly brave."

CHAPTER 2

AUGUST 24TH, 1894, EAGLE CREEK, MONTANA

There were some mornings that Bartholomew King had to pinch himself. Today was most certainly one of those. There was a haze of mist over the mountains as the sun came up that made the world look completely ethereal and utterly breathtaking. He watched as birds flew overhead and a majestic stag stalked purposefully across the meadow a short distance down the mountain. The Eyrie Hotel was quite possibly located in the most beautiful place on earth.

But he did not have time to stand around enjoying the view. In no time at all their guests would be coming downstairs into the breakfast room, and they would need him to arrange their day trips and evening plans. He smoothed down his jacket and went inside, ready for the day ahead. Inside he checked the busboys' uniforms, straightening jackets and hats before sending them off to their posts to pre-empt the customers' needs.

He waited by the stairs to greet people as they came down the stairs. As always, it was Major Danvers who was the first to descend. He greeted Bart with a smart salute. Bart never saluted back. He'd not served in the military and felt it would be disrespectful to do so. But he did always stand at attention. "Good day to you, King, fine morning for it."

"I couldn't agree more, Major," Bart said escorting him into the breakfast room. "And what will you be doing today? Is there anything I might help you with?"

"I thought I'd take a walk up to the waterfall. It is quite spectacular up there, and so rarely anyone else around. I'd have thought that a place like that would have everyone clamoring to see it."

"I think many are put off by the long walk from the track," Bart said. "If you don't have stout boots, it can be a little tricky."

"Nonsense," Major Danvers said shaking his head. "It's no harder than tackling your stairs there."

Bart chuckled. "May I arrange for a packed luncheon for you, Major? I believe the cook has been making some of her famous scotch eggs."

"How can a man say no to that kind of an offer?"

"I'm not sure, Major. It surprises me when they do. I myself can never pass up a scotch egg."

"Never known anywhere else that makes 'em. Perfect little balls of egg and sausage, all in a crispy shell. Utter heaven. I shall have to get the recipe before I leave – and pray my own cook can recreate 'em when I return home."

Bart gave him a polite bow, just from the shoulders, and departed to greet the next guests as they arrived. The breakfast rush went by in a flash. Bart took orders, flattered and offered suggestions as to what people might do that day, and as they all disappeared back to their rooms, or out on their adventures, he took a few moments to breathe slowly and quietly.

"There you are," Mr. Hemsley, the hotel's owner, said coming in without knocking first. "I have to go away again, blasted family wedding. I'll be away for at least a month."

"The Eyrie will be safe in my hands," Bart assured him.

"I know that, or I'd not have hired you. Best maître d' in the business. Don't you ever leave me, Bartholomew. This place hasn't ever run so smoothly since I took you on."

"Glad to be of help, Sir," Bart said with a grin. "Whose wedding is it this time?"

"Youngest niece, Sarah, Belinda – oh, I don't know which of 'em it is. I only know that I'll be talked about endlessly if I'm not there."

"Your youngest niece is Grace, Sir. She very much liked the painting above the mantel in the breakfast room last time they came here. It might make a very thoughtful wedding gift."

"See, that is precisely why I keep you around," Mr. Hemsley said with a grin. "What'll we put in its place?"

"I have a lovely new work by a local artist in mind, of The Eyrie itself. He was asking quite a steep price for it, but I think it would be perfect."

"Beat him down by at least fifteen percent," Mr. Hemsley said. "As long as I feel like I've got a bargain, I'll be glad to look on it every day."

Once his employer was gone, Bart got down to the real work of running the hotel. This part wasn't so much fun, keeping the ledgers, ordering all that they needed, haggling by letter and telegram with suppliers to get the best prices. He was good at his work, and he enjoyed most of it, especially since he'd come to The Eyrie. The hotel was as busy and expected as high standards as any he'd ever worked in, perhaps Mr. Hemsley even demanded they provide even more for their guests. It gave him a real challenge every single day, but every day that passed was another day closer to the one when he'd have to leave.

And he didn't want to leave here. He'd come to truly love this little, out-of-the-way town. He'd chosen it for its remoteness, as much as for its beauty. But as Eagle Creek had begun to grow his anxieties had grown with the town. More people here, from all over the country meant there was more chance someone might recognize him, and he could not afford for his past to catch up with him.

Shaking off his anxieties for now, he carried on with his work until his friend, Peter Algood, called on him, just before the busy lunch rush. "Well, if it isn't our romantic honeymooner," Bart said with a smile, shaking Peter's hand enthusiastically.

"We were married some time ago now," Peter reminded him. "I think the honeymoon is long over."

"It is only over if you let it be. We had a couple here, just last week, celebrating fifty years together – and I swear they were the most romantic couple I've ever seen."

"I think it would be nice if we could have had a little more time for romance," Peter said with a wry smile. He and his new wife had been faced with a number of troubles before the ink had been dry on the record in the church register.

"Make time for it. Bring Jane up here for dinner, take her up to the waterfall. It's wonderful at this time of year."

"We keep saying we'll do that, and simply haven't found the time," Peter admitted. "Mrs. Albert's been finding things so much harder, and Jane has had to do so much more in the boutique. She's always so tired when she gets home."

"That's hard for her," Bart said. "I wish there was something I could suggest."

"I think Mrs. Albert needs to sell us her share of the business, or at least let Jane make more of the decisions in running it. She'd hire a new seamstress in a heartbeat, but Mrs. Albert won't hear of it, keeps swearing she'll be back at work in no time. But if her joints are this bad in the warm, dry weather we've had this summer, what will they be like in winter?"

Bart nodded. Mrs. Albert was a lovely woman, but she could be very stubborn. He hoped that Peter and Jane would find a solution that would help Jane and salve Mrs. Albert's pride, but he knew that it would be hard. "I'm sorry," Peter said, shaking his head. "I shouldn't have burdened you with this. You are frighteningly easy to talk to."

"It is why I'm good at my job," Bart joked.

"It must be."

"But there must have been something other than Effie Albert's joints that brought you up here today?"

"There was. Jane wondered if you would like to join us for supper on Thursday night, she knows it is your night off."

"Will that not be too much for her?"

"She was insistent. She fears you don't spend enough time with people who aren't your customers and I think she has a point."

"She probably does," Bart agreed. "And I would be delighted to join you both. Thank her very much for the invitation."

The rest of the week passed quickly, and as his night off drew closer, Bart couldn't help worrying a little. He'd quite purposefully not made many friends since his arrival in Eagle Creek a few years earlier. People who wanted to be friends wanted to know about the past, where people had come from and what they'd been doing, and he didn't like talking about it much. But, when Peter had come to Eagle Creek and stayed at the hotel, they had immediately struck up a bond, perhaps because Bart had never expected the rather busy New York businessman to ever move to a backwater like Eagle Creek.

He wondered if he could perhaps send word to them that he was unavoidably detained at the hotel but knew that he couldn't always make that excuse. No matter where he'd been, there had always come a time when people grew too curious about him. And he longed to have friends, to feel like he belonged somewhere. He'd not felt that in a very long time. But could he risk it? Would it not cause trouble – not just for him, but for them, too? He didn't want anyone to get hurt. He never had.

How he longed for connection, though. To have just one person who he might call a friend. It seemed that Peter wanted to be that person. Could he trust him with his past, or would that be a step too far, even for the kind and forgiving man Bart knew Peter to be? Peter had forgiven his twin for his often-unexplainable behaviors over and over again, and he'd even forgiven the men who had tried to ruin his life. Not that he hadn't gotten his revenge, but he'd done it by being successful, by doing good things with the wealth he had built, rather than trying to ruin anyone else. If anyone could forgive him for his past, it was Peter Algood, Bart was sure of that – but would it be asking too much even of him?

He knew that he did not have to find out, at least not just yet, but would it hurt more to lose a friend once he was even more fond of him than to never really become friends at all? It was a question he'd asked himself many times over the years, and until now he'd chosen to not make friends for fear of their loss, but it might already be too late with Peter. Bart had liked him from the start, and Jane was such a sweet lady, with a warm heart and a clever eye for color and pattern. She'd helped him to redecorate many of the suites in the hotel after he'd found her moving things around during her own stay there some years ago. She'd sourced the right fabrics and told him which went best with which furniture. He'd need to call on her services again, soon, as some of the older suites were looking tired and needed refreshing.

But could he bear losing them? Because he knew that he would. He couldn't stay here much longer, no matter how much he loved the place, or how many friends he might make here. Eventually, he would have to move on. He had been so blessed to have been able to stay here this long, it was the longest he'd remained anywhere since he was a boy. Could he let himself hope that he might be able to stay? That he might never be found? And how would his friends react if they knew the truth? Knew that he'd been lying to them all along?

He'd be a pariah. No matter how kind Peter or Mr. Hemsley might seem now, they'd not understand that. No man could.

Fighting against his own better judgment, he made his way down the mountain to the Algood's tiny cottage. He knocked on the door tentatively and stepped back off the porch to wait. It was opened within moments by Peter who grinned and shook his hand warmly. "Good to see you," he said happily. "Come inside."

The house was small, and the front door opened onto the kitchen directly. The room smelled of roast beef making Bart's mouth water. Jane came down the stairs and greeted him with a sisterly peck on the cheek. "I am so glad you're here," she said. "It has been such a long time since I've seen you."

"I was honored to be invited," Bart said honestly. "And something smells wonderful."

"Supper has been cooked for us by Cook," Jane said. "I was surprised to find her here in my kitchen when I returned from work, but she found out we were entertaining, decided that I am working too hard, so let herself in to prepare a feast for us all."

"Mrs. Denny's cook?" Bart queried.

"Yes," Jane said.

"I should talk to her about working at the hotel if this tastes even half as good as it smells," Bart joked.

"You'd never get her to leave, she's as loyal as they

come, but she'd probably come and train your cooks for you. She likes passing on her skills and her recipes."

"Now that is something I may have to negotiate with her," Bart said as Peter handed him a glass of whisky.

The meal was delicious, and the company was even better, and when he came away at the end of the evening, Bart was even more torn than he'd been before. But he'd also come away knowing that his lifestyle had caused him to miss out on something even greater than friendship. Love. He'd never known it in his life, so hadn't known that he was going without, but the more loving couples he saw at work, and having watched Jane and Peter together tonight, he knew that it was something he longed for more than anything.

But it was the story of how they had met that had most made him think. Jane had forgiven Peter for so much, and still loved him. She could so easily have pushed him away forever, but she hadn't – because of love. Maybe, if he found the right woman, if she loved him enough, he might one day be able to tell her the truth – and perhaps he might get as lucky as Peter, and be forgiven for all that had gone before?

CHAPTER 3

AUGUST 25TH, 1894, EAGLE CREEK, MONTANA

R uns With Horses, The Eyrie's Crow stable manager was unwell. Bart sighed heavily as he tried to find someone on his staff who could drive to Eagle Creek in his place to pick up the new guests arriving today. There simply was nobody who could be spared from their regular work. He would have to do it himself, though he barely had the time to breathe when the hotel was so full. Handing Eddie Dobley, his faithful clerk, a list of things that would need to be done in his absence, he picked up his driving gloves and made his way out to the stable yard.

Fred Kipsey stared at him wide-eyed and stood to attention as Bart approached. "Fred, there's no need to be afraid of me," Bart told the boy. "We're all a team here. You'll learn that soon enough."

"Yes, Sir," Fred said quickly. Bart was sure he would have saluted him if he'd thought it might impress. The lad had only started work a few days earlier. He seemed very eager to please.

"I'll judge you on how well you help me to get the carriage ready, not on how formally you address me, you know."

"Yes, Sir."

Bart couldn't stifle a chuckle. "Have you always been so polite, Fred? Or am I truly so frightening?"

"I'm a little nervous, Sir, but my Mom always said I was to be polite to my elders, to do as they tell me."

"She raised you well, no doubt, but deference and respect are not the same thing. I'd rather win your respect than have you defer to me just because I run the hotel." Fred's lips curved into the slightest of smiles, but it seemed he still did not trust Bart's word. Bart frowned, trying to think of a way to get his point across. "Imagine if I were to kick one of the horses, would you let me do it or would you try and stop me?"

Fred frowned. The question was a difficult one for him to answer, obviously, but Bart wanted him to think it over carefully. From all Runs With Horses had told him about the new stable lad, Fred would do anything to protect an animal in his charge. Bart wanted to know that he would do what was right, no matter who was asking him to do wrong.

"Would you stop me?" Bart asked again.

"I would not want you to hurt the horses," Fred said shyly. "But they are yours, it is not my place."

"Wrong," Bart said. "In theory, Mr. Hemsley, the hotel owner paid for them, so it makes the animals his and not mine. However, in practice, the animals belong to our guests, and they trust us to ensure that the animals they ride and drive while they are here are happy, healthy and well-cared for. If an animal is abused, will they be a happy, well-behaved animal for our guests, Fred?"

"It is unlikely, Sir. An abused horse will fear anyone who raises their hand or their voice to them – or even near them."

"Quite. And so, what is best for our animals is what is also best for our guests. So, I ask you again. If you saw me kicking a horse, what would you do?"

"I would step between you," Fred said with a tentative smile. "And I would try and remind you of this conversation."

Finally, Bart saw a glimmer of the intelligence and cheek that Runs With Horses had told him of. "Running a hotel, Fred, is all about making sure our guests are happy. Though we all have different roles, and some may seem more important than others, this is simply not so. I cannot do my job without everyone else doing theirs, and they cannot do theirs if I do not do mine. So, my name is Bart, and I am glad you are now a part of our little family here." He held out his hand. Fred tentatively held out his. Bart shook it solemnly, then gave the boy a wink. "Always come to me, Fred. Whether you have concerns or wish to tell me something good, there is nothing too big or small that I do not wish to hear about, if you think I need to know it."

"I shall, Sir. I mean, Bart," Fred said.

Bart grinned. "Now, Fred. Runs With Horses is unwell. So, you will be in charge here in the yard. I need to know that you can manage that. If you do not think you can, tell me now, because I will need to call someone in to help out if you think you need help."

"I can do it. I like the horses, they like me, and though it is busy, I can manage."

"You'd be able to harness the grays and get the carriage ready? You'd not leave guests waiting if you drive to town to fetch the new guests?" Bart asked lightly.

The boy blushed, his neck and face glowing at being so easily caught out. Even his ears glowed red. "I would need help to do that," he admitted.

"Never be ashamed to admit you need a hand," Bart assured him. "We all do. So, I'm here. Tell me what to do."

"I couldn't," Fred said aghast.

"The stable yard is your domain, yours and Runs With Horses. The hotel is mine. Would you know how to keep a ledger? Or know how much flour is in the pantry at any time?"

"No, how could I?"

"Then how am I to know what to do to get the carriage ready?" Bart teased.

"But you do, Sir, don't you?"

"I do, but you could not know that, as you've never seen me do so. So, as the horses, their tack and all the vehicles are your responsibility today, would it not be wise to tell me how to do something you've not seen me do before?"

Suddenly, what Bart had been trying to tell the boy seemed to sink in. His eyes widened in wonder. "I see what you mean, Bart," he said, a little more confident than he'd been just moments before. "So, first we need to shine the harnesses."

Bart followed Fred's directions. Soon the carriage was ready, the horses in the shafts, and everything gleamed ready to make a good first impression upon their new guests. And Bart knew that the stable would be in good hands in Runs With Horses' absence. Even though he was extremely busy and could barely spare the time, he did not regret a moment of the time he'd spent here with Fred. He had the measure of the lad now, and Fred was now much more relaxed in Bart's company, too. He knew that there were many who'd frown at his style of managing a hotel, but Bart found that when you trusted people to do their best and tried to ensure everyone was valued for their contribution to the enterprise, that they worked harder and with more pride in what they were doing – however menial a task it might seem. A good hotel could lose its reputation all too easily, and it was usually over tiny things left undone or done badly. Bart knew that every tiny smudge on the brasses, every crumb on the carpet, every frayed piece of riding tackle could be the difference between their guests enjoying their stay or telling all their friends how terrible it had been.

He drove quickly down the mountain. The train would arrive in just fifteen minutes, and he did not like to keep the guests waiting. It made a terrible first impression to leave them standing outside the station. Occasionally guests had mentioned that this had happened, most often in the winter, which had only added to the guests' discomfort. There wasn't anything much worse after a long train journey than having to stand around in knee-deep snow, waiting for a sled that did not come. Bart had vowed it would never happen again.

While he waited in Eagle Creek for the train to arrive, he hurried across the street to the general store. A pile of news-papers stood just inside the door and Bart picked up a few copies of each one to put in the lobby of the hotel. He took them back and stored them under the driver's bench of the carriage, keeping the Montana Gazette out to read while he waited. He flicked through the pages, reading the articles that interested him carefully, and skimming those that did not. He liked to be relatively well-informed of both local and national news. The Eyrie catered to wealthy clients from all over the country, after all, and guests often liked to chat. If he could mention something pertinent to their home county or state, it often impressed them.

In the middle of the newspaper were pages of advertisements. From the announcements of births, marriages, betrothals and deaths columns to those wishing to buy or sell something in particular. He rarely bothered with them and turned the pages quickly. The final page of advertisements was always filled with matrimonial advertisements. Until he'd come to Eagle Creek, Bart hadn't much thought about those, either. But since being here and knowing how many of the inhabitants of this little town had found love there, they had come to fascinate him. And after his time with Peter and Jane, he found himself wondering if they might be the answer to his own loneliness.

He just wanted to have someone to write to, someone with whom he could be himself. Someone to share his hopes and dreams with. She did not have to want to marry him. In truth, it might be for the best if they never met in real life at all. But he longed to have someone or something that was constant in his rather nomadic life. For, even if it was not yet time, he would have to leave here soon and say goodbye to everyone and everything here.

But all of the women who advertised wanted husbands. He was not sure if he could ever take such a risk. He could not ask a woman to have faith in him, to trust him, if he could never confide in her why they must always keep moving on. And any woman worth having would demand to know. He did not want a simpering doll who would just do as he told her. He could think of nothing worse than marrying a woman raised simply to please the men around her. No, if he were to ever fall in love, she would be feisty and brave, fearless and clever. If they were to talk together every day for the rest of their lives, he wanted it to be good conversation – not simply about how well her appointment at the dressmaker's might have gone that day.

There was only one advertisement, among scores of them, that gave him hope that the woman at the other end might possess a mind of her own, though of course it was almost impossible to be sure given just a few sentences, but if he were a different man, with a different life, he might have considered writing to her.

Young Lady of Wyoming seeks a husband. Opinionated, headstrong and occasionally stubborn are words that have been used to describe me. I prefer curious, intelligent and determined. If you would like a wife who will challenge you and be your equal, then please write to Box 326, The Sheridan Bugle.

He had to hand it to her, she did not mince her words. He found that refreshing. So many of the other advertisements all said similar things, about being good cooks, wishing to be mothers and so forth. This young lady clearly had more in mind for her life than anything so dull and commonplace. She sounded sassy and would no doubt know exactly what she wanted from a husband – and woe betide him if a man courting her could not bring himself to offer her just that.

But he had little time to think on it now, as the sound of a train whistle nearby alerted him to the arrival of the train. He jumped down from the bench and smoothed out his jacket and pants, put on his velvet top hat and waited. There was an agreement with the porters that they would bring out any luggage to a wagon parked nearby. Bart's aim was always that the luggage would reach the hotel and be unpacked by the chambermaids before they arrived at the hotel. He liked the guests to feel settled and at home from the very first moment.

He grinned as a volley of young lads with carts ran out of the station building, heading straight for the wagon. Within moments of the train arriving, the wagon was on its way up the mountain, and Bart was still waiting for the guests to emerge. He tipped the porters generously and they all gave him a delighted grin. "Wish you were down to pick up your people more often," one of them said as he pocketed his unexpected windfall and scurried away to help other passengers.

His guests emerged onto the street looking a little lost a few minutes later. Bart greeted them warmly, introducing himself and helping them into the carriage. "I chose an open top today," he told them once they were comfortably settled. "The weather is so fine, and the views are so spectacular today."

He enjoyed pointing out local landmarks as they drove through the town and up the mountain, and grinned to himself as he heard their gasps and mutterings of surprise at the beauty all around them. For a moment, he wondered what the young lady in that advertisement might make of Eagle Creek. Wyoming had some very pretty places, but he'd not been anywhere as lovely, even with all his wanderings over the years. She'd not mentioned it, but was she adventurous? Would she accept a challenge as well as expect him to let her challenge him? He shook his head and tried not to think of her. But even as he'd pulled up outside The Eyrie and got the new guests settled into their suites, he couldn't stop thinking about her and what she would make of all of it.

CHAPTER 4

SEPTEMBER 4TH, 1894, SHERIDAN, WYOMING

The hallway was filled with packing crates and trunks. Mother paced between them anxiously. The wagons that they should have been loaded onto earlier this week had still not arrived, their journey delayed indefinitely by the unseasonal downpours that had made the roads too rutted and unsafe to travel upon. Father had gone on ahead to Billings, to take up his new position. He cared little about whether there was a comfortable home awaiting him and had taken lodgings in a boarding house across from the new bank.

Imogen could understand her mother's frustration, but pacing did little good. They would do better to enjoy their final days here in Sheridan – but Mama had refused to even let Imogen go to supper with Emily last night, in case the weather cleared. Imogen had tried to reason with her, saying that the wagons would not come in the evening, so a supper invitation would be quite reasonable to accept, and Emily did only live three doors down from them. Mama had been scandalized at the idea of Imogen running along the street, hitching her skirts up to keep them out of the puddles, and so Imogen was trapped in this cold, empty and echoing shell of a house with her anxious and increasingly snappy mother.

It wasn't the way she would have wished to say goodbye to the only place she had ever considered to be home. She had made friends here in Sheridan, and Mama wouldn't even let her say her goodbyes properly to them. It was all so terribly unfair. All because Papa refused to stay in one place – and she did not doubt that he could have done so at any time had he chosen to do so. But he had not, and now they would move again to salve his anxieties, though nothing ever could do that.

But the most infuriating thing was that she had heard nothing from her advertisement. She supposed that she had been a little blunt, and that there would be few men interested in a self-confessed opinionated woman, but she had hoped that there might be at least one lonely man out there that might. She supposed that the newspaper might have forwarded letters received in the past couple of days to the house in Billings, as she had told them the date she would be moving. If it had only recently been sent on, it might not have reached its new destination yet, not that Papa would send her a telegram to tell her she had mail. She had to remain patient and calm, two things she had never been much good at.

Mama opened the front door a crack and peered outside onto the street. "Oh my," she said, her voice full of relief. "It seems to have finally stopped raining."

Imogen joined her at the door and pushed it open a little wider. The deluge did indeed seem to have stopped and a few patches of blue had appeared in the sky, but there were still plenty of ominous looking clouds up there, too. "Even if it has stopped raining today, the carters may not be able to get here today, Mama," she said softly. "The roads will still be sodden and hard to pass."

"I know that," Mama snapped. "But they might be passable tomorrow, or perhaps the next day. I just want to be gone from here." She turned and looked back at all the boxes. "I am sick and tired of living this way."

Imogen could easily understand that. She put an arm around her mother's shoulder and gave her an affectionate squeeze. "We'll be reunited with Papa soon."

"Oh him, I'm quite alright without him," Mama said shaking her head. "I just want to sleep in a bed with proper linens upon it and know I don't have to hurriedly pack it up in the morning. To have enough food in the house to feed us for a few days, not just buy what we need twice a day in case we might be on our way at any time. It is just all this waiting. If we must move again, I simply want it to be over."

"We'll be there soon enough, now," Imogen assured her. "Look, I can find enough blue to make a sailor a pair of trousers. Isn't that what Grandmama used to say? That if there was enough for a sailor's pants that it would be a fine day?"

"She did," Mama said with a fond smile. "And you are right, there may just be enough. The seamstress would need to be quite thrifty, though." She moved away from the open doorway and stood in the middle of the hallway, looking sad.

Imogen hurried towards her and embraced her. "Mama, you know that I do not wish to move again, any more than you enjoy all this waiting, but things will work out for the best and we'll be on our way very soon now. I'm sure of it."

"You aren't still mad?"

"Oh, yes, but at Papa, never at you, Mama. He doesn't have to accept these roles. And he isn't the one who has to pack everything up and make him a new home every time he decides it is time to move on. I am angry that he puts us both through this so often."

"Your father is a complicated man, with an important job."

"A job he could do in one town for the rest of his life, as his peers all do. He has chosen to uproot us over and over, and for what?"

"You know what, because the bank asks it of him."

"Is that really true, though, Mama?" Imogen asked. "Could he not have said no? Would they have given him his papers and turned him out? I cannot imagine that Uncle Luther would do such a thing. He is my godfather, after all. Papa is clearly of value to the bank, so I doubt that he'd lose his position if he said he wished to stay in one place. We stayed in Deadwood for many years."

Mama gave her a look that told Imogen she was asking questions that she shouldn't. But she was a woman grown, and she was tired of the kinds of platitudes they had been giving her since she was a girl. Papa moved because he wished to, but he hadn't always wanted to. Why would nobody ever talk about what happened in Deadwood, for Imogen was sure that the robbery there was what had changed her father.

"We don't talk about Deadwood, Imogen."

"I know, but perhaps we should. Perhaps if we talked about it, Papa would finally be able to put it behind him." She stared at her mother and gestured at all the crates surrounding them. "Do you truly wish to go through all of this in another few years? For you will."

"We will. I promised to love and obey your father, Imogen. And so I will do just that. If he asks it of me, it is my duty to do as he wishes."

"But do you not long to stop moving? To find a real home?"

"My home is wherever he is, where you are," she said

sadly, but Imogen didn't believe her. She knew that her words had hit home. Mama hated this almost as much as she did. She would never admit it to Papa, though.

"What if I weren't here anymore? Would it still be home? Just you and Papa in another big house you barely get to make your own before you have to leave it?"

"No, that would not be home," Mama admitted quietly.

A young boy bounded up the steps to the open front door. He looked a little confused, as if he should knock, but not knowing where to. He eventually settled on the door-frame. "Yes?" Imogen said, moving quickly back to the door.

The lad reached into a satchel he wore over his shoulder and pulled out a single letter. "For Miss I. Potts," Imogen took it from him and stared at the handwriting. Her address was printed in neat, blocked handwriting, and was clearly from nobody she knew. She turned it over and saw that the return address was the office of the newspaper she'd placed her advertisement in. Her heart skipped a beat and she felt a swarm of butterflies take flight in her belly.

The lad rummaged in another pocket of his satchel and pulled out a smaller envelope, a telegram. "And this one for Mrs. C. Potts." Mama nodded to Imogen to take it for her. The lad tipped his cap then turned and ran to make his next delivery, whistling a merry tune.

"It's from Papa," Imogen said, shutting the door behind

the boy and handing the telegram to her mother who opened it and blanched.

"Your father wants to know why we are so delayed, and whether I will be there for an important dinner tomorrow night."

"But he knows that the weather prevented us from traveling, I sent him a telegram myself," Imogen said, surprised by her mother's reaction to just words on a page. Papa wasn't actually in the room berating her, but her fear of letting him down clearly was.

"What if I do not make it in time? We'd need to leave right away to be sure I can be there on time," Mama fretted.

"We cannot ensure that, unless you go on ahead on the train today. I can follow with our things when it is safe to do so," Imogen said practically.

"But you're just a child. I can't expect you to manage a move such as this."

"Mama, you might not have noticed me growing up, as you pandered to Papa all these years while I did so, but I can assure you that I have – and that we have done this often enough that I know exactly what needs to be done. Go to Papa, be there for him as he wants you to be."

Mama placed her cool palm against Imogen's cheek. "We've not always done right by you, have we?" she asked. "But somehow, you have become a very lovely and very capable young woman. I do know that."

Buoyed by her mother's compliment, Imogen helped her

to pack an overnight bag and found one of her mother's favorite evening gowns in one of the trunks. She packed it into a suitcase, carefully wrapping it in velvet so it would not crease. Mama pulled on her coat and hat then hugged Imogen tightly. "You truly are sure you can manage?"

"I am truly sure," Imogen said as her mother kissed her cheek. "I will see you in a few days."

There were almost no vehicles on the roads still, so Mama would have to walk the quarter of a mile to the train station. Imogen watched from the top step as her mother hurried along the street, waving cheerfully when Mama turned to give her a worried glance. Once she was out of sight, Imogen went back inside and went up to her room, where she sank onto her unmade bed and pulled out the letter from the newspaper.

She opened it and realized that there were actually two letters enclosed. One was from the newspaper asking if she wished to place the same advertisement in another issue, and the second from a gentleman in Montana. She smiled to herself. Someone had actually responded. She could hardly believe it as she unfolded the letter and stared at his rather hurried scrawl.

Dear Young Lady of Wyoming,

I must confess that this is the first time I've ever replied to an advertisement such as yours, and I have no idea what I should say, so if this seems in any way improper, or you simply do not like the sound of me, then please do feel free to never reply. There is no need to be polite.

I am not sure why it was your advertisement that made me stop and think that I must write, I only knew that I wanted to. From the moment I saw it, I could not help wanting to know more about the woman who confessed to being curious, intelligent and determined (and letting me know that others are not always so flattering).

I had not thought that I was looking for a wife. I am by nature quite a solitary man, despite being a maître d' in a hotel. The Eyrie is not quite like most hotels, though. It is set high up on a mountainside, where the eagles fly and all manner of wildlife roam. I have never seen a place so beautiful, so untamed – and yet so peaceful and bewitching. I fell in love with it the very moment I arrived here.

But the nature of my work means it is unlikely that I will be able to stay for long. Hotel work is not always kind to those who seek an established home, sadly. I say this to you now, for I do not wish you to think I might keep such a thing from you. I wish our correspondence, should you wish it to continue, to be as honest and as open as your advertisement was. I would not want you to think that you might come to live in Eagle Creek and never leave it again. It is the kind of place that would break your heart to leave – at least, I know that it will break mine to go when the time comes.

Eagle Creek also has another rather individual feature to it, and that is the number of people here who found love using advertisements in the newspaper. It is quite peculiar to look around and see happy couple after happy couple as you walk along the street, knowing that they met because of a few lines of text in a newspaper. I wonder if their success and happiness, despite rather daunting odds in many cases, was what made me think that perhaps I might find a little of their luck rubbing off on me.

I do hope you will write back to me. I cannot wait to see what you will write when you have the ability to write as many words as you please, and even if you find I am not to your taste as a possible suitor, it would please me greatly to make a friend.

Yours, most hopefully
Bartholomew King

CHAPTER 5

SEPTEMBER 26TH, 1894, EAGLE CREEK, MONTANA

D*ear Mr. King*

Apologies for the delay in responding to your rather intriguing letter. My family was in the process of moving from Sheridan to Billings. So, rather unexpectedly, I find myself not far from you, as I understand from the people here that Billings is not even a morning's train ride away from your beloved Eagle Creek.

I must confess, that what I have seen of Montana so far has been quite lovely. Billings is like many towns though, busy and full of earnest people going about their business. And I have seen many towns in my short life, though unlike you I have never chosen to be on the move.

My father is a banker. I understand that he is excellent at his job, so very good in fact that every time a new branch of the bank that he works for is opened, my father is expected to go and open it, to train the staff, and ensure that it is running smoothly before we have to move to another town, to do it all over again.

I do not wish to seem dismissive of you, so early in our correspondence, but I am not sure that I will ever wish to lead the manner of life that my mother has been forced to endure. I would most certainly never wish to put children through the loneliness that not fitting in anywhere they go brings. So, if you are still inclined towards moving onwards, this may pose a problem for me.

Yet, as you were intrigued by my advertisement, I am intrigued by your candor and wish to find out more about you. Perhaps we might forget, for a while at least, that we were brought together by my advertisement, and simply write to one another as friends – as you suggested? We can see what else might come to pass as we do so.

So, I shall tell you a little more about myself. I am told that I am tolerably pretty, though I could not possibly comment. I have long, dark brown hair, a little like the color of a ripe horse chestnut. I am of average height and have freckles all over my nose, and dimples (that I despise) in my cheeks when I smile. I am told my features made me a quite adorable child, and perhaps that was why I was permitted so much more leeway then, than I am now. No matter how pretty I might be, as a young woman my opinions should be kept to myself now, or so I am told!

I dance but have rarely had the chance to socialize often enough to be sure if I do so as well or worse than any other young lady. I enjoy painting, but have no talent for it at all, and am a passable rider. I am prepared to stand my ground in an argument, even against my so-called betters, which has gotten me into all manner of trouble in school over the years and at my parents' soirees. I am often sent to my bedroom before guests come now, for what was perhaps endearing or amusing to my parents' friends and my father's colleagues when I was a pretty little girl, is not so appealing in a grown woman.

Tell me more of yourself, please? I should very much like to see if the picture I have in my mind of you is correct.

Yours most eagerly

Imogen Potts

Bart had to admit that this letter amused him even more than her advertisement had. Miss Potts was most certainly a character, and one he very much wanted to get to know better. He was glad that she wished them to become friends, for he knew that he would come to very much look forward to receiving her letters. He could just about imagine her as a small girl, challenging all around her to prove their arguments. He doubted if she would have let them get away with

53

lying to her, and he knew all too well how difficult adults found it to be confronted by the innocent questions of a child. He saw it here in the hotel almost every day.

He smiled to himself and tucked her letter away in his jacket pocket, as Mr. and Mrs. Halbard and their son Julian acted as living proof of it. Julian was a curious boy. He asked why about everything, and he was not one to be put off by an adult simply saying 'because.' He wanted the truth, and he would not stop questioning until he got it. It made Bart wonder why his parents did not simply start with telling the boy what he wished to know, rather than going through the often painfully long process of trying not to answer him.

He could understand not giving children answers when you did not have them yourself, but Bart did not think it made a person seem foolish if they did not know the answer. He thought it better to admit to gaps in his own knowledge, rather than pretend to have information he did not have. But few people seemed to feel the same way. It seemed they would rather tell a child nothing or lie to them than admit they did not know.

He approached the couple cautiously. Julian wanted to know how the pastries for his breakfast seemed to have so many layers, and why they flaked the way that they did when he bit into them. This was a subject Bart could help him investigate, at the very least. "Mr. Halbard, Mrs. Halbard, I hope you don't mind my interrupting you, but I wondered if Julian might like to take a tour of our kitchens and see the pastries being made?"

They gave him a look of utter relief. He'd not brought attention to their lack of knowledge, or offered the answer to Julian himself, and they could take him on the tour and perhaps learn something interesting themselves. "Would you like that?" Mr. Halbard asked his son.

Julian's eyes were full of delight. He had a wonky grin, and it was most endearing. He deployed it on Bart and his parents. "Can we go now?"

Mr. and Mrs. Halbard nodded at him happily. "If you wish to see them making the pastries for breakfast, we would do well to hurry," Bart said, reaching out a hand to the boy. He took it and Bart led them towards the stairs that would take them downstairs to the large, cool pastry kitchen.

The cooks were busy, but as Bart entered the kitchen, they all stopped and gave him a nod of recognition. He waved at them to get back to work and led Julian towards a small office at the back of the kitchen. Inside it, was a large dark skinned lady and a wiry white man, poring over a recipe on a desk. "Cook, Monsieur Colbert, I'd like to introduce you both to Julian Halbard and his parents. Julian is most interested to learn why his breakfast pastries taste so delicious, why they have layers and why they flake when he bites into them," Bart said with a smile as he pushed the boy forward a little.

Cook beamed at him. "Well, aren't you the curious chile," she said in her thick southern accent. "You'll want to ask Monsieur Colbert about those. He's from France, where he learned how to make 'em."

Monsieur Colbert did not look quite as pleased to see an intruder in his kitchen, but he rallied well. "I will return shortly," he said, his voice still heavily accented despite being in America for more than twenty years. "Will you wait for me, Madame Cook?"

"I'll be here, chile. I'll just take a few words with Mr. King, here."

Monsieur Colbert took Julian and his parents out into the kitchen. They could soon hear him as he took him to each station in the kitchen and explained with passion what each cook was doing. He found an avid learner in young Julian, who asked sensible questions as Monsieur Colbert explained each step. Cook grinned. "He pretends he doesn't like the young ones, but he's good with 'em," she noted.

"I wasn't expecting to see you here today, Cook, though I am always glad to know you've been. It always adds a little something to our menus."

"I wanted to see you, on Miss Marianne's behalf and we needed to keep it a secret. My being up here would raise fewer eyebrows, if you know what I mean?"

"Well, not entirely," Bart admitted.

"It is Mr. Delaney's 70th birthday in two months. Miss

Marianne wants to throw a big party for him, invite lots of his old New York friends. But obviously, that means we need somewhere for 'em all to stay."

"I can check our availability," Bart assured her. "But November is often quiet, except for Thanksgiving, so I doubt it will be a problem."

"Thank you. Miss Marianne'd like to hire your dining room, too? I'll gladly come and help Monsieur Colbert with the buffet."

"It all sounds like it will be quite the party, and I will be delighted to keep it secret from Mr. Delaney. He deserves a fancy party after all he's done for the young people locally."

"We think so," Cook said with a smile.

Young Julian had reached the end of his tour and was being given a chance to sample some pastries fresh out of the ovens. His face was a picture of rapt enjoyment, his parents looked unusually relaxed and happy. "So, did you enjoy your tour?" Bart asked them all.

"It was wonderful, and very kind of you and Monsieur Colbert," Mrs. Halbard said. "We've all learned a lot."

"It is very simple, yet very complicated," Mr. Halbard said, nodding his head. "And the end result is delicious."

"I am so glad you like 'zem," Monsieur Colbert said proudly. "I learned from my Papa, and 'e learned from 'is Papa. We have been *boulangers et pâtissiers* for as many generations as anyone can remember."

"Thank you, Monsieur Colbert, for your time," Bart said. "And though I am sure there is much more to learn, Julian, I fear we must leave the cooks to their work now."

Julian frowned but nodded. "I have had the most wonderful time. I would very much like to become a baker when I am older."

"He wanted to be a soldier just last week," Mr. Halbard said with a chuckle. "But I wouldn't complain if a son of mine could make anything this tasty."

Bart saw the family out onto the terrace and wondered if they had learned the lesson he'd hoped to teach, that it was better to answer the boy's questions and ask for help to do so if needed. Only time would tell. But the little family looked happier than he'd seen them since their arrival, all because Julian's curiosity had been indulged, just a little.

He returned to his work and was soon lost in the accounts ledger. His head swam with numbers and quantities as he neatly made the necessary entries for the past two days. The hotel was thriving, but the cost of sugar seemed to have risen rather more than he would have expected it to recently. He made a note in his pocketbook to contact the suppliers and find out what was causing the change.

As he put the small notebook back into his pocket, his hand brushed Miss Potts' letter. He pulled it out and read it again. It made him smile again, and he pulled out a sheet of paper and began to write a reply. As the words flew from his pen, he was surprised at how easy he found it to tell her things that he'd never tell anyone in person. It was oddly liberating to write to someone you'd never met, and profoundly personal. As he let his thoughts pour onto the paper, he found himself telling her all about his past. When he caught himself, he shook his head and balled up the letter and threw it into the fire. He watched it crinkle up, crackle, and burn to ash, and wished it were so easy to erase what had happened.

He sighed. No matter how delightful it might be to have someone to write to, he could not forget that he was Bartholomew King now. There were parts of his life that were locked tightly away, and they had to remain that way. He could not ever tell her the truth, or anyone else for that matter. The consequences were too great to contemplate. He had to be more cautious.

More carefully, he tried again. This time it was harder, as he sifted through his thoughts carefully, making sure he gave nothing of his past away. There was enough to talk about without that. He did not need to tell her of the first fifteen years of his life. So, he told her of the hotels he had worked in, how he had gone from being a bus boy, to the desk clerk, and the day he finally got a job as a maître d'. It was easy to talk about his work. He loved it and always had.

From the first day he'd walked into a hotel, all those years ago in Denver, Colorado, he'd known it was where he would be able to turn his life around. Hotels were strangely impersonal. The staff had to be efficient and see to their clients' every need, but their own personality and their own life mattered not at all. They kept their customers' secrets, and their own – and so a boy who wished to leave his past behind had found a place where he could be whatever he wanted to be. And in his case, that had been nobody at all.

CHAPTER 6

OCTOBER 3RD, 1894, BILLINGS, MONTANA

Imogen rather liked Billings, or rather she liked the world that surrounded it. She took rides outside of the city almost daily, trying to forget that she was lonely by racing against the wind. There was so much space here, and everything was so green, the sky so very blue. Their new home was most definitely the biggest house she had ever lived in, with vast gardens she could get lost in when things got too much. Her bedroom was pretty and the bed most comfortable. She'd not suffered a bad night's sleep since their arrival.

But she missed Emily and her other friends in Sheridan. She had so rarely stayed anywhere long enough to make real friends, and she now knew how hard it was to leave them behind. In particular, Emily had been like a sister to her, which had eased her perpetual loneliness more than she had even realized. Most of the places her father had moved them to had been lonely. Even when she had been invited to events, Imogen had never felt a real part of Society, as they never stayed long enough for that. She'd not had that luxury until they moved to Sheridan, where she had finally felt welcome and wanted by her peers.

Billings was possibly one of the nicest places she had ever lived, yet she did not know how to go about making friends here. There didn't seem to be the regular social events that young people were expected to attend here, though there had to be something, somewhere. She simply did not know where to begin looking for it. She had been too old to attend school for many years now, so could not meet anyone in her daily life, and though she had offered her services at the church, they had told her they had enough volunteers to do the flowers, run the Bible classes on Sundays for the children, and for other things that might need willing hands. It made her feel rather useless, and her days began to blend into one another with no feeling of purpose to fulfill her.

Mama worried about her, and fretted over Papa, and there seemed to be a never-ending round of dinner parties that her parents had to attend, but Imogen was never invited, not even to the ones held in her own home. She was lonelier than she had ever been, and it seemed that there was no way to change that. So, she retreated into her books and her rides, and prayed that something would change soon.

As she rode back into the city that morning, she decided to extend her walk and go through the park. She'd seen a billboard poster for an art exhibition in the pavilion. She doubted she would meet anyone there, but it might at least distract her for an hour. She hitched Barney, her bay gelding, to a post outside the pretty, white-columned pavilion and went inside. A man in burgundy and gold livery stood at the door taking people's coats. Imogen handed him hers and followed an elderly couple ahead of her into a large, high-ceiling room with plain white walls, with elaborate plaster moldings.

The pictures on the walls were quite spectacular. The scenes were all of the same place, a mountain town. Imogen picked up a brochure and read about the collection. She smiled to herself when she saw the name of the town. Eagle Creek. Mr. King's home. If these pictures were in any way an accurate representation of the place, it was no wonder he loved it so. It was stunningly lovely, from the babbling creek to the vast heights of the eagle's mountain top home.

And then there was the picture simply called The Eyrie. It showed a collection of simple-looking buildings, but it was the beauty of all that lay around it that made her catch her breath. No wonder he enjoyed his work so very much. A young man approached her. "It is a hotel," he said. "You can stay there."

"I know, I am acquainted with the maître d'."

"You know Mr. King?"

"Not in person, but I have had reason to write to him a little. Has he seen this picture? I'm sure he would love it very much."

"He has, and he did. He purchased it to hang it in the hotel," the young man said with a smile. "My name is Edgar Greenslade. I have the honor of living in the town, and I painted these pictures." He gestured around the room.

"You are a lucky man to live somewhere so beautiful," Imogen sighed. Eagle Creek was the kind of place she had always dreamed of when she'd pictured a home, somewhere where she might stay and build a life. "Is it truly this lovely?"

"I fear that my lowly talents don't do it justice," Mr. Greenslade said with a rueful smile. "Perhaps you should visit, it is barely a short train ride away. I have been traveling in and back every other day of the exhibition. It is a rather lovely ride, with wonderful views from the locomotive as you travel."

"I have been told that it isn't far," Imogen said. "It would be nice to meet Mr. King in person someday, too."

His words echoed around her head as she viewed the rest of the paintings. If it truly was such a short distance to Eagle Creek by train, why should she not go there one day? She doubted that her mother would notice her gone, and if she did Mama would probably assume that Imogen was just enjoying a longer ride than usual, or that she was tucked away in a library somewhere. But would Mr. King welcome her? They'd barely written one letter each to one another.

When she returned home for lunch, there was a letter from Mr. King waiting for her on the hallway table, but no Mama. Imogen suddenly remembered her mentioning a luncheon with the wives of Papa's clerks. She sat alone in the breakfast room to take her lunch. It was smaller and less imposing than the dining room, and she felt a little less alone in there, surrounded by Mama's many plants. While she waited for the maid to bring her tray, she opened her letter, wondering if she would ever dare tell him how receiving it at this very moment had been so reassuring to her.

Dear Miss Potts

Thank you for your frank and rather delightful letter. I look forward to receiving many more of them in the future. As I cannot make a promise to you that I will never move on from Eagle Creek, I am happy to continue writing as friends with no more purpose than sharing our thoughts and the moments in our lives that bring us happiness, or even sadness should those arise.

I am very glad that you are enjoying Billings. It is a funny city, just twelve years ago it barely even existed, but with the growth of the railroads it expanded very quickly. There was some thought that Coulson would be the place that would benefit most from the railway, but Magic City sprung up instead, and Coulson has faded away.

Thank you for your description of yourself. In similar style, I will tell you that my eyes are hazel, my hair is brown, like yours. I am tall, but not so tall that people have to crane their necks to talk to me. I have to dress very formally for my work, and so when I escape from the hotel, I tend to don the more comfortable denim trousers and Stetson of the cowboy. I am told I am reasonably good looking but I could not possibly comment as to whether the people telling me have good taste or not!

I enjoy dancing and have little concern about the fact that I am terrible at it. I am too clumsy to ever be a good dancer, but I am enthusiastic. I once tried to learn the violin from an old fiddler in the mountains, but it turned out that I have no ear for music, only for a lively beat!

I enjoy walking in the mountains here. I have seen so many wondrous things, but the most spectacular are the eagles. The way they swoop overhead and then suddenly dive to take their prey is something I doubt I will ever tire of seeing. It takes my breath away every single time.

This may seem a little presumptuous of me, but I have business in Billings on October 5th. Would I be permitted to call upon you? Perhaps we might meet for a walk in the park, or for lunch at The Grand? I will be there to discuss some matters with my employer, Mr. Hemsley who owns it and runs it. The dining room is very good indeed.

Please let me know by telegram, if you would like to

meet in person. If not, I do understand. I shall simply look forward to your next letter.

Yours, most hopefully

Bart King

Imogen chuckled to herself. The timing of his invitation could not have been more serendipitous, to arrive on the very day she had considered asking if she might visit him in Eagle Creek. She was glad that he did not seem to be too concerned by the idea of a long and drawn-out campaign of letter writing, that he wanted to meet her in person. She knew that she wished to meet him – though she wanted to see Eagle Creek even more.

She finished the soup and bread that the maid had brought her and declined a dessert before hurrying to the telegram office to wire that she would look forward to his arrival. At last she would have someone to talk to. She had missed it so very much. As she walked slowly back home, she prayed that they would get along, and that they would find much to talk about. She so desperately needed a friend, and even if he did not live in Billings, he was close enough that they might meet regularly if they got on well.

But, as she climbed the steps to her front door, she was gripped by panic. Whatever should one wear to a meeting such as this? She did not want to be overdressed, though she knew that The Grand was rather an upmarket establishment, as she did not wish Mr. King to think she placed a greater emphasis upon their meeting than she did, that she might secretly be hoping he would fall in love with her at first sight. She knew all too well that she was simply not that kind of a girl. Young men simply did not see her and jump straight to thoughts of marriage, though she was not unattractive. She supposed she was just a little too different, a little too forthright, and a lot too bookish for most.

She ran up the stairs to her dressing room and flung open the doors of her armoire. Inside it were all manner of dresses, skirts and blouses. She needed an outfit that she would wear to meet with a friend for lunch, but one that was just a little more flattering to her figure and coloring than if she was meeting Emily or another girlfriend.

She took out dress after dress, holding it up against her body and gazing at it in the cheval glass before throwing it onto the chair behind her. Within an hour, the chair was fairly groaning under the weight of them all and Imogen was staring at it, shocked that she owned so many gowns – and still had not found one that felt like it might be perfect for her meeting with Mr. King. There had to be something in here. She began to try them on properly, before she put them back into the armoire.

She realized quite quickly why there were so many that she barely remembered. Some simply did not suit her at all, and others were so old that she could barely fit in them anymore. As she took them off, she put the ill-fitting dresses in a pile to one side. She was sure that the maids would be delighted to have them and would amend them to suit themselves.

As she gradually tried everything on, she found a beautiful cream silk blouse that she hadn't noticed in her initial panic. It was simple, with a bow at the collar, and would look quite lovely with the brooch that her father had bought her for Christmas last year. But what could she wear with it? It would need a high-waisted skirt, one that would nip in tightly to show her curves. She had a navy blue one somewhere, she was sure of it. She rummaged through the pile on the chair, then thumbed through the dresses hanging back in the armoire, finding it right at the back of the cupboard. She pulled it on and fastened it, then exhaled loudly. It was perfect. Simple, yet understated elegance. Ideal for lunch with a complete stranger.

CHAPTER 7

OCTOBER 5TH, 1894, BILLINGS, MONTANA

Bart was a little distracted during his meeting with Mr. Hemsley. His mind kept wandering, rehearsing the things he might say to Miss Potts when they met in just a few hours' time. "Am I boring you?" Mr. Hemsley teased.

"I'm sorry, Sir," Bart said, shaking his head and trying to refocus on the charts laid out in front of them.

"Somewhere you would rather be?"

"In a way," Bart admitted. "I have been writing to a young lady, and she lives nearby. I shall be meeting her for lunch."

"Well, I hope that your luncheon goes much better for you than this meeting is going for me," Mr. Hemsley said drily, then grinned. "It's not like you to be distracted by a woman, King. She must be rather special."

"I honestly don't know, but her letters are certainly fascinating."

"Try and stay with me for just another half an hour," his employer begged. "Then I'll want to hear all about it over tea this afternoon, before you head back."

Bart nodded his agreement, and the two men went back to discussing Mr. Hemsley's plans for The Eyrie. They involved all kinds of things, from a refurbishment of the grand hallway and the dining room to showing local artists' work in the breakfast room. Some of his ideas Bart could agree would be totally in keeping with The Eyrie, but others he felt wouldn't suit the hotel there, even if they were very successful here in Billings. "I can't agree to themed events. The Eyrie is a place where people come to get away from it all, to experience the peace and quiet and the magnificence of nature," he argued.

"But they work wonderfully here."

"I'm sure they do. You hired me because I have worked in many different places," Bart reminded him. "My experience says that you can do those sorts of things in city hotels, and even in hotels that are barely outside of a big town or city – but The Eyrie is one of a kind. There is nowhere like it, and we need to preserve what makes it special – that there is no insistence that people join in with anything at all, that they are simply left alone to breathe and to be."

Mr. Hemsley nodded. "You are probably right. I've never known anyone to have such a head for our business as you do. But doesn't it get dull for all of you up there? With nothing to do?"

"Oh, there's always plenty to do," Bart corrected him. "And no, it is never dull there. But we attract a different kind of guest at The Eyrie. If you wished to encourage that, perhaps you should be advertising to the wealthy but adventurous types. We could hire trained mountain guides who can arrange expeditions for our guests. At the moment, we only take them on day hikes, but there are many who would like to experience more time in the wilds."

"A wonderful idea," Mr. Hemsley said rubbing his hands. "Will you look into hiring someone? I shall draw up some advertisements for the newspapers and we can look them over when you come next month. We could aim to have it up and running for next summer."

"I shall put the word out locally. There are a few young men I can think of who might be suitable. One is Crow, would that be a problem?"

"Not at all. Might even add to the experience for some, meeting a real live Injun' in the wild." Mr. Hemsley looked delighted by the thought. Bart frowned. His employer often meant well, but his enthusiasm could push him over into the realms of bad taste and even occasionally could cause offense without meaning to. He was a kindly man, though, and thankfully tended to listen to well-reasoned advice.

"I'd rather we didn't advertise it that way. It shouldn't become a gimmick. And it might upset people if they come and are taken out by someone who isn't Crow. Keep it simple, Sir. I think that would be for the best."

"You're probably right, my mind jumped straight to posters of gun fights and such, but of course we cannot do that, though it would be mighty popular."

"I don't want to ruin years and years of cooperation between the Crow and the people of Eagle Creek and the nearby towns," Bart said. "And even more importantly, I don't wish to take anything from the charm and grandeur of The Eyrie itself. Some places need gimmicks and things to keep people interested, our hotel simply doesn't. It sells itself because it isn't trying to be all things to all people."

"Well, you are always fully booked, so you're doing something right," Mr. Hemsley said happily.

He pushed a picture of another hotel in front of Bart. "It's in Livingston. What do you think of it?" he asked.

Bart looked at the pictures and the description and pursed his lips. "It looks like it needs a lot of work," he said finally.

"I know, but the location is great, don't you think? I can always knock down what's there and start again. Livingston is growing fast. It has a railway station and is right on the Yellowstone, so there's great fishing up there."

"It is a little risky, taking on a place like this, but if anyone can make it work, it is you, Sir."

"I was rather hoping I might convince you to help me get things up and running over there?" Mr. Hemsley said hopefully.

"I'd not want to leave The Eyrie," Bart said, though he knew that he might have to do so, sooner or later. He wasn't lying, though, he didn't want to leave the hotel or the place that had become the only home he'd ever known. He truly loved it there, and if he could stay there until his dying day, that would make him happier than almost anything else in the world. But he knew that to hope for such a thing was foolish and complacent of him. He would have to leave someday.

"And I'd not ask it of you. You're the best man to run that place, no doubts in my mind, but your help would be mighty useful in finding the right man, another Bartholomew King perhaps, to run this new one?"

"I'll think on it, if you buy the site," Bart countered which made his employer smile.

"Good lad."

He pulled out a gold pocket watch and checked the time. "Well, my boy, if you're taking a young lady to lunch, you'd best hurry or you'll be late meeting her." Mr. Hemsley grinned. "I hope it goes well. Come and see me before you go back to Eagle Creek, tell me all about it."

Bart agreed and left the office. His stomach was suddenly churning. He doubted he'd be able to eat a thing. He made his way through the narrow corridors that housed

75

the kitchens, storerooms and offices that kept the hotel functioning and ran up the tiny, spiral staircase that would take him up to the rear of the grand lobby. He closed the hidden door behind himself and stood quietly under the stairs, scanning the room for Miss Potts.

It was one of the things he enjoyed about his work, watching people as they passed through the lobby of a hotel. You saw all manner of people, doing all manner of things. Today there was an elderly lady sitting with a young boy at one of the tables to the right of the main desk. She was clearly delighted to be spending time with him, though he did not seem quite so happy about it. She was lavishing him with affection, while he fidgeted uncomfortably in the chair and frowned as she tried to caress his cheek.

A young family sat not far away. The mother looked exhausted, and the father was trying to keep his twin sons entertained by teaching them how to play chess against one another, but as soon as the bell sounded to say that the dining room was open, the two boys were up on their feet, racing to be first into lunch. The father gallantly offered his wife his hand and helped her to get onto her feet, then kissed her hand tenderly before tucking it through his arm. It was rather heartening to see that even after many years of marriage, and two rather riotous young sons, they still found a moment to share their affection.

But the person who interested him the most was the

young lady who had just entered through the front door. One of the bellboys took her coat and the maître d' approached her and bowed decorously. She must have told Mr. Donal that she was here to meet with Bart, because he turned and waved towards him. Bart hurried forward, noticing that her description had not done her justice. She did indeed have chestnut brown hair that gleamed like silk under the soft lights, but she was more than passably pretty. There were pink rosebuds in her cheeks and as he drew nearer, she smiled at him, and he got to see the full charm of her dimples.

"Miss Potts?" he asked, giving her a polite bow. She held out her gloved hand and he took it and kissed the air above it.

"Mr. King?" she confirmed.

Mr. Donal had discreetly left them alone. Bart was impressed by how silently the man had moved. But he was not here to think of the hotel or its running, at least not for now. He smiled warmly at Miss Potts. "At your service," he said.

"Well, I'm rather hoping that you'll get to sit with me, rather than wait on me," she teased. "I didn't come all this way to talk to myself."

"Indeed, you did not. How was your journey here?"

"Much quicker than I expected it to be, and as lovely as you said. I can hardly wait to travel back again, to see it all from another angle." She blushed suddenly as she realized what she had said. "I did not mean to imply that I am in any hurry to get away from you."

"I did not think that you meant that," he assured her as he offered her his arm. "Shall we go in? I have it on good authority that there is a roast rib of beef for lunch today, and we most certainly do not wish to miss it."

"Then lead on, for I am famished and am very partial to roast beef," she said, her dimples flashing again as she grinned broadly.

Bart watched Miss Potts from the corner of his eye. He enjoyed seeing peoples' reactions to the opulence and grandeur of some hotels, and The Grand was one of the most luxurious he'd ever seen. She seemed impressed by it, but not overwhelmed and that told him that she was used to such places. He knew that her father was a highly respected banker, and so she had probably seen many grand homes.

The head waiter sat them down at a table by the window, overlooking the gardens. Much of the autumnal color had already faded, winter often came early to Montana. But the gardeners had planted a number of bushes that had colorful stems so that even once their leaves had fallen, they offered some interest to the eye, all the year round. "Thank you," Miss Potts said as Bart held out her chair and she sat down and laid her napkin in her lap.

Bart took the seat opposite and waited while the waiter poured them both a glass of water. "A glass of sherry?" he asked Miss Potts, who nodded happily.

"Very good," the waiter said and left them alone.

Bart suddenly didn't know what to say. But thankfully, it seemed that Miss Potts was not so tongue-tied. "Is your hotel like this inside?" she asked.

"It is Mr. Hemsley's hotel, as is this one, but no. The Eyrie has a character all its own."

"I'm glad, this is a little ostentatious for my liking," Miss Potts said, then clapped a hand over her mouth. "I am sorry, that is probably very rude of me to say something like that."

"Not at all, I enjoy writing to you for your candor," Bart admitted. "It would be a shame if you were more guarded in person."

"My mother frowns upon me being so candid. A young lady should not be so opinionated, apparently."

"It must be hard to feel that you are disappointing her."

"I have grown used to it. Perhaps it is why she never invites me when they have guests for dinner, she is afraid I might say something I shouldn't."

"You are not even invited when such events happen in your own home?" Bart asked, surprised by such a thing. Surely, a young lady began to learn the skills she would need in Society within her own four walls?

"Then she wonders why I have not yet found a husband," Miss Potts said, seemingly unconcerned by her lot. "But when I am not allowed to meet anyone, it does make it all rather difficult."

"So, that is why you took matters into your own hands?"

"Partly. But mostly because I am so very tired of moving all the time. We never stay anywhere long enough for me to make friends. I am tired of it. As a young woman there are not many options available to me, but marriage is one. It seemed a reasonable place to start."

CHAPTER 8

OCTOBER 5TH, 1894, BILLINGS MONTANA

He really was rather handsome, and disconcerting, with his sparkling, almost golden eyes and impossibly firm jawline. Though he was clad in a business suit, he was every inch the cowboy. Imogen tried to pull herself together. She was being altogether too open, far too quickly. He did not need to hear all about her miserable life. "I'm sorry," she said as the waiter brought over their schooners of sherry. "I'm a little nervous and I tend towards blurting out everything all at once when I am nervous."

"Not at all, do not ever apologize to me for being yourself," he assured her kindly, his eyes twinkling with amusement.

"Tell me of yourself." She encouraged. "I know you have traveled a lot, but where did you start? Do you have any family?"

"My father died not long after I was born, he was a soldier. My mother was with child when he was killed in an Indian raid, and she died in childbirth. My grandmother said it was because she was broken-hearted. I lived with my grandparents until they passed and then I was on my own."

"How old were you?"

"Just nine years old."

Imogen gasped. She had been complaining about not staying anywhere long enough to make friends, and Mr. King had lost everyone he loved and who should have loved him while he was still a child. "I am even more sorry for all I said earlier, now."

"Don't be," he assured her. "I survived and made something of my life, and that is what matters."

"I suppose it is. It must have been very hard for you, though. It makes all you have achieved even more impressive."

He blushed at that and ducked his head away. Imogen thought it rather sweet. But they were both saved from saying anything further for a moment as the waiters wheeled a large tureen of soup towards them and ladled generous servings into their bowls. The soup was rich and thick, and smelled delicious. "Do you wish to say grace?" she asked Mr. King.

"If you do," he said.

"We thank thee, our Father, for this delicious food before us," Imogen said quickly. "We are thankful for our blessings and offer you our gratitude. Amen."

"Amen," Mr. King repeated softly and picked up his spoon and began to slurp his soup noisily.

She laughed. "I do hope you are trying to impress me," she said.

"Just showing off my impeccable manners, I raised myself, after all." He stopped slurping and began scooping the hot soup from the far edge of his plate and sipping at it silently.

"You taught yourself well," Imogen noted. "I don't mind the slurping. I have a terrible tendency towards spillages. And as I am wearing a light blouse today, I will no doubt get something down me."

"You were raised in luxury, you should have better table manners than me," he teased her.

"I know. It is no wonder I am such a disappointment to my mama."

"I'm sure you are not," he said kindly. "Perhaps she is just worried for you."

"You know, I think it might be that she does not wish me to leave home, to remain tied to her and Papa forever. I have been company for her throughout all the moves, a task that has no end. If I am not there, what will she have left to do with her time?"

Mr. King nodded sagely but did not comment. It was a strange thought, and one that had only come to Imogen now, as she sat opposite this very charming man. If Imogen had found it hard to make friends wherever they had moved to, then there could be no doubt that Mama had found the same problem. Having actual friends was very different from being expected to socialize with strangers, the wives of people Papa worked with. Imogen could think of nobody who filled that role in her mother's life, except herself. If Imogen found a husband, she would leave home. Mama would have nobody to stay with her when Papa went on ahead somewhere, nobody to help her pack their lives up again, and nothing much to do when Papa was busy at work. She and Mama had been each other's support and only constant companions. Mama would be lost without her. But now was not the time to think about it.

"How long will you be in Billings?" she asked Mr. King.

"Until this afternoon," he said with a slight frown. "I have already dealt with the matters I needed to."

"That is a shame. There is a play on at the theater tonight, I had rather hoped to attend, but one cannot go alone, and I have met nobody here yet."

"I am sorry," he said softly as he pushed away his empty soup dish.

She finished the last mouthfuls of her own, wishing he might consider staying overnight, but she could not bring herself to actually ask him to do so. But as she laid her spoon in the dish and glanced over at him, she noticed that he was grinning to himself. "What is it?" she asked anxiously checking her blouse for a spill.

"No, you have managed your soup beautifully," he said. "But I know of a young lady, who has a similar problem to your own. Her father owns this hotel, and the one in Eagle Creek, and others all over Montana and Wyoming. They are constantly traveling between them all, and I know she finds it hard to make friends, too. Perhaps I might arrange a meeting with her for you?"

"Would you? That would be wonderful, especially if we actually get along."

"If you will excuse me for just a moment," Mr. King said, getting up from the table. "I shall see if she can meet with us after lunch, if that would suit you?"

"It would be perfect," Imogen said, a little taken aback at his kindness. He hurried through the dining hall and disappeared. She waited, tapping her fingers on the crisp white tablecloth. A waiter appeared to clear their dishes. She watched as he balanced them up his arms rather than stacking them. He made it look terribly easy, but she tried doing so with their side plates once he was gone, and even with such small dishes it was very hard indeed.

Mr. King returned with a smile upon his face. "She will join us for dessert, I hope that will suit you?" he asked. She nodded to him as the maître d' approached their table with the enormous joint of beef. He carved thick slices, brown and crisp on the outside and succulently pink on the inside, as the waiters heaped their plates with crisp roast potatoes, vegetables and a rich sauce made from the juices of the roast.

Imogen took a deep sniff of her plate. Her mouth had never watered so much. She could hardly wait to begin. But she waited for him to take a bite first. She did not wish to seem over-eager. Young ladies weren't supposed to have hearty appetites. He took a bite and smiled. "As good as ever," he said happily.

"You eat here often?"

"I come to Billings every month or two, depending upon whether Mr. Hemsley is traveling somewhere else or not, to discuss his plans for The Eyrie and to talk him out of most of them," Mr. King said with a chuckle.

"You tell your employer what he can and cannot do with his own hotel?"

"I do, because otherwise he would turn them all into this," he said gesturing around them at the opulence of the vast dining room. "He thinks every hotel should offer exactly the same level of luxury and the very same services. It is my job to remind him that different hotels attract different people, so what is needed here in the city will not be what is wanted in Eagle Creek, for example."

"I see, you save him from himself."

"I try to," Mr. King said with a grin. "But I am lucky to

be employed by him. He lets me run The Eyrie much as I wish to."

"You said it isn't like this hotel, but what is it like?"

"Altogether simpler, yet just as comfortable in every way. We have clean, bright walls – none of the ostentatious coving and large paintings. The furniture there is comfortable but modern, rather than the elegant, historical pieces he favors here. Everything at The Eyrie is about showing off what is outside, rather than what is inside, for that is what makes it what it is."

"I so hope I can come and visit it one day," Imogen sighed.

"I do, too. I should very much like to show you around," he said, blushing a little redder this time as he admitted it.

Imogen wanted to take his hand and clasp it tightly. He liked her, and he wanted to see her again. She wanted to tell him how happy that made her, but she did not. She kept her delight inside and took a bite of her roast beef so she wouldn't have to respond to him just yet. They ate in silence for a few minutes, and despite what had just passed between them, it was peculiarly comfortable. It seemed that she had at least found a friend.

Their meal complete, Mr. King got up and went into the lobby. He returned moments later with a pretty young lady, she was perhaps a year or two younger than Imogen, with kind eyes and a shy smile. "Miss Imogen Potts, may I introduce you to Miss Joanna Hemsley?"

Imogen stood up and offered her hand. "Delighted to meet you," she said.

The two women shook hands gingerly. "And you," Miss Hemsley said in timid voice. "Are you quite sure you don't mind me intruding upon your luncheon?"

"Not at all," Imogen assured her. "Please take a seat, I understand we have apple pie and cream for dessert. It should be here any moment."

"It is my favorite," Miss Hemsley said, "and of all my father's hotels, the pie here is definitely the best."

"I understand you have to travel around a lot?" Imogen said.

"Yes, my father is an ambitious man. He wishes to have hotels in every city of the country one day."

"From what Mr. King has told me, he's made a fine start on making good that ambition. It must be hard always traveling, though. I have had to do the same, for my father's work, too."

Miss Hemsley seemed to brighten when she realized that she was talking with someone who understood, and for a few minutes the two young women shared their stories, almost forgetting that Mr. King was still seated with them. "How rude of us," Miss Hemsley noted when she looked up to see Mr. King leaning back in his chair, watching them with a smile on his face. "We've quite left you out of the conversation."

"I don't mind at all. I have achieved my goal. For it

seems that the two of you will have much in common and will be able to call on one another often once I am gone."

Conversation continued to flow, this time including Mr. King, and all three were reluctant to part when the time came to end their meal together. "I apologize to you ladies, but I must leave you now, as I promised to call in upon your father, Miss Hemsley, before I leave, and I have to catch my train home. But Miss Potts suggested a trip to the theater this evening, if you might be interested, Miss Hemsley?"

"The Shakespeare at the Rialto?" Miss Hemsley asked, her eyes open wide.

Imogen nodded. "Yes, I could get us tickets on my way home if you would like to attend?"

"I have wanted to see it for weeks, but Papa has not had the time to take me. I should be delighted, but I will leave you both now, as I am sure you wish to say your goodbyes alone." She gave them an understanding nod and as she turned to go, she gave Imogen a cheeky wink.

"She is charming," Imogen said as she tucked her arm into Mr. Kings' once Miss Hemsley had left the dining room. Together they walked through the tables, nodding and smiling at other guests still eating.

"She is, and the apple of her father's eye, but since her mother passed away a year ago she gets a little lonely as she follows him around everywhere. I don't think I've ever seen her so at ease with anyone, she is terribly shy."

"Well, I shall be glad to be company for her when she is

here in Billings," Imogen said happily. "I cannot thank you enough for thinking of us both this way."

"It has been my pleasure," Mr. King said as they entered the lobby together. "I do hope that we will meet again soon."

"I do, too," Imogen said, trying to keep her fervor from her voice. "Perhaps I might come to Eagle Creek? Miss Hemsley might be encouraged to join me, perhaps." She hoped that by offering up a chaperone that he might more readily agree, though she would really have much preferred to have him all to herself.

"That would be lovely," he said softly. "Write to me soon, we shall make arrangements."

CHAPTER 9

OCTOBER 10TH, 1894, EAGLE CREEK, MONTANA

art had enjoyed his time in Billings much more than usual and was looking forward, impatiently, to the next time he would be called upon to meet with Mr. Hemsley there. Miss Potts had been just as she was in her letters, warm and funny, and very easy to pass the time with. To think that he had feared that they might struggle to find things to talk about! They had hardly stopped talking, and not once had Bart feared that he might have to lie to her about his past, as he'd been easily able to avoid the parts of his story that he'd rather nobody knew about.

The hotel was busy, but he'd already started to look into the idea of running explorational trips into the mountains. It wouldn't suit all of their guests, many people simply came to enjoy the views and to rest, but there was a core group of visitors that enjoyed walking in the mountains and might be interested in a guided service that might take them further afield than they could go when staying in the hotel overnight. He had decided that it would be prudent to try it out with guests he knew he could trust to give him their honest opinions in early May – if he could entice enough of them to come along.

Writing the letter to them, though, trying to outline an experience he had yet to fully define was harder than he'd thought it would be. He needed to be sure of what would be happening first, and that meant he had to find his guides. He needed men who were both skilled at running camping expeditions, and who knew the area around Eagle Creek inside and out. And that meant a trip to the Crow Village. The Crow often went on hunting trips, as well as to their annual horse fair. They were used to packing up entire villages and moving onwards at a moment's notice. And nobody knew the territory here better.

He took one of the horses from the stable and rode up the track that led him over the mountain and down into the valley beyond. Normally when he came this way, he dallied a little, enjoying the views and the moments of peace away from the busyness of the hotel. But today he did not have time to spare, if he intended to return before dark. It was already past noon, and it would take more than an hour's ride to get there.

He urged his mount forward on the flatter parts of the path, but let the sure-footed animal pick its own way down the steep, rocky parts. Since the early summer, most of the horses at The Eyrie were from the herds of The Crow, and they were hardy beasts with excellent natures, calm and placid enough for the most nervous riders, yet they could all go fast and had excellent stamina to suit those who wished for a mount with a little spirit.

Mr. Hemsley had been reticent to change all of the animals in his stable when Bart had suggested it in the springtime, but with so many guests needing to go into town to the public stables in search of an animal with more speed if they wanted that, they were losing money and goodwill. When he'd stocked the stable originally, Mr. Hemsley had chosen safe animals, who would be unlikely to throw a rider. He hadn't wanted people to blame the hotel, should accident or injury occur. But people wanted what they wanted, and they would rather leave directly out of the hotel than have to travel into Eagle Creek first before they set off for a day of adventure. And it cost a lot of money to stable horses not their own when guests wished to keep the same animal for more than a day.

The air was definitely growing colder. Bart could feel a touch of ice in the wind as it cut against his cheeks. Winter would soon be upon them and there would be snow all around them for many months. Bart didn't mind the cold, he even rather liked the snow, but the dark mornings and long nights sometimes made him feel a little lonely. He often watched as couples and families would crowd around the fire in the evenings at the hotel, often playing games or just reading together and it made him wish he had someone to go home to at the end of a long day, someone who would read to him. He didn't really remember what it was like to be a part of a family, he'd been alone for so very long now.

The wind had whipped up and was whistling past his ears loudly as he reached the Crow Village. He dismounted and entered on foot, nodding politely to people as he passed by on his way to the home of Many Birds and his son, Walks With The Sun. The lad was busy hammering shoes for one of their horses in a small smithy. "Are you not working in town anymore?" Bart asked him with a smile.

"Jonas helped me build my own smithy here," Walks With The Sun said proudly, looking around his small domain. "He says I'm good enough at these sorts of things to be trusted here alone, and it saves my people time as they don't have to go to Eagle Creek."

"I don't see many horses that have been shod here," Bart said looking around.

"The older ones, they don't hold with this sort of thing," Walks With The Sun said with a grin. "They say a horse can take care of his own feet, but when I've shown men like my father and my friends the benefits to the horse of good hoof care and a well-made shoe, well, they're starting to come around."

"How much longer do you have of your apprenticeship?"

"Only another year and a half."

"And will you continue to work with Jonas once you are finished?"

"He hopes I'll have enough customers here. He's proud that one of his apprentices has their own smithy before they've finished their training, but I hope he'll always be pleased to see me when I need his advice."

"I am sure that he will. He is very fond of both you and Jake. He'll miss you."

"I shall miss him."

"Is your father here?" Bart asked.

"He's meeting with the tribe council. Chief Plenty Coups called them in a little over two hours ago. They'll probably be finishing up soon. You could walk over to the council lodge to meet him."

"Thank you, I will."

The council lodge was right at the heart of the village, with a large open space outside it where the tribe held social events and important meetings that concerned the entire village. To be voted onto the council was a huge honor for any man, and Many Birds' joining the venerable elders of the tribe must have happened quite recently, for he'd not mentioned it to Bart before. But Many Birds was quite a modest man and he'd probably not think to do so, either.

Bart entered the council lodge as it was too cold to wait outside. There was a small outer chamber with a roaring fire. Bart warmed himself by it. He could hear a murmur of voices from the council chamber next door but could not hear any one particular voice. It amazed him that The Crow seemed to manage their affairs with so few raised voices. Bart had seen the town council in Eagle Creek discuss matters, and he'd definitely have heard every word of that, had he been in the building next door, let alone in a chamber separated only by thick hide walls.

Bart waited for fifteen minutes and was contemplating leaving so he would get back to the hotel before dark, when the council members began to drift out. Some gave him odd looks, one old man gave him a malevolent stare, but Many Birds and Chief Plenty Coups both welcomed him warmly. "How may we be of use to you, Mr. King?" the chief said once he'd embraced Bart.

"I was rather hoping that I might, in a way, be of use to The Crow, for once. I need to employ a couple of young men."

"Well, we are always glad to see anyone who will offer our young men work," Plenty Coups said with a wink. "What will they be doing?"

"I have an idea to run expeditions, for the guests. Camping overnight, trekking into the wilder parts of our beautiful territory," Bart explained. "I can think of no better guides than The Crow."

"My son's best friend, Rises With Joy, is an excellent climber and tracker," Many Birds said. "He had a place at the college, but none of the trades they offered there suited him. He needs to be outside."

"He's as much a part of the landscape here as the mountains themselves," Plenty Coups agreed. "And there is Helps with Honor, he's not the tracker that Rises With Joy is, but he can break camp and re-erect one in the flash of an eye."

"They sound perfect for what I have in mind," Bart said. "Would you be able to send them to me at the hotel, tomorrow if they are interested? I would like to meet with them and get their ideas."

"I shall call on them both," Many Birds said with a smile. "They'll both be glad to have work, but even happier that they don't have to go into town for it. They belong out here. Like you do, Mr. King."

"I'm not sure I belong anywhere," Bart said with a smile, though he was secretly rather touched by the compliment.

"Oh, I think you've found your place," Chief Plenty Coups said sagely. "You just have to decide to follow your heart and not your head."

Feeling a little perturbed by the uncanny way that the chief seemed to be able to look into his soul, Bart made his goodbyes and set off back to the hotel. Dusk was drawing in as he left his mount in the stables and he was glad to have made it back before it grew too dark to see. A small pile of letters waited for him on his desk. He warmed his hands by the stove for a few minutes before sitting down and picking up his letter knife.

He put the bills in one pile to be paid the next day, the letters of introduction from the staffing agencies in Billings he'd written to asking if they could find him an experienced housekeeper in another, and he smiled to himself as he recognized Miss Potts' handwriting on the final one. He cut it open with extra care and unfolded the letter. Its slight scent of roses wafted up from the paper. Bart wondered if she'd sprayed the paper intentionally, or if it was just something that had rubbed from her wrists as she wrote. He held it to his nose and breathed in the heady aroma.

Dear Mr. King,

I cannot thank you enough for inviting me to lunch with you. I had the most wonderful time, and I am more than grateful that you introduced me to dear Joanna. We have been having the most wonderful adventures together.

We went to the play I told you about that very evening. It was wonderful, the actors were some of the finest I have ever seen. Joanna had never seen a Shakespeare play in the theater, though she had studied them so often that she knew every line by heart. Can you imagine? I am terribly impressed, and very happy I was able to take her to see it. She said it came alive for her in a way it never had before. We will be going to every performance we can together now!

I must confess that I was terribly nervous about meeting

you, but it was wonderful, wasn't it? You do not need to agree with me, of course, but I hope that you enjoyed yourself as much as I did? I can think of few people I have found it so easy to converse with, and none that I felt I could simply be my truest self with before. And now, I have two of you.

At least, I hope I do, and that your asking me to write to you was not your way of fobbing me off quietly, so you do not have to write to me again? But you did say that you wished to make arrangements for me to come to Eagle Creek, and I am hoping that you truly meant that. For Joanna and myself have hardly talked of anything else.

Of course, she has been there before with her father, but she talks of it in similar terms of delight and rapture as you do. I think she would much prefer to stay there while her father travels between his hotels, but he insists that she accompany him everywhere. She is considering placing an advertisement of her own, so she might not have to travel anymore! Her saying so made me feel terribly guilty, as if I had perhaps put the idea in her head, but she assures me that she has been thinking that it is time she found a husband, and her father seems to have little intention of looking for one for her.

But back to our visit. Would you mind if we came on Friday the 19th? I am not sure I can wait any longer. I meant to wait a little longer before writing to you and I could not, I am writing this just two days after our meeting. I know I

*should feign disinterest, but I have never been much good at
that. I so long to see your mountains.*

*Write to me quickly or send me a telegram. Please tell
me that you will be glad for us to visit you?*

Yours most excitedly

Imogen Potts

Her words made Bart smile. She was so enthusiastic
about life. Given all the time she had spent alone, how often
she'd felt out on the edge of everything, she still had such
hope that things would be different for her. She truly made
the most out of her life, in whatever way she could. It
impressed him and made him wish he'd perhaps been bolder
in his own life, but Miss Potts did not have the stain of his
past hanging around her neck like a noose, just waiting to be
pulled tight. Bart rubbed at his neck. There was not a day
that went past that he didn't feel it chafing at him, and there
was not a single night when as he tried to sleep that his last
moments on a gallows did not fill his dreams.

CHAPTER 10

OCTOBER 19TH, 1894, EAGLE CREEK, MONTANA

Imogen could barely bring herself to wait for the train to come to a stop in the tiny station of Eagle Creek. She turned the handle and pushed the door open and gasped as she saw the train still moving over the gravel bed of the line. She stood back and held on tightly to her suitcase. Finally, the train came to a groaning halt, and she jumped down onto the platform, then turned to offer Joanna her hand. Her friend was a little more hesitant, but they were soon running through the station and out onto the street of the town Imogen had heard so much about.

Eagle Creek was like nowhere she'd ever been before, yet it was exactly like every small town that she'd ever passed through on her many travels. A long, single street where all the shops and other enterprises a town needed ran for over a mile. No doubt it had been all there was, once, but now there were streets behind Main Street, businesses had set themselves up with workshops away from the hustle and bustle of the town, and it was surprisingly busy.

They seemed to have arrived on market day. Imogen knew she should wait at the station for Mr. King to collect them, but her impatience to see everything was winning over any glimmer of pragmatism she might possess. "Oh look," she cried, skipping towards a stall selling woven baskets of all sizes. "I must buy one for Mama."

Joanna frowned, shook her head, then gave in to Imogen's obvious delight. "We should wait," she cautioned as she followed her friend.

"I know, but Mr. King will find us. Perhaps we should leave word with the station master?"

"I'll go," Joanna said with a smile. "You buy your basket. I'll find you in a moment. Do not go too far." She gave Imogen the kind of look one gave a small child. It made Imogen laugh.

She turned back to the stall. There didn't seem to be anyone around, then Imogen saw the derriere of the stall-holder sticking out from under the table. "Excuse me? How much for this lovely rainbow-colored one?" she asked politely.

The person emerged from under the table and Imogen was surprised to see a rather wizened-looking Indian lady.

The woman smiled at her, her teeth sparkling white. "I am glad you like it," she said, taking the basket from Imogen. "One dollar, thirty-five, for such a pretty lady."

"That seems remarkably good value for such a well-made item. Did you make it yourself?" Imogen took out her purse and counted out the coins for the woman.

"Not this one, but many of them. The ladies of The Crow like to make colorful things." She directed Imogen towards a small table to the side of all the baskets filled with beaded jewelry, purses and other small items. They were exquisitely made, and the patterns were very intricate.

"The Crow? That is the name of your people?"

"Yes, we live the other side of the mountain."

"And do all these images have special meanings?"

"Some do, some are just beautiful," the lady said.

She glanced over Imogen's shoulder and smiled at someone behind them. "Enjoy looking. I shall return in a moment."

But Imogen turned too, when she heard the amused voice of Mr. King. "Good day to you Strikes The Iron, how lovely to see you here today. Another fine display of Crow beadwork and baskets, I see."

"Mr. King, how can I help you and Miss Hemsley today? I have some of those bracelets you liked so much last time you were here, Miss Hemsley."

Miss Hemsley politely looked at the bracelets as Imogen turned to smile at Mr. King. "I am afraid that Mr. King and

Miss Hemsley are here to fetch me, rather than to buy one of your lovely things," Imogen said apologetically. Strikes The Iron chuckled and nodded her head knowingly as she looked between Imogen and Mr. King.

"Good day to you, Mr. King," Imogen said, suddenly feeling a little shy.

"I do hope that you haven't spent every penny of your allowance on Strikes The Iron's lovely baskets, Miss Potts," he said with a warm smile of welcome.

"Strikes The Iron, that is your name? It is quite unusual."

The Indian lady smiled at her. "There is a story as to why it became my name," she explained. "Perhaps, if Mr. King ever brings you to our village, I will tell you the story. Crow names all have a story. The story is more important than the name to us."

"What a lovely thing," Imogen said. "I doubt there was anything more to my naming than that it was a name my parents could agree upon liking."

Strikes The Iron smiled. "Mr. King, please bring your friend and dear Miss Hemsley to visit with us in the village. We would be delighted to welcome her."

"I'm afraid she'll not be here long enough this time as these two lovely ladies will be leaving to return to Billings in just a few short hours, but perhaps it is a trip we can plan for another time," Mr. King said apologetically.

"Oh, we must," Imogen said fervently. "I would so love

to see how you make all these beautiful things and hear your name story."

Mr. King ushered her and Joanna away from the stall. "What would you like to do?" he asked them. "I have brought the carriage so we might go up to The Eyrie for lunch, but would you perhaps like to see more of Eagle Creek first?"

"I would, though I can hardly wait to see your hotel, too."

Mr. King smiled indulgently at her. "As a woman, you no doubt wish to browse every market stall so, if you will forgive me, I will leave you to do so while I call at the postal office. I have a number of telegrams and packages to send. Shall we perhaps meet outside the station in half an hour?"

Imogen and Joanna nodded happily, linked arms and began to meander amongst the many stalls. It was very impressive how many were there, and the quality of the goods on sale. There were farmers selling their produce, ranchers selling calves and steers, sheep farmers selling wool and mutton and even a stall selling honey, candles and furniture wax all made from the products of the gentleman's hives. She purchased some of the honey for her father, who loved to slather it on bread for breakfast every morning, and she purchased her mother a lovely, lace shawl from a young woman set up opposite the church. She also couldn't resist a new hat from the milliner's shop, or some delicious looking pastries from the bakery.

As they wandered along, Imogen also took note of the shop windows, in particular the dressmakers'. Their window was by far the prettiest, with a fine display of beautifully draped fabrics and a gown that might more likely be found in a fashionable store in New York. "That is lovely," Joanna said. "Mrs. Albert was good, but since Mrs. Algood came to work for her, the gowns are spectacular. I've had a number made here."

"And you always look quite lovely," Imogen said sincerely. "I had always assumed that you perhaps got them made in Chicago, or somewhere further east as they are always so fashionable. Next time I come, I shall definitely be calling upon them."

The clock above the town hall struck the half hour. "We must hurry and meet Mr. King," Imogen said. "And finally, I shall see The Eyrie in all its splendor."

Mr. King was waiting patiently beside an open carriage. He smiled as he saw Imogen's many packages. "I see the traders have done well this morning," he teased.

She flushed. "Well, everything looked so wonderful. I know I shouldn't have bought so much, but most of the things are gifts for others and not for myself."

He offered her his hand and she climbed into the carriage. He tucked a thick fur blanket around her knees and tucked a hot brick by her feet, then helped Joanna up and bundled her up warmly, too. "I thought you'd want to see as much as possible, but there is a chill in the air today.

I think we may even see some snow before the month is out."

"I cannot imagine how perfect Eagle Creek would look in the snow," Imogen said with a sigh as he took his seat on the driver's perch.

"If you are up early enough to see it before everyone else, it is quite idyllic, I suppose," Joanna said. "But the snow soon turns to slush – and then freezes into hard ice. It is quite treacherous."

"Have you been here often in the winter?" Imogen asked her.

"Three times, I think," her companion said thoughtfully. "It is beautiful up at The Eyrie, but you can barely leave the hotel as the snow is so thick. I have to bring a lot of books with me when we come."

"I don't think you've been here since we purchased the sleighs, have you?" Mr. King asked her.

Joanna shook her head. "Papa told me about them, of course."

"Well, they are wonderful. We have smaller sleds, pulled by dogs, for the more adventurous guests, so they can continue to explore wherever they wish, and the horse-drawn ones which come down to the town daily, and take people out for rides along paths that we clear as much as we can. It has changed the winter experience completely."

"I can imagine, and it sounds much nicer than staying in by the fire," Joanna agreed. "I shall have to come with Papa when he visits before Christmas, perhaps. Do they still have the night market, with the mulled wine and cider a few weeks before?"

"We do," Mr. King said. "Perhaps you might like to come and purchase some more gifts, Miss Potts. It is a very convivial evening, with music and dancing."

"It sounds quite wonderful. Perhaps you might book us a room in the hotel so we might attend?" she said, looking at Joanna who nodded eagerly.

"I shall check our availability as soon as we return," Mr. King assured her. "But in the meantime, perhaps you might like to see what is here now. You've already missed the deer in the woods as we turned onto this road."

"There was a deer? Why did you not mention it before?" Imogen cried, turning to look back behind them.

Mr. King laughed. "No, they tend not to come down so close to the town," he assured her. "But I wanted to remind you that you came here to see the town, not simply to plan your next shopping trip."

"You are quite mean," she said, pouting just slightly, but she couldn't stay mad at him for long as he began to point out all manner of flora and fauna. He was very knowledge-able, and she found listening to his passion on the subject of his home utterly fascinating. She could listen to him talk endlessly.

"You know, I never think of there being much to see at

this time of year," she told him. "But there seems to be an abundance of activity here."

"All the animals are stocking up, preparing for winter. It is their busiest time as they scavenge for the last nuts and berries they can find," Mr. King said.

"The squirrels are funny, aren't they? The way they look around to be sure nobody is watching them before they take a nut or try and bury it. What happens, do you think, if they forget where they hid their stash of food?"

"They think of that," Joanna said with a smile. "Because the landscape has so few features in the snow, they bury their nuts in many places, so that there is always a good chance they will find something when they dig."

Mr. King drove them around a bend and pointed ahead. "Your first glimpse of The Eyrie," he said proudly.

"Oh my," Imogen said with a happy sigh as the collection of buildings emerged. They had been designed and built most carefully, in keeping with the simple log cabin structures common in the mountains, and even in the town itself. A large wooden platform looked out over panoramic views of the mountains, and down into the valley below. But the most magnificent thing of all were the three eagles circling overhead.

They were high over the heads of the small party in the carriage, yet it was clear just how magnificent they were. Their vast wingspans held them in the current until they spied their prey and dived with pinpoint accuracy, rising with something small and furry in their cruel talons. It was barbaric and brutal, but breathtaking. "Oh my," Imogen said again, shaking her head. "I don't think I have ever seen anything quite so spectacular in my life."

Mr. King and Joanna smiled indulgently at her. "You will see that sort of thing two or three times, at least, every day here," Joanna said. "But it certainly does not ever get dull."

"It definitely does not," Mr. King agreed.

CHAPTER 11

OCTOBER 19TH, 1894, EAGLE CREEK, MONTANA

Miss Potts made lots of polite comments as he gave her the tour of the hotel, but it was clear that though she was impressed with it, she would much rather be outside, enjoying the incredible views. He was incredibly thankful that the sun had come out for her first visit, and though it was cold, the sky was blue and only occasionally marred by fluffy white clouds. He tried very hard to ensure that he included Miss Hemsley in everything, though it would be all too easy to just talk endlessly with Miss Potts.

He simply could not remember ever having had such a connection with anyone. They could talk about almost anything, and they laughed together all the time. She was so funny, so quick and she reacted with good humor to his teasing. So many young women were all too serious, he had found, some even putting on a show of disdain for everything around them – but not her. She was happy to show her delight, and the expression on her face when she saw something wonderful made his heart skip a beat, so wide-eyed and full of excitement was she.

They dined out on the deck, wrapped up warmly in furs and with hot bricks at their feet. The meal was delicious, and Bart couldn't help wondering if the inimitable Cook, the Denny's cook, had been in this morning, teaching his own cooks some of her secrets, for he was sure that their beef pot pie had never tasted so delicious before now. But then again, it could be that he was simply having the most wonderful day, and everything seemed to be better than it had ever been before.

"Thank you for this," Miss Potts said, as she pushed away her dessert bowl. "It has been the most wonderful afternoon, but perhaps it would be prudent for Joanna and myself to return to Eagle Creek shortly. We don't want to miss our train home."

"The time has flown far too quickly," Bart said sadly. "But I shall call for the carriage to be brought around." He beckoned to one of the waiters and whispered in his ear. The lad nodded and hurried off out of sight.

"When will I see you again?" Miss Potts asked, and Bart

felt a sudden pang of guilt. He longed to say that he would do all he could to travel to Billings to see her within the next week or two, but a part of him knew he should not let either of them get too emotionally attached. He needed to be cautious. He did not wish to cause Miss Potts any hurt, and he feared that if they grew closer, things could only end in disaster for them both.

"I shall be busy here until after Thanksgiving," he told her, truthfully. "I doubt I'll be able to get away."

"Then perhaps we might travel here again," Miss Potts said, turning to Miss Hemsley who nodded eagerly. "You must have some time to yourself, at least occasionally?"

"Before Thanksgiving, and while preparing for Christmas?" Bart said, trying to keep his tone light and playful. "I should be so lucky. But we could arrange a room for you to come for the Christmas market, if you'd like to come to that?"

Her expression reflected all that Bart felt inside, she was clearly disappointed that she would not see him again for so long, but she was trying hard to be reasonable and understanding of his predicament. "We would like that, very much," she said with a forced smile. "Wouldn't we, Joanna?" Her companion nodded happily.

The drive back into Eagle Creek was a rather somber affair. Miss Potts gazed out at the landscape with sad eyes, and though he and Miss Hemsley tried to maintain a jolly conversation, it felt forced. Bart hated that he had been the one to ruin the special time that they had enjoyed but, in his heart, he knew it was for the best if Miss Potts did not grow too attached to him. She longed for a stable home, a husband who would take care of her. He was not sure he would ever be able to offer her what she wanted, though he longed to be able to. He could think of nobody he would rather spend every day of the rest of his life with.

It was painful waving goodbye to them from the platform. Miss Potts looked so sad as she gazed out of the window. Bart could see Miss Hemsley comforting her as the train left the station and was glad that she had a friend with her to lessen the blow of their parting. He did not know how it had all happened so swiftly, but it seemed that she had feelings as strong as his own, and that was not a good thing.

He walked out of the station slowly, lost in his thoughts, but as he pushed the door open a wanted poster on the wall beside it stopped him in his tracks. He let the door swing shut and took a few steps closer to the poster on the notice-board. Bart would know those dark eyes anywhere, and the sight of them, here in Eagle Creek, brought a chill to his bones. Marty Fitzgibbons was clearly still alive and was wanted for robbing a bank just across the state border, in Wyoming, as well as other crimes. He'd clearly not mended his ways and was drawing closer to Bart after all these years.

So far, he'd been able to outrun his past, but it looked like that might be about to change. In all these years he'd heard nothing of the leader of the little gang he'd once been a part of. He'd come to believe that Marty must have been killed when the sheriff and his deputies had caught them in the act of robbing the bank in Deadwood, but the wily devil had gotten away somehow. Bart had no clue how he'd been keeping watch and there had been nowhere to run, once the sheriff and his men had arrived.

Bart drove up to the hotel at breakneck speed. His heart was racing. He would have to leave immediately. He could not risk drawing Fitzgibbons here, and he most certainly did not wish to be caught for a crime he'd barely even committed all those years ago. The bank in Eagle Creek would be just the kind of place that Marty had always liked the best, full of money and gold. If it wasn't already on Fitzgibbons' list of targets, it soon would be. Bart couldn't bear to think of him coming here and taking everything that the kindly people around him had worked so hard for – and the thought of him hurting Byron Macomber and the clerks at the bank, or putting Sheriff Hale and his volunteer deputies at risk, pounded unrelentingly in his skull.

There was nothing he could do to stop Marty, if he'd decided that Eagle Creek was ripe for the plucking, but he could protect himself. He could run, this very night, and never look back, as he had done so many times before. Leaving the carriage outside the back door of the hotel, he hurried to his rooms and pulled out a traveling bag from under the bed and began stuffing things inside it. He grabbed his shaving things from the washstand and stared at himself in the mirror above it. He could only barely make out the features of the boy he had once been. Would Marty even recognize him now? Why should anyone else see that scared lad in the man that he had become?

He had so much to lose here. Eagle Creek was his home, the only one he had ever let himself have, and he'd not meant to let this town slip into his heart any more than he had any of the others. Yet somehow it had, as had the kindness of the people here. He'd barely let himself make any real friends, but he knew that everyone in town would turn out for him if he needed them. And now there was Peter, and Mr. Hemsley, and Miss Potts – and suddenly it was impossible for him to just up and leave.

How could he just go in the middle of the night and not say goodbye to his friend? How could he leave at one of the most important times of the year at the hotel and leave Mr. Hemsley without anyone to run it? How could he break Miss Potts' heart and his own by leaving before he knew what could be between them? It would be cowardly to go, but it put every one of them at risk if he did not. And he could not bear it if they came to despise him if the truth came to light.

So, what should he do? Should he stay or should he go? Neither was an easy choice. Neither was without risk. So, he asked himself another question, whilst looking himself square in the eyes in the mirror. What did he want to do? The answer to that was much easier. He wanted to stay. He wanted to continue his courtship of Miss Potts, and perhaps one day make her his wife. He wanted to make The Eyrie the envy of every hotelier in the land. And he wanted to raise children who loved this place as much as he did.

But there were so many reasons that his hopes were unreasonable. If the truth came to light, the worst that could come to pass would be that he was tried and hanged for his youthful crimes. But if Fitzgibbons found him, the noose might seem a welcome respite. Bart had failed the gang. He'd not been able to alert them to the danger, and he had fled once he'd seen that the game was up. The lads who'd been caught were too stupid not to tell the sheriffs everything, and so Bart had been in no doubt that there was a wanted poster with his face on it somewhere, even if it was long forgotten now.

He sank down onto his bed and cradled his face in his hands. What was he doing? He had no proof that Fitzgibbons had even crossed into Montana. What reason did he have to come here? Surely, if he'd even bothered to look for Bart in the past, he must have given up hope of finding him by now? And he needed to remember that he was no longer a frightened boy, but a man in the prime of his life. Marty would be getting older, slower and his strength would be fading. There was no reason to think that Marty himself was any risk to Bartholomew King, at all.

Could he wait it out? Bart wasn't sure. The chances that everything would work out for him as he wanted them to, meant he had to at least try. If he didn't, he'd always regret it, he knew that. And leaving Miss Potts and the life he led here would be the biggest regrets of his life. But would he lose them anyway, if the truth came out? Would anyone here forgive him for his lies and deception of them for all these years?

He unpacked his bag and shoved it back under the bed. He put his things away neatly then went downstairs and took the carriage back to the stable yard. He unhitched the horse from the shafts and rolled the carriage back into its stall, then removed the animal's harness and brushed him down. These simple acts helped to soothe him, and his thoughts slowed. With each stroke of the brush, he was more certain that it was time to stop running. If he had to face the consequences for that, so be it. But he would not keep living his life in fear, always looking over his shoulder for the danger that might come.

He had to have faith that all he had done to change his life since those days counted for something. He had made something of himself, despite his pitiful start in life. And he prayed that those who knew him and trusted him would remember the man he had become, and not condemn him for the boy he once was. He knew that their good opinion of him would matter if he ever found himself in front of a judge.

Miss Potts' lovely face danced through his thoughts, and he prayed, especially, that she could forgive him. Part of him longed to tell her the truth now, so that there were no secrets between them, but he could not bear the thought of losing her. He had certainly not intended it to happen and had never expected to fall so hard and so fast, but he knew that he loved her with all his heart. He could not lose her, not yet, and he never wanted her to look at him with anything other than the delight they had shared today.

CHAPTER 12

OCTOBER 30TH, 1894, BILLINGS, MONTANA

"Have you seen those terrible posters everywhere?" Joanna said as she took the seat opposite Imogen in the tea rooms. Imogen gave her a puzzled look. Joanna pointed towards the notice board behind the counter, where a number of wanted posters had been pinned.

"Oh, those. They always seem to make men look meaner and more dangerous than they possibly can be, don't you think?"

"I don't know. We were held up by a highway bandit once, when I was traveling with Papa some years ago," Joanna said and shuddered at the memory of it. "They looked even meaner than those posters do."

Imogen nodded. "My father's bank was robbed when we lived in Deadwood. I didn't see them, I was far too young and was at home with my mother, but the poster of the gang leader was particularly frightening, if I remember rightly." She glanced back at the posters behind the counter. "I know it is probably my mind playing tricks upon me, but I'd swear that one of those men was the one I was so afraid of back then. But they probably all look somewhat alike. He'd be unlikely to still be at large, surely, after all this time?"

"You'd hope he'd have been caught long ago. But there is something about the one in the middle's eyes. They chill me to the bone."

"That's the one that looks familiar to me," Imogen said. "The way Papa always described him, and the image of him they put onto the posters gave me nightmares when I was a girl, it was as if he were the devil incarnate to my impressionable mind – and I think to Papa's, too. He's never been the same since."

"That is sad. Is that why you move around so much, do you think?"

Imogen nodded. "I think my father never really got over what happened. He blames himself, and so doesn't ever wish to have the responsibility of running a branch himself again or stay anywhere long enough for robbers to strike." She paused for a moment, thinking how to explain something that made so little sense to her. "You know, he is so well studied on matters of security, and he ensures every bank that he gets set up has the very best equipment, staff and procedures in place to manage anything that might occur. You'd think that knowing all that and knowing that everything is as secure as it can be would put his mind at ease, but it never does. He is always sure that there is more to be done."

"That sounds oddly tiring, to always be so alert to danger."

"It is, I think. And he barely sleeps, and eats like a bird. But it seems to work for the bank. The branches he establishes are the safest in the plains and the northwest."

"Any employer would be glad of that."

"They are, but I know that Mama and I are sick of always moving onwards. It is hard to be a woman, always following a man around that way."

"And we must do so," Joanna said and sighed. "But you have Mr. King now, and I cannot imagine him anywhere other than Eagle Creek and The Eyrie."

"I certainly do not have Mr. King," Imogen protested, as an image of his smiling face banished almost all other thoughts from her mind. It was so hard to remain worried for her father or concerned for her mother when she thought about him.

"But you do hope to make him yours," Joanna teased.

Imogen felt her face flush and it annoyed her that she could be so easily distracted by a man. She nodded and sighed like the silly girl she'd become. "Oh, I most certainly do hope that," she admitted. "But I fear that there is a long road to tread before I can even begin to hope that there might be a proposal. I always feel that he is about to tell me something, and then he doesn't. His letters always hint at his moving around a lot, and I fear that the next one I receive will be telling me that he must go to Canada or to Texas or somewhere equally foolish."

"I do hope not," Joanna said, looking surprised she would say such a thing. "My father would be heartbroken if he were to leave. Mr. King is quite his favorite, you know – and Papa rarely trusts any of the people who work for him as he does Mr. King. He visits them all, all the time – but since Mr. King came, we've barely visited The Eyrie at all."

"That is quite a compliment."

The maid appeared with a tray of sandwiches, cakes and other sweet treats, a pot of tea, a bowl of lemon slices and a jug of milk. Imogen smiled at her as she put each item down on the table, then bobbed a curtsey to them. "Thank you," Imogen said softly, which made the girl blush as she hurried away.

"I wonder if anyone else ever notices her," Joanna said, as Imogen picked up the pot.

"Lemon or milk?" she asked.

"Lemon, please," Joanna said picking up the tiny silver tongs that sat in the small bowl of lemon slices and added some to her cup. "Do you want some?"

"Yes, please." Joanna added some to Imogen's cup, too, and then Imogen poured the hot, golden liquid into the cups.

Joanna added a lump of sugar to hers and stirred it vigorously. Imogen simply dunked the lemon slices four times, then squeezed her spoon against them. She picked up her cup and took a sip. "Delicious."

"I do not know how you bear it without sugar," Joanna laughed.

"I've not got much of a sweet tooth, though I could eat the entirety of one of the chocolate cakes they make here."

"All sixteen slices?"

"All sixteen. It is quite the most delicious thing. But I'd probably feel rather queasy after just two, so I doubt that I will ever attempt it."

The two young women giggled as they helped themselves to the dainty sandwiches. They ate in companionable silence, and then resumed chattering for a few moments before taking a slice of cake each. Their weekly teas had come to mean a lot to them both. They were happy occasions when they planned their excursions for the week. As they finished their food, they both pulled out their day planners from their reticules and opened them ready.

Today, Imogen had news of an orchestra from London, in England, who were touring all of America. "They are supposed to be quite wonderful, my mother even said that they were sublime," Imogen explained.

"It sounds perfect. Shall I get us tickets? I believe it is my turn."

Imogen nodded. "And there is the exhibition at the museum," she said. "It closes on Friday, so if we mean to catch it, we should go soon."

"Would tomorrow suit you? In the afternoon?"

"I have an appointment, I'm afraid, with Mama. But I could manage Wednesday at any time."

"Wednesday morning would suit me best," Joanna said. "I have to have lunch with Papa at the hotel afterwards. Would you care to join us?"

"That would be lovely, if you think he wouldn't mind?"

"He'd be delighted. He is growing very fond of you."

"I'm glad. I rather like him, too."

They soon realized that there was not much of the week left, as Joanna would be attending Mrs. Walton's card party on Thursday evening and the Haverham's ball on Friday, neither of which Imogen would be permitted to attend. While her parents seemed happy to let her go to an afternoon tea with Joanna, or to the theater or a concert occasionally if they got tickets for a matinee performance, Imogen knew that they would never permit her to go to any evening functions, either with or without them. But since becoming friends with Joanna, her now dear friend had done all she could to ensure that Imogen met as many of their peers at the many afternoon events they were free to go to. Imogen finally felt as though she had friends and was not alone.

Their planning for the week complete, they put their planners away and returned to the most important part of their meeting. Gossip. "Did you hear that Samantha Goode is to be wed," Joanna said, shaking her head. "Her father chose for her, poor girl. The man is an oaf, with bad breath and his buttons are always bursting as his belly is too big."

"Poor Samantha, and she is so quiet and timid, she'll never even think to protest. I am so lucky that my father does not seem to wish to marry me off – though I fear that may be because Mama has talked him out of it. I often think she wishes to keep me close, for I am her only friend. I worry she will come to be envious of you, as we spend so much time together and she is all alone in that big house."

"She has not led an easy life, has she, your poor Mama? Have you told her about Mr. King at all?"

"What is there to tell?" Imogen asked. "At the moment we are little more than correspondents."

"Have you not heard from him since our visit?"

"No, though I console myself that he did say that he was very busy. I keep wondering if perhaps my last letter has gone missing, and that is why I have had no reply yet, but then I begin to fret that he no longer wishes to speak to me, that his fobbing me off about another visit before December was his polite way of saying he doesn't really like me."

"I think we can discount the latter," Joanna assured her. "He clearly cares for you a great deal. He was so full of delight the entire time we were in Eagle Creek. I've never seen him that way. If I am honest, I had always thought him a little taciturn, and very reserved until I saw him with you."

"Do you truly think so?" Imogen begged. "I thought we got along well, and I know that I certainly feel more for him than I should, but I was so worried that I might have been caught up in my own daydreams."

"He definitely was as caught up in the moment as you."

"Oh, I do hope so," Imogen said with a heavy sigh. "I find it hard to think of anything but him. I like him so very much."

"Well, worry no longer, for I am sure that he likes you very much, too," Joanna said firmly. "But you must not fret if his letters take longer to arrive than you wish. Even though they should not take long to arrive from Eagle Creek, there are many things that can cause a letter to go missing. You must be patient, dearest heart. It will come, and December will be here in no time at all."

"You are right, of course. But I have never been the patient type."

They paid their bill and walked out onto the street, to take their now traditional walk in the park together. Joanna tucked her arm through Imogen's, and they crossed the street. The park had vast, iron gates with gilded flowers and leaves artfully created by a very talented smith. Imogen had always liked them, but suddenly she realized she had seen something similar in Eagle Creek. "Aren't these the same as the ones on the trade college gates?" she asked Joanna.

"You know, they are very alike. I know the town council paid a lot of money to have these made. I wonder if they asked Mr. Gilpin to make them for them. He is by far the best smith in the state."

"A mystery for us to solve," Imogen said happily. "I wonder who we can ask."

"My father could probably find out for us," Joanna said. "He has friends on the council."

"Then I charge you to find that out, and to ask Mathew Tindall for a dance on Friday at the Haverham's ball."

"I couldn't, it would be improper," Joanna protested.

"But the problem with being proper is that he is too shy to ask you, despite most certainly wanting to, and you being too polite to break the rules is that you will never get to dance together," Imogen teased.

"He is terribly shy, isn't he?"

"More so than any man I've ever known," Imogen said. "But the way he looks at you, and when you say hello to him his little ears flush bright pink. It is quite sweet, really."

"I do like him. He is very handsome, isn't he – though most people would never notice because he is so quiet."

"He does have very fine features."

"And he is very kind."

"So, are you going to ask him to dance or not? Because you obviously like him a lot, too."

Joanna giggled. "I'm going to ask him," she said boldly.

"Then might I suggest that you wear your blue velvet? It

sets off your eyes beautifully, and swirls most becomingly when you dance," Imogen said with a grin.

"I shall. And you should wear your red. I wish I had the coloring for such a bold color, but it suits you perfectly." Immediately after she had said it, Joanna clapped her hands over her mouth and gave Imogen an apologetic look.

"If only my Mama and Papa would agree to my attending such an event," Imogen said with a heavy sigh. "I should so enjoy getting to dance with every eligible young man in the city. It would be a nice distraction, so I might forget that I am pining for a letter from Mr. King."

Joanna gave her arm a supportive squeeze. "He'll write," she said softly. "I know he'll write."

"I do, too. But I still wish I could come to the ball as well. It is so dull being the only young lady that isn't permitted to attend such functions in all of Billings."

"If only there were something I could do," Joanna said sadly. She grinned from ear to ear.

"What is it?"

"I might not be able to do anything, but I am certain my father might," she said mysteriously. "Trust me, you shall go to the ball, Cinderella."

CHAPTER 13

OCTOBER 31ST, 1894, BILLINGS, MONTANA

T hankfully, Imogen did not have long to wait. When she went down for breakfast Mr. King's long-awaited letter had finally arrived. It sat on a tiny silver salver by her place setting. Her father sat at the head of the table, buried in his newspaper, tutting and drawing breath through his teeth at all the scandalous and terrible things happening in the world. Her mother was eating toast and jam delicately, watching her husband nervously for signs that anything he was reading might worry him enough to declare that it was time to move again. Imogen felt sorry for them both, so trapped by father's fears. She could hardly remember the last time any of them had been happy.

She helped herself to a boiled egg and some toast that she buttered thickly and dipped into the runny yolk. Her mother frowned at her for being so childish, but there was nobody there to see her. If there had been, Imogen would have used a spoon. She would never embarrass her mother. But she did not understand why she was supposed to act on ceremony when there was nobody to see her. She ate her egg with relish and took another – in part to spite her mother who was still glaring at her.

"Mama, is it not enough that I must be perfectly turned out and have impeccable manners in public, must I really bear the weight of your disdain when eating my breakfast?" she teased.

"You are such a hoyden," Mama said, but her frown softened and she almost smiled. "I don't know how we will ever convince anyone that you are well-mannered."

"As you rarely let me meet anyone, I don't think we need fear that."

"I think it may be time for you to accompany your father and I to some of his functions," Mama said tentatively, glancing over at her husband to gauge his reaction to the suggestion. "You can be quite well behaved when you wish to be."

"Haverham's ball," Papa said without looking up from his newspaper. "She should come with us to that."

Imogen looked at him, stunned, then at her mother.

Mama gave her a genuine smile. "You mean it?" Imogen asked. "I am to come?"

"Can't disappoint a man like Hemsley," Papa said grumpily, putting down his newspaper and standing up. He yanked down his vest and took his jacket from the back of the chair and put it on. "He says his daughter will need a companion there."

Imogen beamed and vowed to thank both Joanna and her father for this most wonderful intervention into her dull and monotonous life. But she knew better than to make a fuss over it. She accepted her father's dutiful peck on the cheek as he left for work without getting up from the table, as her mother did.

"We shall go to the dressmaker's this morning," Mama said once the front door had slammed behind Papa. "You deserve a new gown, rather than having to wear that red velvet again. I cannot tell you how delighted I am that he has finally seen sense, that in order for you to find a suitable match you need to go out and be amongst people. He is so afraid harm will come to you. But this is a wonderful start."

Imogen was a little surprised by what her mother had just said. Had Papa been trying to protect her, by keeping her from becoming a part of Society in the towns and cities that they had lived in? Was it just another of his ways of trying to cope with his own fear? Suddenly, his reticence to have her join them anywhere, even at dinners in their own home made more sense to her. If she did not go anywhere, or see anyone, then nobody could harm her. She shook her head a little sadly. She had been forced to miss out on so many things that other young women took for granted. "I am still surprised he let me make friends with Joanna, and even with Emily."

"I confess that I never told him," Mama said. "You needed to have something, and a few visits to the tea shop in full daylight hardly seemed dangerous to me. I wasn't expecting you to start gallivanting all over the country, though. You need to be cautious, my dear. There is only so much that I can keep from your father."

"You knew that we went to Eagle Creek?"

"I knew you went somewhere, for I found the stubs of your railway ticket," Mama said. "You need to be more careful when you send your clothes to be laundered, my darling."

"I wish there was time to go to Eagle Creek now, and to have a gown made there," Imogen said with a sigh. "Their dressmaker is so much better than the one here."

"Perhaps we can go and visit her another time. I just pray that nothing happens that makes your father regret giving you permission this time. If anything goes wrong, he'll not let you out of the house again, you know that don't you?"

"I do," Imogen said. "I shall be well-behaved, polite. I shall dance with whoever marks my card, but I will not show favoritism towards anyone."

"I don't think he fears you finding a suitable husband,

Imogen. More that in a crowded place, anything can happen."

"I am hardly likely to be kidnapped during the Haverham's ball."

"I know that, and you know that – but it does not stop your father from fretting over the possibility of it happening."

Imogen nodded, but there was nothing more she could say to that. Her father was so overly protective of her that such news was not really a shock to her. He saw bandits round every corner, and it had ruined not only his own life, but his family's too. It was sad, and infuriating all at once.

"I shall call the carriage for ten o'clock," Mama said as Imogen got up from the table. "Do not be late."

Imogen nodded, then hurried into the hallway, and began to head upstairs to change, having almost forgotten the letter she had been waiting so impatiently for. She ran back into the breakfast room and picked it up. Mama shook her head and gave her an indulgent look. Imogen grinned and went upstairs, a little more slowly this time. Once in the privacy of her bed chamber, she opened the letter and began to read.

Dear Miss Potts,

I am terribly sorry for the tardiness of my writing to you. It has been extremely busy at the hotel. I do hope that this letter finds you well.

For myself, I am tired but glad to be so occupied. It is rarely quiet here, there is always something to do, but when we are particularly busy the time flies by so quickly – and that means that I am closer to seeing you again, for Mr. Hemsley wishes me to come to Billings again in two weeks' time – and I do hope that we will be able to meet while I am there?

I am sorry I do not have time to write a long letter this time, but I want you to know that you are in my thoughts all of the time. I am so very glad that I replied to your advertisement, and that we have met. Our meetings have brought some much-needed joy into my life.

Yours, most earnestly

Bart King

It was short, but the sentiments it contained did not need pages of honeyed words to be conveyed. He would be here in Billings shortly, and he thought of her often – as she did him. He had brought joy to her life, too, and it made her heart sing to know that he felt that way, too. Her day had started so wonderfully well, that she feared that it could only get worse from here. But she dressed quickly and went downstairs to meet her mother in the hallway.

Mama cast her eye over Imogen and gave her an approving nod. "You'll do," she said.

"We are going to the dressmakers," Imogen pointed out as they stepped out of the house onto the street. "Not to a Society affair."

"Imogen, when will you learn that as a woman you are always on display. There will be others at the dressmakers.

Some of them may be influential to your future, some may have sons or grandsons that they wish to marry a nice, well-mannered young lady. Remember that."

"But what if I do not wish to be married to their sons and grandsons?"

"Then you must be polite to them, because they have the power to invite you to all manner of events where you might meet someone you do wish to marry."

Imogen didn't say a word about having already found the man she hoped to wed one day as they climbed into the waiting carriage. Mama would not think writing to a complete stranger was a suitable way to find a husband. "I promise to be the perfect, demure lady," she assured her. "But it is all such nonsense. Surely, it would be better for everyone if we actually got to know each other as we are – rather than some pretty fiction?"

"Pretty fictions make the world work, Imogen," Mama said wearily. "Sometimes, they are all that can."

The two women sat in silence in the carriage. Mama's words echoed around Imogen's head. She had always despaired at how so many things seemed so unreal in her world. Mama would invite people into their home that she barely tolerated yet would seem to be their best friend in the world. Nobody spoke of her father's anxieties and moods, they were glossed over as being utterly normal for a busy man, in such an important role. And young ladies were supposed to be quiet and well-behaved, talented, and educated just sufficiently to find a husband, after which they might do as they pleased – and woe betide them if their husband came to despise them because they were not the winsome young lady that they thought they'd married. Mama was right that pretty fictions were all around, but she wasn't so convinced that they made the world work, only that they gave the pretense that all was well.

A young woman with her aunt were already in the dressmaker's shop when they arrived. She was being fitted for a riding habit. Imogen nodded to her politely as the dressmaker pinned the hem, while Mama chatted with her aunt. Imogen wandered around the store, looking at the bolts of fabric and letting her fingers trail over the ones she liked. Imogen liked for her clothes to be comfortable, to feel soft against her skin. She could not bear to be clad in highly starched, scratchy fabrics – no matter how fashionable they might be, or how well they withstood a day's wear. A particularly fine claret velvet won her heart, but she doubted whether Mama would approve.

When she turned back, the dressmaker had finished her pinning and the young lady had returned to a small cabin at the rear of the shop to dress in private. The aunt settled their bill, and when the young lady was ready, they left the store with a friendly wave. The dressmaker turned to Mama. "How may I be of help to you today?"

"It is very late notice, but my daughter needs a ballgown,

to be ready by Friday night. Would that be too much to hope for?" Mama asked sweetly.

"I think we can ensure she is the belle of the ball in that time," the dressmaker said, pulling out a tape measure. She swiftly took all of Imogen's measurements, and only then wrote them down in a tiny notebook hanging from her waist. "I noticed you looking at the fabrics, did you see anything you particularly liked?"

Imogen pointed to the velvet. "An excellent choice, especially with your lovely dark coloring," the lady said pulling the bolt of fabric down onto the counter. "It is quite my favorite in the entire store. I am so glad you didn't ask for one of the muslins or taffetas, they are so much harder to work with and it might have been much harder to have them ready on time for you."

"It should be modest," Mama said, as the dressmaker showed them a sketch book of possible ballgowns. "Nothing too ostentatious."

Imogen put out a hand to stop Mama from turning the pages as she saw the gown she longed for. It was off the shoulder, framing the shoulders and while it exposed her cleavage, it was tastefully done. A tightly nipped in waist, thanks to a fitted bodice and a full skirt that would billow as she turned and would flatter Imogen's womanly curves without drawing too much attention to her. "What of this one?" she asked hopefully.

Mama frowned. The dressmaker smiled. "This would

suit you perfectly," she said. "In fact, I have a gown that is quite similar to this, that I made for another young lady who decided that it didn't suit. I think that it would fit you, though it isn't in this lovely velvet, but in a deeper red still. It might need a nip and tuck here and there, but it would most certainly be ready in time."

"May I try it on?" Imogen asked excitedly.

"Of course," the dressmaker said. "Go through and get undressed, I shall bring it through."

Five minutes later, Imogen emerged from the changing room and stood nervously in front of her mother. "Well?" she asked, as Mama circled around her, tutting and tapping at her lip thoughtfully.

"It is quite lovely," Mama said eventually, tears in her eyes. "But when did my little girl become a woman? Have my eyes been so very tightly closed to the passing of time?"

CHAPTER 14

NOVEMBER 9TH, 1894, BILLINGS, MONTANA

"**A**m I boring you?" Mr. Hemsley asked Bart, as his attention drifted again.

"Not at all, Sir," Bart assured him. "I am sorry."

"I believe that you are having luncheon with my daughter and her friend again shortly, on completion of our meeting," Mr. Hemsley said with a grin. "Things are going well for you and Miss Potts?"

"I hope so. We seem to enjoy one another's company, and I cannot wait to see her again."

"That is as it should be my boy. I felt that way about dear Joanna's mother. And I would give everything I possess now to have even one more day with her. Will you ask her to marry you?"

"It has barely been a couple of meetings," Bart said cautiously. "I do not wish to scare her. But I would ask her tomorrow if I thought that she would say yes."

"Then ask her, and you'll find out. Because I hear that you might have some competition. Miss Potts was quite the belle of the Haverham's ball the other week and has had young men sending their calling cards ever since." Bart felt a pang of jealousy at his words but did not say a word.

"I can perhaps send someone down to bring Joanna to me so you can have a few moments of privacy, should you wish it?" Mr. Hemsley added with a wink.

"I think I should at least present myself to her parents before doing such a thing," Bart said with a smile. "Perhaps next time I am in the city? I should like to think that if our connection is as I believe it to be, that no matter how many young men call on her, Miss Potts will be true to me."

Mr. Hemsley grinned at him. "I'm not sure I'd take the risk."

Bart didn't want to be so cautious, and the mention of other young men calling on Miss Potts to court her had made him even more sure of the depth of his feelings for her. He hadn't liked the idea of other men calling on her at all. But he wanted to do everything right. And he had to be sure that he had a future to offer her, before he recklessly and self-ishly took her as his own. He would not ever wish to trap her in a life spent looking over her shoulder, in fear of what might be lurking there. She'd lived with caution and fear for long enough, and when she was finally free of her father's home, she deserved to live her life without any more of that.

Yet, Bart was not sure that he would ever be able to offer her that life. It seemed like there was a new story in the newspapers every day about Fitzgibbons and his raids. And he was drawing closer, the last bank he'd targeted had been in Montana, just across the border, south of Billings. Bart didn't know if he should warn Byron Macomber that the bank in Eagle Creek was just the kind of target that Marty had always liked best, or if he should keep his mouth shut and his head down. He didn't know the Macombers that well, or many other people in town whose money would be at risk, but he didn't want to see anyone in town harmed by Fitzgibbons.

But there were pictures of Marty everywhere now. Seeing his eyes staring out at him from every public place had brought all his fears that his secrets would be found out to the forefront. He knew he'd be hounded out of town, at best, though it was more likely he'd find himself up before a magistrate. He knew he should move on, but he couldn't bear the thought of it. Not just because of Miss Potts, but because of Eagle Creek, The Eyrie, Mr. Hemsley and everyone there who had welcomed him and made him feel like he had a home there if he wanted it.

Bart had always hoped that nobody had given his name

to the sheriffs, and in all these years, he'd never seen a poster with his own name and image upon it, though he'd spent his entire adult life moving on in case anyone was still looking for him. But he'd realized in the past weeks that his concerns had not really been that the law men would find him. He knew now that he had been worried that Marty would – because Marty would not ever forgive him for failing to warn them in time, and then abandoning them all to their fate. He had just been a scared boy, but Fitzgibbons wouldn't care about that.

His meeting with Mr. Hemsley finished, he made his way downstairs to the dining room where Miss Potts and Miss Hemsley were already seated, waiting for him. He greeted them politely and took his own seat between them. "I hear that you both had a wonderful time at a ball recently," he said, teasing them both just a little. Miss Potts blushed becomingly, and Miss Hemsley ducked her head down, so he couldn't see her face. "Come now, it cannot have been that bad?"

Miss Potts took her friend's hand and patted it affectionately. "Joanna fears that she made a terrible fool of herself."

"I did," Miss Hemsley protested, looking up, her expression one of deep shame.

"You cannot have done anything so very terrible," Bart assured her.

"I asked a boy to dance."

"A man, a very nice man," Miss Potts explained. "Who,

sadly, is not a very good dancer. He trod on her feet and tripped over her dress, dragging them both onto the ground. Joanna is sure that everyone was watching, and that Mr. Tindall will never speak to her again."

"I can never show my face in public again," Miss Hemsley said dramatically.

"I cannot imagine that it was as bad as you think, and he was the one who actually made you fall, so I would imagine that he feels terrible about that," Bart said reasonably, as Miss Hemsley suddenly ducked her head down under the table. "Now what is the matter?" he asked.

"I'm not here," she whispered up at him. "That's him, over by the French doors, with his parents. I shall wait until he is looking elsewhere and will slip away."

"You're being silly, Joanna," Miss Potts said. "And it is already too late, he has seen us and is coming over."

"He isn't, you're just saying that," she hissed back.

"No, she really isn't, if your Mr. Tindall is a tall, slightly hunched gentleman with sandy hair." Miss Hemsley nodded that his description matched the man she was trying to avoid. "You may wish to be seated properly when he gets to the table in a few moments," Bart said trying not to laugh. However silly it might seem to him, it was a delightful distraction from all of his own concerns, for a few moments at least.

Miss Hemsley took her seat once more and nervously smoothed her hair and dress as they waited for the rather awkward looking young man to draw closer to the table. "Good day to you, Miss Hemsley, Miss Potts," he said bowing to them.

"Dear Mr. Tindall," Miss Potts said, beaming at him. "How lovely to see you again. Might I introduce you to our friend, Mr. King?"

Bart stood up and offered the young man his hand. "My pleasure," he said.

"Thank you," Mr. Tindall said shyly. "I am terribly sorry to interrupt, but might I have a few words, in private, with Miss Hemsley?"

"Whatever you wish to say, you may say it in front of Imogen and Mr. King, they both know of our mortification," Miss Hemsley assured him.

Mr. Tindal flushed as red as a beet. "Oh, my. Well, of course, you were there, Miss Potts."

"It truly wasn't as bad as either of you think it to be," she assured him. "Virtually nobody saw it, at all. You were both up on your feet again so quickly."

"I do wish I could believe that, Miss Potts, but my own friends have been teasing me about it endlessly ever since."

"I'm sorry, perhaps you need nicer friends," Miss Potts said solemnly. "Mr. King, perhaps we might take a turn around the gardens, before we place our orders for dinner?"

"I should like that," Bart said and moved to help her up, then tucked her arm through his. It felt so right for her to be on his arm that way and he had to remember to keep his face impassive, when all he longed to do was beam like a besotted fool. Miss Potts mouthed something at Miss Hemsley before they made their way across the dining room and out into the fresh, chill air.

"I should have thought to bring my coat," she said shivering a little as she turned to peer through the window. "I can't make out what they are saying."

"Perhaps you should give them the privacy that Mr. Tindall requested?" Bart said with a grin as he removed his jacket and placed it around her shoulders.

"Won't you get cold?" she asked him as she pulled it tight around her. "It is so lovely and warm, though. I'm not sure I could give it back."

"I will quite probably catch my death," he said with a smile. "But frostbite will be worth it to have your scent on my jacket on the way home reminding me of our time together."

"You flatter me too much," she protested.

"Perhaps not enough, if you have been receiving young men in my absence," he said as lightly as he could. He did not want her to think him jealous, even though the thought of her in another man's arms made him want to rip the fool's eyes out.

"Ah, you have been listening to gossip," she said with a smile. "But I can assure you, that though I have received more than fourteen calling cards, I have yet to send an invitation to tea with Mama to anyone."

"You cannot possibly know how glad I am to hear that."

"I thought it only fair that you be the first of my suitors to meet me with my family," she said a little shyly. "I think they will think anyone else to be second best if they have you in mind."

"You want me to meet them?" He was both flattered and panicked all at once.

"If you would like to?"

Bart wasn't sure what he wanted. Or at least, he knew what he wanted, but wasn't sure what he could dare to let himself actually have. He did not wish to give Miss Potts hope where there might be none, but he still couldn't bring himself to break away from her friendship, even though he knew that it would be for the best – at least for her – if he could. She deserved so much more than him. She deserved someone who did not have a tawdry past, and an uncertain future. But he couldn't say no to her. He couldn't walk away.

"I should like that," he said softly, reaching out and pushing a stray strand of hair behind her ear. She smiled nervously at him but did not step away.

"I'm glad, for I said that I would be bringing someone home for afternoon tea. I'd have had to beg Joanna to come with me if you'd said no."

"I do need to get the train home, remember," he said softly.

"I know, but there is a train that stops in Eagle Creek that leaves just after seven o'clock. You don't have to hurry back to the hotel for anything today, do you?"

"I don't now," he said. She'd snared him most easily, but he wasn't inclined to struggle to break free. She truly had captured his heart, and he would do anything she asked of him.

And so, he had the answer to many of the questions he'd been mulling over ever since he'd met her. He would stay and fight for a life with this wonderful, funny young woman. He would face the consequences of his actions, and if he lost everything, then at least he would know that he had stood firm, done his best, and not run away from everything because it was too difficult to stay. The reward of her love would be worth it, and if he lost her that would be the harshest punishment that any magistrate could hand down to him.

CHAPTER 15

NOVEMBER 9TH, 1894, BILLINGS, MONTANA

A s they approached the front door, Imogen turned to Mr. King. "I feel like I have all the butterflies in the world trapped in my belly," she admitted.

"Snakes for me," he said with a nervous smile. "Lots of writhing and wriggling."

"Ew," Imogen said. "That sounds even more unpleasant than all these flapping wings. Now, Mama will greet you warmly, she will be polite and do all that is expected in such a situation as this. Do not expect her to make jokes or discuss anything more challenging than the weather."

"Small talk only," he said, nodding. "I understand."

"Be polite, but not obsequious. Be generous, but not overly so. Flatter her, but not unreasonably."

"Temper everything," Mr King said and grinned. "You do remember what I do for a living, don't you?"

She laughed. "I do. Of course, you know better than I do how to talk to women like my Mama."

"Not your mama, though. You have specialist knowledge that I shall put to very good use."

"Are you ready?" she asked him.

"As I will ever be," he assured her.

Together they entered the house. Imogen took Mr. King's coat and hung it up on the coat stand by the door and laid his hat and gloves beneath it. She took off her own and hung it next to his and placed her hat and gloves in a hat box on the stand. She took his hand and led him across the grand hallway, her heels click-clacking loudly on the checkerboard tiles on the floor. She led him into the sunny front parlor, where Mama was sitting on the floral sofa, reading a book. "Mama, he agreed to come," she said, hurrying forward and pressing a kiss to her mother's cheek. "Mr. King, may I introduce you to my Mama?"

"I am charmed, Mrs. Potts," Mr. King said bowing over Mama's hand and kissing the air above it.

"I shall wait until I have got to know you a little better before I make such a decision," Mama said a little tartly.

"As you rightly should," he agreed. "I could not help but notice the garland in the hallway as we entered, it is quite lovely. Did you do it yourself?"

"I did," Mama said, blushing a little at his praise. "It is such a small thing, but I like to do it."

"However did you get all those beautiful blooms at this time of year?"

"There is a wonderful man in the market," Mama said. She took great pride in arranging her flowers, and they brought her great joy, but Imogen had not told him anything about that. It was impressive that he'd picked up on something that Mama could talk about with him happily for many hours.

"You must give me his name, I would be glad to have a man that can source such lovely flowers as a supplier for the hotel."

"Imogen told me that you run a hotel. Eagle Creek, was it?"

"Yes, it is called The Eyrie, for it is where the eagles nest, right at the top of the mountain."

"You should see the eagles, Mama," Imogen said. "The way they swoop and dive. It is quite breathtaking."

"I still haven't forgiven you for lying to me about your trip there," Mama said with a frown. "But I must confess that I should like to see eagles flying in the mountains."

"Perhaps you should accompany Miss Potts on her next visit, for the Christmas market, if you would permit her to come," Mr. King said warmly. "You could stay at the hotel, perhaps for a couple of nights even, so I can show you both a little of the town and the area around it."

"Wouldn't it be awfully cold and hard to get around in the winter?" Mama said drily.

"It can be cold, but if you are warmly dressed and have a good guide, it is possible to enjoy Eagle Creek in winter. We have many guests who only come in the months when the snow lies thick on the ground, because it is so very beautiful."

"Do you have snow there now? We had a few flakes overnight, but nothing settled," Imogen asked him.

"We do, it is quite thick up by the hotel, but only a fine dusting in the town. I'm sure by the time I return there will have been more, the clouds looked heavy with snow when I left this morning."

"Oh, please say we can go, Mama," Imogen begged her mother. "Joanna said that the Christmas market is a wonderful event, with all sorts of stalls selling wonderful gifts and there is mulled cider and wine."

"And there is usually a roasted pig, done on a spit. It is delicious with some sage and onion stuffing and apple-sauce," Mr. King added.

"You could meet the lady who made the basket I bought you for your birthday," Imogen added. "She will be selling Crow baskets and jewelry there."

"It is a lovely basket. You know, I always wondered where you had found such an unusual gift," Mama said with a slight chuckle. "I cannot stay angry with you that you lied to me about it, you are a woman grown after all. I think it took your father and I a little while to see that."

"You just wanted to keep me safe. I understand."

"And can I trust you to keep my daughter safe, if I send her to you?" Mama asked.

A strange look clouded Mr. King's handsome features, but he nodded resolutely to Mama. "I will do all I can to ensure she is kept happy, safe, and well. And we have the finest sheriff in the state in Eagle Creek. Nate Hale is a fine man, respected by all who know him, and feared by those who do wrong."

"Well, that is reassuring, given all the dangers you read about in the newspapers these days," Mama said. "And of course, Miss Hemsley will be going with you?"

"Of course," Imogen assured her. "Though won't you come, too? You would love it there. I know you would."

"I must stay here and take care of your father," Mama said softly. "Though perhaps I can convince him to take some time off work in the spring, and we can come and see your mountains then – if the two of you are still courting, of course."

"Will I meet Mr. Potts today?" Mr. King asked her. "I would very much like to reassure him that my intentions towards your daughter are honorable."

"He will be working late, no doubt. But I shall assure him of your intentions," Mama said.

But even as she said it, the front door slammed. She

stood up and hurried out of the room. "You're doing very well," Imogen whispered.

"Thank you, I don't think I have ever been so scared of anything. She can be quite formidable, can't she?"

"She has to be, living with Papa."

Mama returned a few moments later. "Your father has gone upstairs to change and to freshen up. He will return shortly. I am so glad that he was able to get away in time to meet with you, Mr. King."

"I must confess that I am too. I may have need of his advice," Mr. King said, surprising Imogen a little. She gave him a quizzical look.

"Why would you need the advice of a banker?" she asked.

"Not for me, at least not particularly, but a friend of mine runs the bank in Eagle Creek, and I am sure that he would be grateful for some of your husband's advice on safety and security. As you said, there is so much crime reported in the newspapers these days that it is wise to be prepared for all eventualities."

"I am sure he would be delighted to offer you his opinions," Mama said with a smile. "Now, I shall call Betsy to bring our tea and fetch you Mr. Walcott's card, so you may call on him about the flowers. He is terribly helpful. Just tell him that I sent you and he'll treat you very well indeed."

"Thank you," Mr. King said. "That really is most kind of you."

Once she was out of earshot, Mr. King turned to Imogen, his face slightly pale. "So, how do I impress your father?"

"His greatest concern is safety. Just talk about that, and don't mention Deadwood."

"Deadwood?" His brow furrowed. "Why would I talk about Deadwood?"

"You wouldn't, because that was where it all happened, the bank was robbed and his secretary, Miss Kelly, was killed."

"Someone was killed? You didn't mention that before." Mr. King said, his face pale and eyes wide.

"Don't mention it," Imogen urged, glancing over her shoulder. "Don't even mention South Dakota, even if he asks you where you've lived in the past – if any of them were in the Dakotas, do not mention it."

There was no time to explain further, as Papa appeared. He looked pale and tired. Imogen hurried to greet him. "Good afternoon, Papa, I am so glad you could come and meet Mr. King."

Mr. King reached out a hand and Papa shook it, staring into Mr. King's eyes. His eyes narrowed, his brow furrowing as if he were trying to remember where he might have seen Mr. King somewhere before. "Have we met?" he asked.

"I don't think so, Sir," Mr. King said a little nervously, his deep, rich voice catching a little, something Imogen had never heard him do before.

"Your face is very familiar, but I see so many faces,"

Papa said, shaking his head and moving to take his usual seat by the fire. He beckoned them both over. "Come, sit down."

Imogen took the seat beside her father and Mr. King sat opposite them, on the seat beside where Mama had been sitting earlier. "Mr. King has to leave by half past six," she explained to her father. "We thought you might not be able to get away from the bank in time."

"It was a quiet enough afternoon," Papa said, taking her hand in his and holding it tightly. "And what manner of man would I be, if I could not take time to meet a young man that wishes to court my daughter?"

"A busy one," Imogen teased him. He smiled at her fondly, and reached out and cupped her cheek gently. It was rare he was so tender with her, and she cherished the moment.

"I was just saying to Mrs. Potts, before you arrived, that I can assure you that my intentions are entirely honorable, Sir," Mr. King said earnestly.

"I should hope so, too. My Imogen is a priceless jewel. I'll not have anyone snatch her away who doesn't deserve her."

"I will do all I can to prove my worth to you, Sir."

"You see that you do."

Mama returned and handed Mr. King the card she had promised, as Betsy appeared with the tea tray. Mama poured and Imogen cut them generous slices of cake. Mr. King complimented Mama on the cake but didn't go so far as requesting the recipe. Imogen smiled at that, after all Mr. King had an army of cooks working for him, and though Mama had served them a fine spread, it could not hold a candle to the food on offer at The Eyrie. Every so often, Papa gave Mr. King's face a searching look, as if he was still trying to figure out where they might have met before, but he clearly came up with no suitable conclusions. The tea was delicious, if the company had become a little strained with Papa's unexpected appearance.

When the time came for Mr. King to leave, Imogen walked him to the station. "I am sorry for that," she said, nodding back towards the front door as they walked down the street. "He's not an easy man."

"No, I suppose not. But you said he was involved in a robbery in a bank in Deadwood?"

"Yes, I told you about it in my letters, that it was why we had moved around so often."

"You never said it was in Deadwood," he pointed out. "I'd have remembered that, for I lived there once myself."

"Really, then perhaps Papa had a reason to think he'd met you before," Imogen said.

"I doubt it, I was there for only a short while, as a young boy. I doubt we were even there at the same time."

"We left there in early May, 1875, it is etched in my mind, as my life was never the same again," Imogen said sadly. She was so lost in her memory of that time that she did not see Mr. King blanch and gulp nervously.

By the time she returned to the present day and tucked her arm through his, he had recovered his composure, and she smiled up at him. "I shall miss you terribly," she admitted as they drew closer to the station.

"At least we know that we shall see one another in just a month's time," he said warmly. "I will apologize now, for I may not have much time to write between now and then. But know that I am thinking of you in every moment I have spare, and that I am looking forward to receiving you and Miss Hemsley for the Christmas Fair" He bent his head and pressed a kiss to her forehead. His lips were soft and cool against her warm forehead. She reached up and touched the spot with her fingers. It tingled where his lips had been and sent shivers through her entire body.

"Stay well, Mr. King," she said.

"Perhaps you might consider calling me Bart, if you think that we are familiar enough with one another now?"

"I should like that, Bart, and you may call me Imogen."

"Imogen, take good care of yourself and if you don't have them ensure you have some fur mittens and a warm hat for your visit." He beamed at her, then disappeared into the station.

CHAPTER 16

DECEMBER 7TH, 1894, BILLINGS, MONTANA

"She is not to go," Papa shouted as he ran down the stairs. "I'll not permit it." His eyes were wild and his movements erratic. He stumbled on the stairs, but kept moving away from them, as if they were coming for him with pitchforks.

"You already gave your permission," Mama called, following him, her face pale and lined with worry for him. Imogen worried for them both and felt guilty that somehow this was all her fault. Her father hadn't suffered one of his episodes in such a long time, and now he was railing and ranting about Mr. King, sure that he was the very devil himself. Holding back tears, Imogen tried to be brave for them both.

Mama caught up to Papa and took his hands in hers and tried to make him look her in the eye. Papa tossed his head from side to side, but though he leaned away from Mama, he did not pull away. "You cannot say no, not now," she said to him softly. "And certainly not because you have a strange feeling about him. You barely know the man."

"She knows him only a little more," Papa said, his tone similar to that of a petulant child. "What does she really know of his past? Who he is? Where he came from?" He snatched his hands away and clasped his head, looking around the hallway trying to see a way out, as if there were men lurking in the shadows, just waiting for him.

"What does any of that matter?" Imogen pleaded with her father. "Surely what matters is the man he is now? And he is good and kind, and decent. He works hard and everyone likes him."

"It matters because he could be quite literally anyone," Papa spat angrily. He looked tormented, overwhelmed as the nightmares that played over and over in his head grew too loud and too insistent for him to ignore them. Imogen had seen him like this so many times, usually not long before they moved on to a new town. But this time, they wouldn't just move somewhere else. He would do all he could to stop her from seeing Mr. King, and Imogen could not bear the thought of that.

It was so unfair that his fears had taken over his reason,

for him, for Mama – but in this moment, Imogen's pity was all for herself. She would not let him part her from Mr. King. She and Mama had done all they could to ease Papa's burden. Over the years, they had found him the finest doctors and tolerated his outbursts. They had moved from one side of the country to the other, and back again to placate his needs. Imogen would do it no more. She had to be entitled to her own life now. She would have liked her family's blessing, but she would follow her heart without it if she had to.

"Don't you care at all that he could have been one of those who robbed the bank all those years ago?" Papa railed at her. "Who killed dear Marta who had never hurt a soul in her entire life?" Imogen shook her head and tried to remember the good man she knew behind the mania. "Imogen, his eyes, they are so familiar to me. You must heed me. I am sure he is there, in my memories of that time."

"Papa he would have been a child," Imogen said reasonably, though she knew that would make little difference. "How could he have possibly been responsible for robbing a bank as a boy of no more than fifteen?"

"Those gangs use lads to look around the places they intend to rob. Nobody takes much notice of a boy, loitering. That's what boys do," Papa said, his voice strangely calm, though his eyes were still wild. "They use them as lookouts, and decoys."

"In which case, why would you remember him, if he was supposed to be so innocuous, so invisible?"

"Because he isn't, is he?" Papa sank down onto the stairs and cradled his head in his hands. "Those eyes are just so vivid. I've never seen anyone with eyes like that anywhere else. I hate it, but I can see every man, woman and child that went near the bank in the week before that robbery. Every image is burned upon my soul, and it plays over and over again. And I am sure that I have seen those eyes before, two days before the robbery – and again on our way to church that morning. He was standing on a corner by the saloon. I'm sure of it."

"Papa, I know you are trying to protect me," Imogen said softly, sitting down beside him and putting an arm around his waist. "But you cannot protect me from the demons inside your head."

"I know, and I hate that I see them everywhere," he moaned.

"You should go to bed, get some rest," Mama said softly, knowing that the worst had now passed. "Imogen will call on Doctor Barnard for some of his sleeping draft, that usually helps, my dearest one." She took Papa's arm and helped him to his feet then led him back up the stairs.

Imogen nodded to her and grabbed her coat. She ran out of the house and along the street, down two blocks where she turned right. Halfway along the street she stopped and knocked on the door of a fine townhouse. The housekeeper, clad all in black opened the door. "Miss Imogen, whatever is the matter?" Mrs. Honey asked kindly. "Is it your father again?" Imogen nodded. "I shall fetch the doctor. He's in with a patient, but he won't want to leave you waiting. Take a seat in the kitchen, it's warmer in there than the parlor."

Imogen did as she was told and went into the empty, but warm kitchen. She warmed her hands by the stove and took a seat in the rocking chair beside it. Mrs. Honey did not return, instead Imogen heard the heavier tread of Doctor Barnard's leather boots on the flagstones. She turned and he gave her an understanding smile. "He's done well, I think this is the longest between episodes yet," the doctor said as he handed her a vial of liquid. "What set him off this time?"

"He thinks that a young man who called on me was present at the robbery. No, that he was a part of it," Imogen said, shuddering at the thought of it.

"I'm sure it will pass, but if some good rest and good food do not help him, you may need to convince him to seek further assistance. I know a fine doctor in New York, who specializes in such conditions, who might be able to help him. It is a relatively new field in medicine, but great strides are being made for many sufferers of the maladies of the mind. I could ask him to come and visit with me for a while, so he might offer his opinion? A case like your father's would be of great interest to him."

"We shall try what has worked before, for now," Imogen said, unsure how either her mother or father might react to the idea of that, a doctor coming all this way might make him feel like an animal in the zoo. Papa would likely reject the idea out of hand, no matter how beneficial the man's counsel might be. Imogen tried to ignore the way that Dr. Barnard had phrased the suggestion, and to consider the merits. She knew that her father needed more help than he had tolerated so far.

"I fear you may be right that we need to urge Papa to see someone who can help him," she said cautiously. "The fear is ruining his life, always replaying those few days over and over in his head, seeing ghosts where there are none. It seems much worse this time than I can ever remember it being before."

"His condition does not just affect him, though, does it?" Dr. Barnard said kindly. "It is ruining yours and your dear mother's, too."

"Sometimes," Imogen said, a little defensively. "But we can manage."

"And if you are to wed? To move away? Who will help your mother then?"

Imogen had not much thought about that lately. In all her need to get away from her chaotic life, she'd simply forgotten how that might affect Mama. She would be alone. She had almost no real friends, no family. If Papa were to have one of his turns, what would she do without Imogen there to help calm him? She shook her head slightly. It was not a thought she needed to concern herself with right now. She had no immediate plans to leave her family, even if she harbored hopes for marriage and a family of her own with Mr. King. He had not yet asked for her hand, and there was no reason to think that he would at any time soon.

"I shall call on your mother tomorrow, and we shall see how he is then," Dr. Barnard said, placing a comforting hand upon her forearm. "We shall do what we can for him, and then when he is well again, perhaps we might consider talking about my friend coming with him then."

"Thank you, Doctor. I shall certainly tell my mother all we've talked about tonight. And thank you for the sleeping draft. I am sure that with some rest he will be himself again."

They all slept in a little later than usual the next day. Imogen was quite surprised when she saw the time on the clock above the mantel. If she was to be at the train station in time to meet Joanna, she would have to leave within the hour. But she couldn't leave Mama, not with Papa like this. She dressed in a plain gown and went downstairs. Mama was still in her dressing gown and nightdress, gulping down coffee from the large silver pot on the buffet, when Imogen entered the breakfast room. "How is Papa?" she asked.

"Still asleep, I thought it best to leave him to rest," Mama said.

"And how are you?"

"I barely slept a wink, but we've survived worse." Mama poured another cup of coffee and sank down into one of the chairs at the table. She stared at the basket of pastries on the table and pushed them away listlessly.

"You should eat, you will need to keep your strength up," Imogen urged her.

"I don't think I could eat a thing. I'd choke on it, my belly is so tied in knots," Mama said a little sadly. "He'd been so well. I suppose I had foolishly hoped that we were beyond the worst of it, that perhaps he might finally have conquered his own mind."

"Mama, you must not torment yourself this way. It is my fault, I should not have brought Mr. King home."

"How could you have possibly foreseen that your father would react to a suitor in this way?" Mama said, taking her hand. "You must not blame yourself, either. Your Mr. King seems a perfectly charming and decent young man." She paused and cocked her head to one side, a quizzical look on her face. "Are you not supposed to be meeting Miss Hemsley at the station this morning? Your trip to the Christmas Fair? I know how much you have been looking forward to it, to seeing him. Why are you wearing such a drab frock?"

"I can hardly leave with Papa like this," Imogen said.

"Of course you can," Mama insisted. "He will sleep for the next few days, then once he is rested, I will ease him back off the sleeping draft and he will try to come to terms with himself again. I think that I will tell Dr. Barnard to invite his friend as soon as he can, whatever your father says. It is time. He will not ruin your life as well as mine. No, you go. Stay for a week, more if you want to. Take the money from your father's desk, there's always plenty in there."

Imogen was torn. She wanted to go, but she felt obliged to stay. Mama seemed so determined, though, in a way that Imogen could not remember her ever being before. "If you are truly sure," she said cautiously.

"I am. One of us should live their life, have some fun. You have had such a heavy burden to carry, for far too long, my dearest. It is time that I stopped leaning on you, and that your father stopped relying on me. It is time we face this, once and for all, whatever it takes."

Imogen embraced her mother tightly. When they broke apart, both had tears pouring down their cheeks. "Mama, he will be alright, won't he?" she asked anxiously.

"I don't know, my darling. I've fooled myself for too long that one day this would follow its course and fade into nothing. It is not ever going to do that. I need to do what is right for us all – even if it makes your father angry with me for a time."

"You fear Papa may need to go away, don't you?"

"I do, but I am hopeful that he will not, that there will be more we can do while he is here, in his home, where he feels at least a little safer – or at least he did."

Imogen kissed her Mama on her cheek. "I am just a short train ride away. You must promise to send for me if you need me. I'll not go if I think you will keep anything from me."

"I promise I will send a telegram if we need you, my darling. Now go, have some fun for all of us."

CHAPTER 17

DECEMBER 8TH, 1894, EAGLE CREEK, MONTANA

Bart paced up and down outside the station, waiting for the train to arrive. He'd been right that with all he had to do in the past month or two, he'd barely had time to stop, but though the time had passed quickly, he'd missed Imogen every single day. She'd sent him jaunty little notes to cheer him up, even though he'd not had time to reply to them, and he longed to tell her how much they had helped him through his work – and the terrible thoughts that had crowded his mind after learning that someone had been killed that day, all those years before.

He'd not known that. Not until Imogen had spoken of it. But in the few spare moments he'd had since his visit to Billings, he'd thought of little else. Marty had always prided himself in those days that nobody ever got hurt when he robbed a bank or a store. Perhaps that fateful day in Dead-wood was when everything had changed, because it certainly seemed that after that day Fitzgibbons had shown little care for people's lives. He'd summoned the courage to ask Nate for more information about the man in the posters, and his crimes had grown more reckless and more dangerous as time had passed.

But though he had been unaware of just how much had changed for Mr. Potts and his family that day, Bart knew that he would have to confess to his part in it soon. It was wrong not to tell Imogen, so she could choose whether or not she wished to continue to associate with him – or if she wanted to see him punished for his role in what had happened. He would not blame her if she did. Yet, he could not bring himself to tell her. He feared losing her so very much, for she had come to mean the whole world to him.

When the whistle sounded, he tried to rid his head of such thoughts. It did no good to dwell upon them, as there was little that he could do now to change anything. Instead, he pinned a smile to his face and rushed into the station to watch the train pull in. He stood right at the edge of the plat-form, making a guard frown at him and try and usher him back a little, but Bart was going nowhere. He did not want to wait for the fog to clear before catching sight of Imogen, he would be right here waiting for her, in the tiny passageway between the train and the mass of smoke and steam. He felt the air displace around him as the train moved past him, slowing to a halt as the pistons stopped their clanking.

Bart's smile softened, no longer did he need to force it, as he saw Imogen's face pressed to the glass in the carriage that had just passed. Just the sight of her made his heart lighter. He hurried to open the door. She smiled as he offered her his hand, but she looked weary. There were lines around her eyes and she seemed somehow less exuberant than he'd been expecting her to be. "What is wrong?" he asked.

"I'll explain in a moment, but I know it is late notice, but is there any chance I might keep our rooms at The Eyrie for a week, not just the two nights we had planned?"

"I'm not sure, but if we can't, I'm sure there will be someone in town who will be glad to put you up," he assured her, as he took her overnight bag from the floor of the train, then helped Miss Hemsley down, too.

"I have a case with me, it was too large to put in the carriage, so it had to go in the baggage car," Imogen said, as she looked up and down the platform for it anxiously.

"I shall fetch it," he assured her. "Why don't you and Miss Hemsley go out and get yourselves settled in the carriage. There are hot bricks, and blankets in there. I'll just be a moment."

She nodded, and he watched as Miss Hemsley put an arm around Imogen's waist and urge her forwards. Something had obviously happened, and Imogen was most certainly not well. He wondered what could possibly have occurred that would have such an impact on a woman as strong and determined as Imogen seemed to be. He vowed that he would not press her, that he would wait for her to tell him when she was ready. He longed to be able to put everything right for her, immediately, whatever it would take, he would do it.

Having fetched her suitcase, he returned to the carriage. The two young ladies were waiting for him, but not inside the coach as he'd suggested. Imogen had her head buried in the neck of one of the carriage horses, while Miss Hemsley stood beside her, looking a little awkward. "Shall we go straight up to the hotel so you can rest, or would you like to see some of the preparations in town for the fair first?" he asked, trying to sound as bright and breezy as possible as he stowed the case on the back of the carriage.

"The hotel please," Imogen said, patting her equine friend's neck, then opening the carriage door. Bart hurried forward to offer her his hand and she took it with a wan smile as she climbed inside. "Perhaps after a nap we might come back down."

He was surprised when Miss Hemsley climbed up onto the driver's perch, rather than getting into the carriage with Imogen. "Did you wish to drive us?" he asked lightly.

"I thought you might like a few moments with Imogen, there are things she needs to tell you."

Bart nodded and gave her a smile of thanks. She nodded back at him and took up the reins. He grabbed a blanket from inside the carriage and tucked it around her legs. "Thank you," she said. "Did you say there was a hot brick, too? I might freeze half to death out here without one."

He grinned and fetched one for her, before climbing into the back of the carriage with Imogen. She was staring blankly out of the window, and jumped half out of her skin as he sat beside her and accidentally grazed her leg with his own. "I'm sorry," she said. "I've been so on edge. I probably shouldn't have come, but Mama insisted."

"What has happened, Imogen? Your letters have been so bright recently and have brought me such happiness. It pains me to see you this way. What can I do to help?"

"Nothing. There is nothing anyone can do." She exhaled loudly. "It is my father. You remember I told you about the robbery that occurred, and how he keeps us moving onwards when he gets afraid. Well, he had one of his turns, just yesterday. I can't help but worry about leaving him and Mama like this."

"What are you not telling me?" Bart asked her, noting that she had barely looked him in the eye once as she explained her woes.

She sighed and turned to him. "He thinks you were there, the day of the robbery, that you were somehow a part of it. He's quite convinced of it. I've told him how ridiculous he is being, that you would have been little more than a child. But he won't listen, and he's driven himself half mad since he met you."

Bart felt his chest contract and his mouth was dry as a bone. He could barely breathe. The moment had come. He had to make his confession. Of course, he'd been preparing himself to have to tell her everything at some point, but not yet. Not now. Not like this. How could he add to her pain and anguish? He'd already been the cause of so much harm to her and her family. Would his confession add to that, or ease her burden? He did not know, though he was certain that she would turn around and leave immediately. He would never see her again, and even the thought of that brought him unbearable pain.

How could she possibly trust him once she knew? Her father was unwell, and it was all his fault. He well remembered the looks that Mr. Potts had given him when he'd joined the family for afternoon tea. The man had been convinced he'd seen Bart somewhere before, and Bart knew all too well that he had. As soon as he'd heard they had lived in Deadwood, he'd known. And Marty had killed someone that day, someone who had no doubt mattered a great deal to Mr. Potts. So, now he had to face up to his past. He had to atone for it. But how? Telling Imogen would not absolve him. Even if she forgave him, it wouldn't ever take away the harms that had been done.

"Miss Potts, Imogen. I don't think that your father is mad at all," he said softly, taking his time over the words, trying to find the right ones, knowing that there were no right words in a situation like this. All he could do was tell her the truth, and pray that she would understand, that she could forgive him. At least it would not be there, waiting, lurking between them any longer.

"Oh, he most certainly is," she said firmly.

"Not about this," he said. "About him thinking I was there, I mean. You see, I believe that I was there and that he did see me back then, because I was in Deadwood at the same time that your family was."

"You were? So, Papa did recognize you. Even after all this time." She stared at him. "You do have particularly unique eyes. He always speaks as though his memories of that time are playing over and over in a loop in his head, as clear as the day they happened, but that he would remember your eyes still seems quite unreal to me. You must have changed so much since then, you would have barely been more than a boy."

"I had just turned fifteen," he said with a rueful smile. "I was much the same height I am now, and though I've filled out a little, my face hasn't changed so very much – and as your father pointed out, I do have rather distinctive eyes."

"You certainly do," Imogen said, this time her smile was soft, as she gazed into them. "Golden eyes."

He closed his eyes for a moment, unable to hold her gaze. "Imogen, I have something to tell you, and you are not going to like it – or me – once I have said it."

"Then don't say it," she said pressing a gloved finger to his lips. "Not today. I've had enough of misery today. Let me have the rest of this day to enjoy the fair and tomorrow you can tell me whatever it is that you think I must know and will make me dislike you. I cannot think of anything you could say that would make me do that, but I am sure you have your reasons."

"You are sure of that?" he asked. "Would it not be better to just get it all done with, all at once? Like pulling a tooth, or yanking out a splinter?"

"I've always much preferred to let a tooth fall out on its own, and to gently ease a splinter out," she said wearily. "We can talk about all of this tomorrow. Tonight, I just want to forget all about it, to dance and have some fun."

He nodded. If that was what she wanted, he would do as she asked. At least he would have one last night of memories. He would do all he could to make tonight perfect. "As you wish," he said softly. "As you wish."

Once they were at The Eyrie, he showed Imogen and Miss Hemsley to their suite, then left them to settle themselves in. He went back down to his office and sat at his desk, staring at the back of the door, wondering how peculiarly the world worked sometimes. Of all the people he could have written to, he had written to Imogen. Their lives seemed bound together somehow, though not in the way he had once hoped for. It seemed to Bart that all he had ever done was to bring her and her family pain. He wished it could have been otherwise.

He picked up some of the paperwork on his desk and

tried to focus on it. But he couldn't concentrate for more than a few minutes at a time. His mind was haunted by the thought of the torment his presence must have caused Mr. Potts, how seeing him again must have dragged up every terrible memory of that day for him. It was no small wonder why the poor man had lost his mind. Bart only hoped that he might one day be able to make it up to the man, somehow.

As the sun went down another fall of snow carpeted the land. Bart ordered out the sleds for their guests to take them down to the town for the fair. He pinned a smile to his face and waved them on their way. Everyone was in festive spirits, some already enjoying a snifter of brandy or port from a hunting flask on their way there. Bart waited impatiently for Imogen and Miss Hemsley to descend the stairs.

They were the last down, but the sight of Imogen, wrapped up in her elegant fur coat, her face a little flushed, filled his heart with both pure delight and poignant sadness. She smiled at him, as if all she'd said earlier in the carriage had never passed between them. She tucked an arm through his, and her other one through Miss Hemsley's. "Are we ready?" she asked.

"Is Eagle Creek ready?" he teased.

"I very much doubt it," Miss Hemsley said. "But I hope they will be glad of our money. I intend to buy all my gifts for Christmas here."

"I shall do all I can to ensure a larger sled on our return journey," Bart promised her.

CHAPTER 18

DECEMBER 8TH, 1894, EAGLE CREEK, MONTANA

I t was lovely to leave her cares and woes behind, if just for a short while. Imogen focused on the feeling of the cold air biting at her cheeks as the sled took them down the mountain. Eagle Creek was lit up with lamps and candles everywhere, making it seem magical and even more beautiful than usual. The stalls that were normally there for the market were mostly missing, instead Main Street was lined with stalls decorated with holly and pine boughs, selling delicious treats to eat, hot mulled cider and wine, and beautiful things that had been made by the people of the town, the farms and ranches nearby, as well as a great number of stalls filled with colorful items made by The Crow people.

As they browsed them all carefully, Imogen was able to lose herself in the moment. Chatting with the stall holders, and the townsfolk, laughing and joking with Joanna and Bart all helped to ease the guilt in her heart and the pain she felt at her father's slide into madness. She purchased something from every stall, keen not to show favoritism, but when she reached Strikes the Iron's stall, she was greeted like an old friend.

"You look tired," the Crow woman told her. "Drink this." She handed Imogen a cup of hot, sweet tea.

"What is in it?" Imogen asked.

"Crow secret," she said with a smile. "But it will help ease your mind and your heart."

"How did you know I am heartsore?"

"Because I know the look, and you did not look this way the last time you were here. You were full of hope and joy that day. Today you carry the world upon your shoulders. I can see how heavy the burden weighs upon you."

"I have been trying so hard not to show it," Imogen said with a sigh. "To forget, as my mother insisted that I try and do, and to have some fun. But it is hard, not knowing how my father is. Fearing that it is my fault that he is unwell."

"How could it be your fault?"

"I brought someone home who reminded him of a time he needs to forget."

"Mr. King?"

Imogen nodded. "My father works too hard. It is how he

copes, by keeping his mind occupied – but because of that he is always tired, and so very on edge. I fear I may have, unintentionally, pushed him over it."

"A healthy mind comes in part from a healthy body," Strikes the Iron said wisely. "But it also requires a healthy spirit. You say your father is trying to forget, always trying to forget. That tells me he lives too much in the past and not enough in the here and now. His spirit must be very tired, too."

"He needs to rest, but he won't, for the nightmares haunt him when he does."

"But the nightmares must be survived, so we can learn from them. Our dreams can bring healing, if we let them."

"I wish he could come and spend some time with you," Imogen said. "I think you'd help him far more than any doctor ever has."

"Bring him here. You are welcome in the Village whenever you wish."

"Thank you, that is most kind, but I fear he would never agree to it. It is hard enough getting him to see a doctor. I cannot imagine how he would react if I told him I wanted him to live with an Indian tribe."

Strikes the Iron smiled so warmly that Imogen felt like the older woman was enveloping her in a motherly hug. "I understand how hard men can be to convince to do anything," she said. "My offer stands though, and always will. For him and for you."

"Thank you, you are most generous."

A small band began to play nearby. Imogen noticed that a dance floor had been erected there, with lanterns hanging from posts at each corner. A number of couples took to the floor, while others stood by and clapped their hands to the music. Bart and Joanna caught up with her. Joanna handed her a cup of mulled cider. "Did you find some more baskets for your mother?"

"I didn't even look," Imogen admitted. "But I came away with something far more valuable, a real friend." She turned and looked back at the stall she'd just left. Strikes the Iron waved at her, then went back to serving her customer.

"Strikes the Iron is very wise," Bart said. "I can think of few people I respect more."

"She certainly is," Imogen agreed. "And I am glad that I got to see her again."

"Now, would you care to dance, Miss Potts?" he asked gallantly, with a bow and a flourish.

"I'd like to drink my cider, but I am sure that Joanna would be happy to dance a reel or two with you," Imogen said.

Joanna nodded her agreement and Bart took her out onto the dance floor. Imogen watched as he whirled her friend around, both smiling and happy. She wondered for a moment what it was that Bart had wished to tell her, but a part of her was already sure that she knew. It was why she'd stopped him earlier, because if he were to confirm it, she would have to decide what to do about it right away – and she wasn't ready.

Not that it much mattered what he said, this trip was not going to give her the escape her mother had hoped for. Imogen knew that coming here was about saying goodbye. She did not want her friendship with Bart to end, it had brought her so much happiness. But his presence in her life would only hurt her father more, and so she would either have to say goodbye to Bart, or to her family. And the most terrible thing about it was that she had no clue which of them she would choose when she was finally pushed to make up her mind.

When Joanna was breathless, the pair returned and Bart claimed her hand, refusing to take no for an answer. The music had changed from the lively jigs and reels to a more serene waltz. Bart held her close, and Imogen let herself imagine what it would be like to dance with this handsome and kind man every day for the rest of her life. She fit so beautifully into his arms and felt lighter than air as he whirled her around effortlessly. He was all she could have ever hoped for when she had written that advertisement, all those months ago.

She smiled up at him and he smiled back, as if they were two untroubled lovers with their lives ahead of them. She wished that this night might never end, that this pretty fiction, as her Mama would have called it, might continue to make her world work. And that her father could remember his own words about not holding a man's past against him. She scolded herself silently. There was no need to borrow misery. There was time for that later. Tonight, she would enjoy every moment.

A lively tune followed, and Bart guided her around the floor, switching tempo as easily as he might from a walk to a run. His sparkling eyes held her gaze and she wished that she could get lost in them forever. How could she have been offered this moment, this connection with him? Why would God show them the love they could have had, if everything they had hoped for was not to be? There had to be a solution, though she could not find one.

He frowned slightly. "Our not talking doesn't seem to be helping," he said softly.

She shook her head. "No, I thought I could forget about it all, for a few hours at least, but it seems I can't."

"I know you are concerned for your father, but do you really think we should wait to talk about this? It is clearly bothering you. You smile and seem to be here with me, but a moment later you are somewhere else, and it is not making you happy to be there."

She sighed. "Perhaps back at the hotel. Let us enjoy the rest of our time here. Hold me, dance with me."

"You're preparing to say goodbye," he said sadly.

"I don't know what I am preparing for," she admitted sadly. "I only know that I don't know what I am supposed to do with what I know – or think I know."

He steered her from the dance floor to a quiet spot away from everyone else. "Imogen, I know you didn't want to hear what I wanted to say, but I think you need to. At least then you'll be worrying about what is real, not what you might be imagining."

"I think I know what you're going to tell me," she said. "I remembered that you said you hadn't always been a good man, that your past was something you'd much rather leave behind you. And my father recognized you. Why would you be so familiar to him if you were just a boy who lived in Deadwood. The town was full of boys. I doubt he'd be able to pick out any of them, even the sons of his own colleagues and friends. But he knew you, some eighteen years after we left there."

Bart nodded. "Yes, he knew me," he admitted. "Because I was there. I was in the bank, looking around for weeks before we did the job. I was there, on the corner, acting as a lookout – a role I failed to do well enough as so many of the gang were taken by the sheriffs. He knew me because I caused his worst nightmares, and my face probably figures in them still."

Imogen nodded. He was right. It was somehow easier hearing it out loud than it had been echoing around in her head all afternoon. Now it was real. It couldn't be unsaid, or unthought. Now, she had to decide what it meant. She raised her hand and cupped his face with her palm. He really was such a beautiful man, and she wished that everything between them was different. But it was not.

"You've not pushed me away," he said with a forced laugh. "Does this mean I might be able to hope for forgiveness?"

"Bart, it isn't for me to forgive you. I was not the bank. My father was not even the bank, though he took the robbery as very much a personal failing of his. You did not take anything of mine."

"I took your father from you. And worse, I took Miss Kelly's life."

"No, you did not," she said firmly. "Do not dare hold yourself to account for how he chose to deal with what happened or for Marta's death. You did not pull the trigger. You weren't even in the bank when any of it happened."

"It isn't that simple though, is it?"

"No, it never is," she said with a shrug. "So, explain it to me – your side of it, I mean. I've heard my father's side for as long as I can remember. Why did you do it?"

"I don't know. I've thought about it every day since then. I could use the excuse that I was a young orphan, and I was flattered that an older man was willing to take me in and give me a family of sorts. But I'm not sure that was true." He paused and bit at his lip. Imogen could see that talking about it was as hard for him as it was for her. But she had to know what he did. She could not make a decision without knowing everything.

"What might have been true?"

He shrugged. "I could say that because we only ever robbed banks that I never thought we were taking anything from anyone personally, but the money and the gold in those vaults belonged to someone. I could say I didn't have a choice, that I did what I had to in order to survive. Maybe it was all of them, but it may have been none of them. Marty always took pride in the fact that nobody ever got hurt – and I didn't know anyone had been until you told me. I knew he grew more violent after that, but the man he became, well he wasn't that way then."

Imogen nodded. "Did you enjoy it?" she asked him. "Was there some kind of excitement or pleasure you took from it all? I know many men say that risk is what fires their blood."

He shook his head vehemently. "All I know is that I never felt comfortable doing those things. I have confessed my sins over and over, done more penance than any priest has ever asked me to do, and I built myself a new life, an honest life. But I have always been looking over my shoulder, waiting for the lawmen to catch up with me, though in many ways I have spent my entire life locked away already, unable to let myself get close to anyone or stay anywhere too long for fear of losing them."

"Yet you let yourself get close to me? You stayed here, in Eagle Creek," Imogen pointed out. "Why me? Why here?"

"I think that having been here, you must see why Eagle

Creek won my heart and made me want to stay. I haven't made many real friends here, but I would count Mr. Hemsley as one, and Peter Algood. I was going to introduce you to him and his lovely wife, Jane, tonight. And why would I not wish to be close to you? You are funny, warm, witty and wise. You have a kind and generous heart – even to those who have done you wrong."

Imogen felt her face flush at his words and was glad of the darkness to hide how much they had meant to her. Nothing he was saying was making her choice any easier to make. If only he had said something that might make her hate him, despise him for being weak – or worse, for being evil. But he was still the kind and gentle man she had come to know. The errors of his past did not change that. In truth, perhaps they were what had made him the man he was – one who never wished to cause others pain again.

The image of her father, railing madly against him last night flashed through her mind. If only Papa could see that Bart was not the sum of a few foolish decisions he'd made as a boy. If only Bart's mere presence did not cause her father such pain. "I don't know what to do," she admitted sadly. "Whatever I do, whoever I choose, someone will get hurt. I will be hurt."

"I'd never ask you to choose me over your family. I know that your loyalties are to them above all," Bart said firmly. "Do not worry for my feelings in this. I do not want to lose you, but I know that given the circumstances, you were never mine to lose. I can learn to accept that."

She laughed a little bitterly. "Your gallantry only makes it harder," she said. "Because you truly mean that. But I don't want to give you up. I want my father to get well, and I want him to learn what I know, that you are not what happened that day. That you did what he should have done from the first, you took responsibility for your part in it all and did all you could to be a better man."

"I have never taken responsibility for my part," Bart protested. "Perhaps I should. Maybe it is time that I did."

Imogen gasped. Was he truly saying what she thought he was saying? "You wish to go to the sheriff and turn yourself in?"

"Maybe I should," he said, as calmly as though he'd just told her that he wished to get another drink.

"You cannot. They'll hang you, you fool."

"They might, or like you the magistrate might see that I have done all I can to atone. But at least I could face your father and tell him that I am sorry."

"You can do that without confessing to a magistrate," Imogen said angrily. "I'll take you to him tonight, if that is what you wish to do."

"Imogen, you know that he will not think justice has been served until I am tried. And I can give the sheriffs information about the leader of our gang. He's out there, now, drawing closer, robbing banks all over the north-west."

"The man on the posters, with the evil eyes," Imogen gasped. "You knew him."

"Knew him, did everything I could to please him. He was like the older brother I never had. He looked out for me, fed me, clothed me, and so I did whatever he told me to do."

"But he's killed a man."

"He's probably killed more than twenty, from the sheriffs' reckoning."

"Why would you not give the sheriffs information about him before now?"

"How could I have done that, without giving myself up, too?

"Yet you'll do it now?" She shook her head and stared at him. "Bart, you're not making any sense."

"I had no reason to do it before – well, I did but I did not have the courage to risk my own life. I suppose I could have sent them an anonymous letter. But I was so afraid for myself that I didn't dare. What if it made them come looking for who sent them the note? What if someone suddenly remembered a boy hanging around with them all those years ago? I was so afraid. And I was a coward."

"Yes, you were," Imogen agreed, though she smiled to soften the blow of her words. "I am glad I have given you courage, but it also seems that I attract lunacy, too. You've barely known me but a few months and you're almost as mad as my father. Promise me you won't do anything rash, Bart? I couldn't bear it if I lost you."

He pulled her into his embrace, and they stood together, still and silent for what felt like a lifetime. If Imogen had hoped that talking would make everything clearer, she had been a fool. She had even more questions, more worries, and more fears now than she had ever possessed. How would they ever unpick this tangled mess?

He pressed a kiss to her forehead. "You know that you have to go home, and I have to go to the sheriff. While he's out there, I cannot just stand by. I've done that for too long. I won't wait until another man gets hurt or killed by Fitzgibbons. I'll not see another family's life ruined by him as yours has been."

"But…" Imogen began to beg him not to, to make him see reason, but he kissed her lips, silencing her. She felt her body melt into his and knew that she could go home, but he would be seared into her memory as surely as he was in her father's. She would never be free of him, and nor did she want to be. Her arms wound tightly around his body, and she clung to him as though they were lost at sea, and he was a raft that might somehow get her safely to shore.

CHAPTER 19

DECEMBER 9TH, 1894, EAGLE CREEK, MONTANA

Bart rose long before the dawn. The world was dark, though the snow on the ground glistened in the moonlight. He'd barely slept. Everything he and Imogen had talked about played on his mind, taunting him. Whatever she had said, he knew that he had been a coward. He could have stepped forward years ago, given the sheriffs information about Marty that might have led to his capture years earlier. He could have saved others lives, and livelihoods. Instead, he had spent a lifetime looking over his shoulder, afraid of what might happen to him. It had been selfish and wrong.

But he had a chance to put that right. He could see no other option but to turn himself in, even if Imogen thought that foolish. Her father's health and happiness had been ruined and a life had been taken by Fitzgibbons and the gang's actions that day. His actions. Imogen's life, and her mother's life, had been changed irreparably from that moment onwards. How many other men, women and children's lives had been ruined by Fitzgibbons since? He could not bear the thought that there would be any more.

He dressed and made his way downstairs to the empty lobby. He left a note to his head clerk saying that he should take full control of the hotel, and that he would return in due course. Eddie was a sturdy, capable sort, if a little lacking in imagination. He'd not falter under the weight of responsibility and would do all he could to ensure that any scandal did not affect the hotel's guests or its reputation. He also wrote a letter to Mr. Hemsley, explaining everything about his past. He did not ask for his employer's forgiveness and kept his tone factual and to the point. He owed him that much. He did not doubt that Mr. Hemsley would be forced to terminate his contract, and he tried to find the words to say that he understood and did not hold that against him, that he was grateful to have had the happy years at The Eyrie he had been blessed with.

Not entirely content with what he'd written, he knew he wouldn't find any better words to say all he needed to, he left both letters on the counter so they would be easily found, then made his way to the stable yard. Even here, it was quiet. The only sound that of the swish of a horse's tail and an occasional neigh. He saddled one of the least popular steeds and mounted up, glancing around him one last time, trying to take in every detail, every scent, every color, every sound, before turning away from it all and heading down the snow-covered trail.

When he reached the town, it too seemed deserted though a few lamps had been lit, their faint light casting a glow over Main Street in odd patches. Everything from the market the night before still filled the street, stalls had been left up and the dance floor stood empty. Bart didn't doubt that there would soon be all the usual faces, out helping to put everything away, neatly, as if nothing had ever happened. He wished that his past was so easily tucked away.

The sheriff's office was closed when he arrived. Nate Hale was probably still having breakfast with his wife and family. It was too cold to just stand around, but he didn't want to disturb the man, so he dismounted, hitched his horse to the post outside, and began to pace up and down. The snow melted around his feet and the damp seeped through the thick leather of his boots, through his thick woolen socks, and made his feet feel like blocks of ice. By the time the sheriff appeared, Bart could barely walk at all, his feet were so cold.

"You're up early," Nate said as he unlocked the door to his office. "What's bothering you? You look pale as milk."

"Something I should have spoken up about years ago," Bart said.

"Well, come inside and tell me about it in the warm," Nate said, with an obvious shiver. "It'll take but a minute to get the stove burning and some coffee on." He went inside. Bart hobbled in behind him.

Nate soon had the stove lit, and as they waited for the coffee pot to boil, Nate pulled some clean socks and a pair of boots from a trunk behind his desk. "You may be glad of these, though they might be a little tight. How long were you waiting, for your boots to be soaked through like that?"

"Long enough, but I didn't mind." Normally, Bart would have smiled at such an observation, there wasn't much that the eagle-eyed sheriff missed, but today he couldn't muster anything more than a frown. His feet felt like they were burning they were so cold. Gratefully he took the boots and socks, sat down in the chair opposite Nate's desk, pulled off his own and put them on.

"You should have come to the house. I'm barely a block away."

"I didn't want to disturb your time with your family."

"But you have something so important to say that you're here at the crack of dawn to say it?" Nate said wryly. "You're a conundrum at times, Mr. Bartholomew King. Kind and polite, but never let anyone in too close. Everyone speaks highly of you – yet none of us really knows you, or anything about you."

"That's why I'm here," Bart said a little nervously. "It's

time you knew everything. And it is time I took the consequences for my choices."

Nate poured them both a cup of coffee and then sat down in his chair. He leaned back and put his feet up on the desk. "I'm all ears for a good story," he said. "You just sit yourself down and tell me everything."

Bart paused for a moment, wondering where to start. But once he started, everything flooded out of him. In moments, Nate had put his feet back down on the ground and had grabbed his notebook and a pencil and was scribbling down everything Bart told him. "You've been running scared all this time?" he asked when Bart finally stopped speaking.

"Yes."

"Well, I don't know how to break it to you, but you needn't have," Nate said. "There was never a warrant for you. Not even a wanted poster. Nobody in the gang ever squealed on you. You could have carried on living your life quietly, if you'd not said anything now."

Bart shrugged. "I needed to do this. Not to soothe my conscience, but to stop what happened to Imogen's father happening again. Surely, there is something in there you can use to catch Fitzgibbons before he hits another bank?"

Nate glanced down at his notes. "There is certainly a lot of information here that I don't think anyone else has, and some of it may prove to be very useful indeed." He leant back and put his feet back up on the desk. "But given all you've said, I'll have to lock you up and take you before the magistrate. Believe me, I don't want to."

"I understand," Bart said. "I came here knowing that. I'm ready to face the consequences of my actions."

IMOGEN AWOKE FEELING tired and grouchy, after an interrupted night's sleep filled with nightmares of Bart standing in a courtroom before a magistrate, her father brimming with glee at his demise, then standing, alone, on the gallows looking out at the gathered crowds, desperately searching for her face. She dressed quickly and hurried down the stairs. She beckoned one of the busboys over. "Is Mr. King here yet?" she asked as nonchalantly as she could.

"He left for town about an hour ago," the boy said. "Said he would be calling on the sheriff and that he might not be back for some time. Was it something important, Miss? I can call for Mr. Dobley, the head clerk. I'm sure he'd be happy to help you. He's in charge in Mr. King's absence."

"No, thank you, but could you arrange for a sled to be brought around as soon as possible?" Imogen said, her heart filled with fear. The boy nodded and ran off. She paced up and down in the foyer until the stable lad appeared and beckoned to her.

"Can this thing go any faster?" she asked, as they set off in the sled at a leisurely pace.

"It's icy, Ma'am," the boy said apologetically. "I'd not want to cause us or the horse any harm."

She nodded, understanding his reasoning. She sat back and tried not to fear the worst, but she could not think of anything else. Why, oh why had he gone to Sheriff Hale so quickly? Could they not have talked more? There was so much unsaid between them. She'd never even told him she loved him. And she did. With all her heart.

Finally, they reached the sheriff's office and Imogen barged in without knocking. A handsome man, with a gold badge on his chest was leaning back on his chair, his feet up on his desk. Bart sat opposite him. He was not wearing manacles. Imogen's heart leapt. Perhaps she had got here in time to stop Bart from being a fool. Both men leapt to their feet as soon as they saw her, giving her polite, nodding bows. It seemed so strange, almost out of place to be here and have them abiding by such social niceties that she almost forgot why she was there.

As she caught Bart's eye, he gave her a look that told her he'd already told the sheriff everything. She shook her head. "You shouldn't have come here," she said sadly.

"I'm sorry, Imogen," he said softly. "But I cannot live with the guilt I feel for my part in your family's suffering. I have to do the right thing."

"This is not the right thing," she protested.

"It is," the sheriff said putting a kindly hand on her shoulder. "His confession, and the information he's given me today will be a great help to us in finding Fitzgibbons and bringing him to justice. That will gain him a lot of credit when he goes before the magistrate."

"It won't stop them from hanging him, though, will it?" she said tears pouring down her cheeks. She felt like her world was crumbling around her faster than she could possibly reach out and push everything back into place. She longed to curl up in a ball and sob, but she could not do so. Not here. Not yet.

"It might," Sheriff Hale said softly, guiding her towards a chair. "And I know there are many people in this town who will speak on Bart's behalf. He's got more friends than I think he knows."

"Will you be one of them?"

"Undoubtedly," the sheriff said handing her a clean, pressed handkerchief to wipe her tears. She took it and blew her nose loudly, making the two men laugh.

"I can't believe you're laughing at a time like this," she said shaking her head.

Sheriff Hale encouraged her to sit, and Bart knelt down beside her. "I know that you are worried for Bart," the sheriff said as he leaned against his desk, "but I promise I will do all I can to help him. As I said he's given me valuable information so we can catch Fitzgibbons, and we need to catch him, Miss Potts. Bart is well-respected here. Everyone knows him and many will be happy to testify that he isn't the boy he was then."

"And I don't think there's a magistrate in the state that hasn't stayed at The Eyrie at some point," Bart added, taking her hands in his.

"What if they had bad soup, or their rooms weren't clean enough during their stay," Imogen said stupidly, giving them both a wan smile.

"Then he's in deep trouble even I can't help him with," Sheriff Hale said with a grin.

"I can assure you, Imogen, that I have never let a magistrate stay in an unclean room, nor has the hotel ever served bad soup, to my knowledge," Bart assured her, his golden eyes twinkling with merriment that oddly didn't feel out of place, despite the desperate circumstances.

Sheriff Hale's calmness was strangely reassuring. He seemed so certain that Bart would face a fair hearing that when she reluctantly left his office, Imogen was sure that Bart had at least a chance of coming out of this terrible situation with his life. But she now faced the problem of having to tell her father he was right, and she feared how he might react if Bart went free. Leaving her things at the hotel, she scribbled a quick note to Joanna, which she gave to the waiting sled boy and walked straight to the station, where she purchased a ticket for the next train to Billings.

CHAPTER 20

DECEMBER 9TH, 1894, BILLINGS, MONTANA

By the time Imogen reached her parents' home, they had already received a telegram to tell them about Bart's capture. Mama flung her arms around Imogen tightly. "I am so glad you came home. To think, he was one of them, all along."

"Mama, he wasn't one of them," she protested, pulling away from her mother's embrace. "He was a frightened boy, doing all he could to survive."

"He was one of them, and your father was right to be suspicious of him."

"How is Papa?" Imogen asked nervously.

"Vindicated," Mama said shortly.

Imogen sighed. How would she ever get her father to see

reason? If her mother was being so stubborn, then Papa would be utterly intransigent. He would no doubt demand the death penalty. All the way here, she had fretted over what she might say to her family. Now, none of the things she had rehearsed seemed suitable. She had so hoped that her mother might remember that she had liked Bart, found him charming even. But it seemed that Mama could be as unforgiving as Papa.

"Where is he?"

"You'll not get him to speak on behalf of that man," Mama warned her as Imogen tried the door of her father's study. "I'm surprised that you would even consider it, given all the pain he has caused us all."

"I consider it because Bart was a boy. He did as he was asked by a man that he was afraid of. The man that might finally be caught because of all Bart has told the sheriff. A man who has killed people with no remorse because they stood in his way. Do you think that a boy could have stood in his way? Do you think a boy would have been able to stand up to a man like that?"

Mama had the decency to look a little ashamed. But Imogen could see that she still longed for revenge – whoever might be the one to pay the price for that. That Bart had put himself forward was enough for her, she would take her pound of flesh. As she entered her father's study, Imogen had few doubts that her father would feel the same way.

"Papa," she said cautiously. The room was dark, and all

she could see of her father was his feet, sticking out at the bottom of his large armchair by the fire. A puff of cigar smoke plumed above the high back of the chair.

"I told you I knew him," Papa said as she took the seat opposite his. He had the most grotesque smile upon his face, it was almost chilling to behold. Imogen shivered, though the room was so warm she could hardly bear it. "You said it couldn't be."

"Because it seemed so fanciful, so unlikely that I should somehow meet someone, eighteen years later, that had been involved in the robbery. It is quite the coincidence."

"The Lord moves in mysterious ways, but he has finally blessed us," Papa said. "I'll be the first to that courtroom to condemn him, and I'll watch him swing with delight." He seemed almost deliriously happy. Imogen could hardly believe that her kind, frightened father could have become this almost maniacal creature, hellbent on the death of the man she loved.

"Is there anything I can say that might make you see the truth?" Imogen begged him. "Bart was a boy. He had no choice. But he didn't rob the bank himself. All he did was stand lookout. He did you no harm, none at all – and he is helping them to catch the man who did. Does none of that matter to you? He has made something of himself. He is a good man. A respected man. He left all of that in his past, long ago. Why can't you? Why have you tormented your-self, and us with it all these years? They did not harm you.

They did not take our money. What did they really take from you at all, Papa?"

"My pride, daughter. As a girl, I'd not expect you to understand that, but I'll wager your Mr. King understands it. I failed the town that day. People I cared about lost everything. I could not hold my head up and say I'd done all I could to protect them, to protect their money – because if I had, that day would never have happened."

"You could have done everything there is possible to do, and it would still not be enough to face down men with guns who will use them without compunction."

"Leave me, daughter. Don't make excuses for him. He knew what he was a part of. He could have come forward before, he could have made a difference before. He did not, and so he is a coward that deserves his fate. I'll not speak for him. I'll not consider his side of this, so don't try and make me. I'll see him hang and be glad of it. It is no less than he deserves."

"So, all these years your words to me meant nothing," Imogen said sadly.

"What are you talking of daughter?"

"You have told me so many times that a man is not the sum of his past, that it is his actions in the present that one should judge him on. You clearly never believed a word of that, did you? You just said it because it made you sound magnanimous. You cannot bring yourself to even consider that Bart is not the boy he was. Your need for revenge and retribution is too great to abide by your own convictions."

"I never meant those words to be applied to criminals," her father spluttered.

"But who else would they need to apply to?" Imogen asked him softly. "Who else needs their past to be overlooked?"

Shaking her head, dismayed and a little ashamed by her father's vitriol and hypocrisy, she fled from the room. She raced up to her own room, slamming the door behind her. She threw herself down onto her bed and sobbed. She had harbored only the slightest hopes that she might get her father to speak on Bart's behalf, but they had been utterly smashed to pieces in their short exchange. She had no doubt that her father would do exactly as he had said he would and would crow delightedly if Bart were sentenced to death – even if that would break her heart. Her father did not care about her feelings in the matter, only his own.

She had always believed that her father had been ruined by the robbery, that he had been taken from her that day because of what happened, but she was suddenly no longer sure that was the case. Had she ever known him at all? Had he always been rude and selfish? Had she been too young to realize that he had always been that way? Had he really just admitted that all that had been hurt was his pride? She did not want to believe that he had made all their lives miserable because he felt he could no longer hold his head high. It all seemed so petty, so utterly nonsensical to her that his reputation meant more to him than her mother's happiness or hers. His spite had festered away inside him, a canker in their midst that could never be excised.

But what did that mean for her now? She couldn't stay here. But she had little money, only what was left of her quarterly allowance – for she didn't doubt that if she left home her father would cut her off without a penny. She had no skills, so finding work would be difficult, and where would she go? Thanks to her father, she'd never stayed anywhere long enough to truly make friends. Could she rely upon Joanna to help her? What if Mr. Hemsley took the news badly and refused to support Bart, too?

All she knew was that she had to be nearby. She could not bear the thought that Bart would face this alone. Even if she had to watch him be sentenced to hang, she would not forsake him. She knew that he could not change his past, but that he was not that boy any longer. He was a good man, a far better man than her father was. He'd not let his pride get in the way of what was right. It might have taken him all this time to do the right thing, but she had to acknowledge that he had done that now. She respected him even more for doing so. And she loved him, with all her heart.

She sat upright and planted her feet firmly on the floor. Surely, there had to be something she could do to help him. There had to be someone, someone who was affected by the robbery that she could speak to, who could be persuaded to see the truth of the matter. Bart needed to have as many people on his side as she could muster. And she knew just the place to start.

DECEMBER 15TH, 1894, BUFFALO, WYOMING

The bank towered over every other building nearby. Imogen took a deep breath before entering. She couldn't help thinking that this trip might be a waste of time, but she knew that she had to try. Bart's trial was in just two weeks' time, and unless Nate and the other local sheriffs somehow managed to track Fitzgibbons down in that time, all Bart had to rely on would be the testimony of those affected, and those who knew him now. She needed to know she had tried everything she could to influence what was said.

She straightened her spine and held her head high as she marched through the main foyer of the bank, past the lines of people waiting to transact their business with the cashiers behind their counters. She went straight to the stairs she'd only once gone up before, when her father had brought her here as a girl. A liveried man stretched out a hand to stop her from opening the door to the stairwell. "I'm here to see Mr. Fortescue," she said firmly.

The man frowned. "One moment," he said. She waited patiently for him to speak to a rather stern looking young man with wire-rimmed spectacles, who was working at the counter nearby.

"He has no appointments available today," the man said on his return. "You'll have to come back another day."

"I'm his goddaughter," she said with an exasperated look. "I'm sure I shouldn't need to make an appointment."

The man looked mollified, but the stern-looking clerk was not convinced. He came out from behind the counter. "Wait here. I shall see if he can see you. It really is quite rude to come without an appointment, he is a very busy man."

"I am well aware of that," Imogen said. "But I simply must see him, so please tell him that."

It took less than four minutes for the clerk to return looking sheepish. "Miss Potts, please accept my apologies. Mr. Fortescue will see you immediately."

Feeling a little annoyed, Imogen climbed the stairs and walked along the corridor to her godfather's office. She rapped on it lightly and entered before being invited. "Good day to you, Uncle Luther."

"And to you, dear Imogen. I must say this is quite the surprise. Sit down, my dear, my secretary will bring us tea shortly."

"Uncle Luther, I'm not here for a social call," she said as she took off her hat and gloves and took the seat opposite his desk. "I'm here because, well, because of the trial."

"The trial?"

"Well, yes. Mr. King's trial, in Eagle Creek."

"He'll be taken back to Deadwood, to face trial where he committed the crime. Did you not know?"

"To Deadwood?" Imogen's heart sank. All Nate's consolatory words about Bart knowing all the magistrates in the state suddenly turned to ash.

"Oh my." Imogen found she could say nothing more, as tears threatened to fall. She gulped them down and shook her head.

Her godfather gave her a quizzical look. "What are you really here for? I would have thought that your family would be delighted that another one of those bandits has been caught."

"My parents are," Imogen admitted. "I can't remember ever seeing my father so ghoulishly happy. I think I preferred him when he was so miserable that he wouldn't leave his bed."

"That is quite the thing to say," Luther said. "Why are you not happy that someone who caused your family such torment has been caught? For I can see by the puffiness around your eyes that you have been crying."

"Almost non-stop," Imogen confessed. "For Mr. King is a friend of mine. A good friend."

"Ah, I see."

"No, I'm not sure that you do. The man that has been caught was no more than a boy when that robbery happened," Imogen told him. "He was afraid and did as he was told by a man who had cared for him like a brother. He had nobody else and knew no better. He has not committed a single crime since. In fact, he has done all he can to become a pillar of his society, a man of worth and substance. He is without doubt a good man – and he handed himself in, despite there never having been a warrant writ for his arrest."

"He still broke the law," Uncle Luther said softly. "A man should pay for his crimes, Imogen, it is the very basis of our legal system."

"He has paid for them, over and over, always looking over his shoulder, never being able to make anywhere his home, or permit anyone close to him for fear of them learning the truth about his past. *His past.*" She stressed the last two words heavily. "He was just a boy."

"Should you not be saying this to your father?"

"My father will be the first man in line to condemn him, you know that, Uncle. But it was not my father who was robbed, it was the bank – and the bank belongs to you. "So, your word supersedes that of my father, does it not?"

"I suppose it does, but what if I am not inclined to speak on behalf of a man who robbed me? Who killed a valued member of my staff?"

"Because he didn't rob you and nor did he kill dear Marta. He wasn't even in the bank. He was just a lookout. Please, Uncle Luther. For me? I've never asked you or anyone else for anything. I've been a dutiful daughter and done as I was told, and lived a miserable and lonely life, because of all this. I will not let one of the few friends I have made die for something he could not have stopped, something he was just a tiny part of when he was just fifteen years old."

"That is the law's choice to make, not ours."

"No, it is the choice of men," Imogen said. "They make the laws, and they remake them when it suits them. If you were to speak of leniency, of forgiveness, that would be taken into consideration, you know that."

"I do, but I was not there. Your father was and he will be listened to, even if the bank itself speaks against the death penalty in this instance."

"But it would count for something," Imogen begged him. "Please, Uncle Luther. You have to stop this. Bart is the finest man I've ever known. He could have not said a word, but what he has told them will finally bring the man who was truly responsible to justice. That has to matter."

"You love him that much, that you are willing to lose your father?"

Imogen had been trying not to think about that. Hearing her uncle say it out loud made the reality of her situation seem bleak and without hope. "Whatever happens, I will lose someone I love," she said simply. "I would rather know they were both alive, though, than have one of them responsible for the death of the other."

CHAPTER 21

DECEMBER 21ST, 1894, DEADWOOD, SOUTH
DAKOTA

The cell at the sheriff's office in Deadwood was not as comfortable as the one Bart had been inhabiting in Eagle Creek. It was damp, with a cold stone floor and a small opening blocked by bars that let in icy cold air, so high up that Bart could not even see out of it if he stood on tiptoe. "You'll be out of here by tomorrow night," Nate had promised him as the Deadwood sheriff had locked him inside when they'd arrived late yesterday afternoon. He'd given Bart an apologetic look, then been hurried out by the Deadwood sheriff.

It had been the worst night of his life. Bart hadn't slept a wink, pacing up and down to try and keep warm, trying not to think about whether he'd be leaving here a free man the next day, or if he'd be taken elsewhere. A dirty, and foul-smelling man inhabited the cell next door. He, too, would be going before the magistrate today, but he seemed happy to tell the world that he'd killed the man he was charged with murdering in cold blood. Bart had heard him muttering to himself all night, but he hadn't engaged the man in conversation. In truth, he seemed half mad, alternating between reckless and prideful boasting of his crime, and sitting hunched in the corner of his cell mumbling something incoherent over and over again.

The sound of heavy boots and rattling keys made Bart's stomach lurch. The Deadwood sheriff was a humorless man, with heavy-set features and a permanent scowl. He unlocked Bart's cell and put manacles onto his wrists and ankles before leading him out to a windowless carriage that would take them to the courthouse. Bart was shackled to the bench and left with a deputy who would not look him in the eye, while the sheriff went to fetch the murderer.

Both his charges settled, the sheriff got into the carriage and sat beside Bart. "His trial will be first, it'll be short," he said grimly, nodding towards the other man who was now singing to himself. Bart didn't doubt that, after all a man who so easily confessed to his crimes would not need much time in court.

"You'll not have long to wait to find out your fate," the sheriff added and unexpectedly gave Bart a reassuring look.

"It's best to know, right? So you don't keep running the possibilities over and over."

"I suppose so."

Bart felt every jolt deep in his bones as the carriage seemed to find every rut in the road between the sheriff's office and the courthouse. When they finally got there, he was taken to another cell and locked in. "I'll come for you when it's time," the sheriff said brusquely. "You've got a couple of visitors. They'll be through in a minute."

Wondering who could possibly have come to see him, Bart waited by the bars. He supposed that it was probably Nate, so he was overcome with delight when he saw Imogen, Joanna and Mr. Hemsley walk along the corridor towards him behind Nate Hale. "How are you?" Imogen asked him, taking his hands through the bars.

"Tired," he admitted. "I've not slept much."

"You look so pale," she said, caressing his cheek. "I can hardly bear to see you this way."

"It won't be for long. You'll be free and back home where you belong in no time," Mr. Hemsley said bravely.

"You'd take me back?" Bart asked him.

"You were a boy," the older man said gently. "I'll not hold a few indiscretions against you. I'm sure we've all got things in our past we're not proud of."

"I know I do," Nate said softly. "I wasn't always a sheriff, and my past helps me to be better at that than I ever would have been without it."

"They always say that to catch a thief you need to set a thief after him," Mr. Hemsley agreed.

"Has there been any news of Fitzgibbons?" Bart asked hopefully. He knew that his hopes for acquittal hung in the balance – if his information about Marty proved useful, it could sway the magistrate's opinion his way.

"The sheriff in Ucross took him into custody yesterday, not long after I left you with the sheriff here," Nate said calmly, as if he were simply passing the time of day. Bart stared at him incredulously. Nate grinned. "Your information helped us to find some of his hideouts. He's strangely predictable, even after all these years, goes to the same spots you told us about between robberies. He really likes the Crazy Horse Saloon in Recluse. We were able to place a man at the saloon who gained his trust enough to be brought into the gang."

"Oh my," Bart said, his knees suddenly weak as the sheriff's words sank in.

"This is wonderful news," Imogen said excitedly. "It has to have an impact, doesn't it?"

"It will help, but word is that Feldman Muldoon is a tough magistrate," Nate said. "He's fair, and he'll hear you out, but to him, the law is the law."

"So, I'd best say goodbye to you all now," Bart said, trying to keep his voice light. "Mr. Hemsley, I trust you to take the ladies far from the court as soon as my sentence is read out. I don't want them here for what follows after."

"I'll not leave you," Imogen said firmly.

"You will, I'll not have you see that," he said. "Don't let your tears be the last thing I see."

"You'd rather it be my father's gloating face?" she said angrily.

"No, I'd rather it not happen at all, but it most likely will – and we have to be prepared for that. I couldn't bear to think of you being haunted by that sight for the rest of your days."

Imogen nodded and kissed his hands. He kissed hers too. "You will not die this day," she said firmly, as if she might wish it into being.

The four of them left Bart alone. He sank down onto the wooden bench at the back of the cell and buried his head in his hands. After all he had done to escape this very fate, here he was, having walked into it willingly. He could not decide who was most touched by madness, himself or his cellmate the night before. But he did not have time to ponder it for long, as the Deadwood sheriff returned and marched him into the courtroom.

The magistrate's chair at the very front of the room was empty, but the benches behind Bart were completely filled with people. Some he did not recognize, but many he did. It seemed half of Eagle Creek had come to Deadwood to see his trial. He wondered if they were on his side, or just here for the spectacle. But there was one face he not only recognized but one that told him clearly that he wished Bart were already dead. Mr. Potts sat in the very front row, his eyes full of hate and spite.

Bart turned away from him. He knew that there was little that he could say that would ever make Mr. Potts change his mind about what his fate should be. He only prayed that Imogen would not lose her family because she cared for him. She had already lost a happy childhood to Bart's actions, he could not bear the thought she might lose the love of her mother and father, too.

Feldman Muldoon was announced and swept into the courtroom dramatically. He looked a little like a bald eagle, with a hooked nose and sharp eyes that missed nothing. He glanced around the courtroom, glowering at anyone who dared to so much as whisper. "I'll have order in this court," he demanded. "Anyone speaking out of turn will be turned out immediately." His gaze rested on Bart, who tried to meet his glare without fear. "We are here to examine the events of the eleventh day of April, in the year of our Lord, 1875. There are likely many versions of what happened that day and memories may have lapsed somewhat given the intervening years, but it is my job to find the truth and to pass judgment."

What followed felt endless. Mr. Muldoon asked him hundreds of questions, many of them repetitive, as if he hoped to trip Bart up. It was exhausting, but Bart told the truth each time so had no fear that the magistrate would catch him in a lie. "You may take a seat," Mr. Muldoon said eventually. Bart gratefully sat down on the chair one of the deputies brought to him. It was a kindness that Bart knew was not often offered to a prisoner. Most men were expected to stand throughout – no matter how long it might last. Bart prayed that it was a good sign, that the magistrate had warmed to him.

"There are a number of people who have approached the court, and we will hear from them all in turn," Mr. Muldoon explained. "Mr. Ansell Potts will be first."

Bart inhaled sharply as Mr. Potts rose up out of his seat. Mr. Muldoon peppered him with a number of questions, too, but Mr. Potts was so incensed that he often got his answers muddled, and he was not clear. It was actually a little painful listening to him. Bart wondered how much of this somewhat frightened, angry and scared man had existed before the robbery. It hurt to see Imogen's tears as she listened to her father fumble over what he wanted to say.

"Do you have anything further to say?" Mr. Muldoon asked him when he was satisfied.

"I have a small statement I wrote, I think it perhaps might speak more coherently of that day than I just have," Mr. Potts said, bravely acknowledging that his testimony had been less informative than he had perhaps hoped.

"You may read it," the magistrate said.

Mr. Potts pulled out a piece of paper from his pocket. He glanced momentarily at Bart, then at his daughter. A flash of rage passed over his face before he turned back to the paper and began to read. His voice was clear, even though he faltered over some of the words, as he denounced Bart and his actions that day, and advocated strongly that Bart should receive the punishment he deserved – to be hanged. Imogen's hand flew to her mouth to stifle a cry. Bart wished he could console her, but he turned back to face Mr. Muldoon.

The magistrate took a deep breath. "We shall now hear from Mr. Luther Fortescue."

Bart glanced around, not knowing who Mr. Luther Fortescue was. A handsome older gentleman, of similar age to Mr. Potts stood up and bowed politely to Mr. Muldoon. Bart had never seen this man before in his life, and wondered why he was there. He glanced at Imogen who seemed strangely happy at the appearance of this stranger and wondered what she had been up to.

"You are the owner of the Deadwood bank, Sir?" Mr. Muldoon asked.

"I am, as well as many other banks in the northwest of our great country," Mr. Fortescue said proudly.

"And were you present on the day of the robbery?"

"No, I was not, but it was my responsibility to manage the aftermath of the robbery, to placate our customers and to manage their expectations."

"You have done this successfully?"

"I believe that the bank managed to limit its losses, and Mr. Potts has been most diligent in ensuring that all of our branches have the very best security measures possible ever since."

"Would it be fair to say that you had not much thought about such measures before the robbery?"

"I will confess that we were a little lax," Mr. Fortescue said. "Looking back, I can see that we were almost advertising how easy it would be to rob us."

"But not anymore?"

"Not anymore."

"So, in some ways you might say that being robbed has improved your bank?"

"In many ways it did," Mr. Fortescue said. "It made us much more aware, and awareness means you can take action, something that Mr. Potts, in particular, now excels at."

"A robbery made him a better employee?"

"In many ways," Mr. Fortescue said. "And I am ashamed to say that the bank rather exploited his fears following the incident, to our benefit."

"You did not encourage him to face his fears?"

"No, I rather think we encouraged him to keep running from them. It gave him more ideas how to prevent further robberies and meant we always had someone we knew would take all necessary measures when setting up a new branch."

"So, do you believe that Mr. Waters should hang for his crimes?"

"No, I do not. I believe that Mr. Martin Fitzgibbons should as the leader of the gang and perpetrator of more than twenty similar robberies, but the boys he used as lookouts? No, I don't believe they should hang for following a man who would beat them in an instant, or worse, if they did not."

"Thank you," Mr. Muldoon said. "You may stand down."

Mr. Fortescue smiled at Imogen as he took his seat. Bart couldn't help noticing the furious glare that her father gave to them both. They had clearly gone behind his back, which meant Imogen had been to visit this very important man on his behalf, to beg him to make this testimony. He wondered how much it might help but didn't dare pin his hopes upon it.

What followed was a parade of people all speaking on his behalf about the man he had become. Aston Merryweather, the town postmaster; Mr. Hemsley; Peter Algood; Nate Hale; Tom Greening; and a number of Montana magistrates who had made the journey to Deadwood to speak on his behalf. Bart could hardly believe how kind and generous all of them had been to take their time to come here, knowing they might not be able to spend Christmas with their families, should his trial go on for more than a day. He would never be able to repay them.

The final witness was the sheriff of Ucross, who spoke of the attempted robbery of their bank and the information that Bart had given to the lawmen of Wyoming, South and

North Dakota and Montana being essential in thwarting it. "Martin Fitzgibbons is finally in custody, thanks to this man," he said to finish.

"Well, that is mighty fine news," the magistrate said. "But does not hold any bearing on this man's actions eighteen years ago. However, I do believe that anyone in their right mind would be fearful of a man like Fitzgibbons, and so would any boy." He paused and looked over at Bart, then at Mr. Potts who was perched on the very edge of his seat, his face full of rage. "Stand up, Mr. Waters."

Bart stood and waited for the magistrate to speak. "This is a peculiar case," Mr. Muldoon said thoughtfully. "I don't think I've ever sat in judgment over a man who offered himself up of his own free will, after eighteen years of not being a wanted man. Yet, he did so. Because it was the right thing to do. His information has led to the capture of the man truly responsible for the crime perpetuated that day, and many others before and since. His friends and colleagues speak of a man who is kind and decent, honest to a fault, who has most clearly learned the error of his ways."

"I am bound by the law," he went on. "But the law cannot be rigid, or it will fail us all, when it cannot bend to take into account that men can change. Mr. Greg Waters was an impressionable, easily led young man – as were we all at fifteen, something we would all do well to remember." He glanced at Mr. Potts as he said it. "He was changed by what happened that day, as were many others – and it seems that good has come out of that for many people. Does that good outweigh the harm? I cannot possibly say, for the harms are personal."

"However, taking into account all that has been said here today about the actual role that Mr. Waters played, and has freely confessed to, in the robbery on the eleventh of April, 1875, I can only hand down a sentence that takes into consideration the man that he has become because of it. Greg Waters, now known as Bartholomew King, I sentence you to one month to be spent in Eagle Creek jail. The time you have already served will be taken into account." With that, he stood up and swept from the room.

Bart hadn't realized that he had been holding his breath, but he gasped for air now. He was to be freed. Not right now, but soon. He put his hands to his throat and took a few deep breaths, glad that he would not be hanging from it the next day. It was over. But as soon as he glanced over at Imogen, who was watching her father storm from the court without so much as glancing her way, he knew that this was barely the start. He might have his freedom, but she would never be free of the pain it had caused her family.

CHAPTER 22

DECEMBER 21ST, 1894, DEADWOOD, SOUTH
DAKOTA

Papa stormed from the courtroom, his face as black as thunder. Imogen frowned. Mama gave her a brief look of compassion then hurried after her husband. She wanted to be able to celebrate this unexpectedly fair outcome with Bart, but how could she when her father was still so angry? How could he truly wish to see a man hang for what Bart had willingly confessed to? It made no sense to her. It was such a small crime, when compared to those of Marty Fitzgibbons, yet her father seemed to want Bart to suffer the same fate that was amply due to the now captured gang leader. It was hard for her to reconcile her quiet, nervous father with the angry and unhappy man that had just left without so much as a word.

"He'll come around," Mr. Hemsley said kindly, patting her on the hand, before hurrying to congratulate Bart before he was taken away again, back to his cell in Eagle Creek.

Imogen followed him, her heart breaking for all she had lost. But Bart would be free soon, and that was the most important thing in this moment. She pinned a smile to her face and embraced him. "At least it is dry and warm in the sheriff's office in Eagle Creek," she said, fussing with the rumpled collar of his shirt.

"And you will be nearby?" he asked.

She nodded. "I have nowhere else to go now," she said sadly.

"I am sorry it has come to this for you," he said softly. "I would never have wished to come between you and your family."

"My father is being unreasonable," she said more firmly than she felt. "He will come to see that, especially once Fitzgibbons himself is tried. He'll understand."

"I do hope so, Imogen. I never wanted this for you, for us."

"I know, and I know I tried to talk you out of this, but you were right to face up to the past. I see that now. It was important for you."

"And for your father," Bart said. "He had to see justice being done – even if he cannot yet accept the outcome. I pray that you are right, that he will soften in time, but what if he does not? What does that mean for us? I will not ask you to choose me over your family."

"You do not have to ask. I shall make that decision myself," she assured him. "And it will hurt whoever I choose, I am prepared for that – though I fear my choice may already have been made."

Nate gave her a rueful smile. "I have to take him back now, it's a long journey and it's for the best that we get on the road quickly."

She watched as he led Bart away. Mr. Hemsley stood to her right, his arm around her shoulder, as Joanna took her hand to her left. Having such good friends meant the world to her in that moment. She was grateful to them for the support they had given her, and Bart. It helped her to believe that not all people would condemn a man for something he'd done as a foolish boy, that many would see the man he had worked so hard to become. She could only pray that in time her father would do the same, for she wasn't sure what she would do if he did not.

They retired to the hotel. Imogen was glad that she had a room to herself and vowed to thank Mr. Hemsley for insisting upon it when she and Joanna had said they would happily share. He had been sure that she would need some time alone, whatever the outcome of the trial, and he had been right. She lay on the bed and tried to think of anything she might be able to say to her father to make him see sense, but she knew there was nothing she could say that would make any of it better for any of them. Too much time had passed. Her father had been too badly damaged by all that happened. But she couldn't let them leave without at least trying to make amends.

She got up and went out into the corridor. There were only two places to stay in Deadwood, and Imogen couldn't imagine that her parents would have even considered the saloon an option, which meant they had to be staying in the hotel, too. She ran down the stairs and asked the clerk for their room number. He seemed disinclined to give it to her. "They are my parents," she told him. "I'm not some stranger."

"I can't," the man said nervously. "I'm not permitted to."

"Then fetch me your manager," she insisted. "I will wait."

The man disappeared into the offices behind the front desk. A tall, thin man with grey hair and bushy eyebrows returned in his stead. "I understand you wish to be given the number of another guest's rooms?" he said. "I'm afraid we don't do that. We must protect our guests' privacy, at all times."

"And as I told your clerk, I am not some stranger seeking to gain access to some stranger's room. I am Mr. and Mrs. Potts' daughter. I simply forgot which number their room is. We arrived so late last night, and I was shown to my room first and we breakfasted in your lovely salon this morning, so I've not had cause to call on them yet." The man looked a little skeptical still, and Imogen knew she was probably offering too much information, but she had to see her parents before they left. She could not leave things as they were.

"It has been a very long day, and I simply wish to bid them goodnight," she continued. "They will worry if I do not do so." It was a very small lie to tell, though much of it was true enough. She waited nervously as the man scanned the page of the ledger of guests then looked up at her.

"I can understand their concern," he said. "In this instance, I feel I may bend the rules ever so slightly. You will find them in room seven."

"Thank you," Imogen said. "I am so very grateful."

She took the stairs slowly, not wanting to seem impatient or in any way out of sorts, knowing that the watching eyes of both the clerk and the hotel manager were upon her. Once out of their sights, she leaned against the wall of the corridor and took a few deep breaths before she sought out room seven. She still had no idea of what she intended to say to her father, and she feared that he may not even let her in to speak at all.

Her heart pounding, she made her way along the long corridor and stopped outside room seven. She paused and exhaled heavily before raising her hand to knock three times on the heavy wooden door. The door was opened just a crack by her mother. "Imogen, you shouldn't have come," she whispered. "Your father is furious."

"I know, and that is why I had to come, Mama," Imogen insisted, trying to push the door open a little wider. "Please, let me in. I have to talk to him. He has to know that I did not side with Bart against him, merely that Bart's need of me was greater in that one moment."

"He will never see it that way," Mama said sadly. "He feels you have betrayed him."

"I know, but I did not. I do understand that he wishes to see the men responsible for that day punished. I do. But Bart was not responsible for any of it."

"I know, he was just a boy. I listened to his testimony and the verdict of the magistrate, too, Imogen. But whether any of that is true or not, your father simply does not see it that way."

Mama frowned, but she came out into the corridor and closed the door behind her. Imogen reached out to embrace her, and Mama pulled her close. "My darling girl, of all the people you could have found to make your friend, why did it have to be him?" she said, shaking her head.

"He is not just my friend, Mama."

"I know, I know. And you are being torn in two by all of this. I am sorry for that, but I don't know what we can do to change it. Your father will not see you. He will not even let me speak your name."

"Is it really so bad? He cannot disown me for being the person he raised me to be."

"He may have raised you to stand up against injustice,

my love, but he did not raise you to forgive anyone involved in the worst day of his life, and certainly would never have expected you to go to Mr. Fortescue as you did."

"But he did raise me to look beyond people's pasts. He never stipulated that there was an exception to that rule," Imogen protested. "And Uncle Luther was the only person I could turn to, after Papa refused to see sense."

"Your father fears that it has made him seem weak, petty even."

"Uncle Luther would not, does not. He understands why Papa feels as he does. He said that in many ways he is to blame for supporting and encouraging Papa's fears, for they benefitted him and the bank so well. I know he feels bad about that."

"Well, that would explain the raise your father was offered just a few days ago," Mama said with a wry chuckle. "He thought it was because of his tireless efforts for the bank."

"In a way, it was," Imogen said. "Mama, I cannot let him leave without speaking with me. It mustn't end this way."

Mama sighed. "You'll find him outside the bank."

"Thank you, Mama."

"I can't promise he'll speak to you, and I fear it will only make things worse if you do – but I know that you have to try. I miss you, my darling."

"I'll write to you, whatever happens," Imogen promised

her mother, as she hugged her tightly once more and kissed her cheek. "Please write back?"

"I shall."

Imogen went back along the corridor. She turned and waved to her mother before taking the stairs down to the lobby. Mama gave her a sad look, then went back into her room. Imogen wondered if they would ever see one another again and wished that her final memories of her mother could have been filled with joy and happiness, rather than all this fear and regret.

She'd not taken much notice of how much Deadwood had changed since she had last been here, but now she could see how much bigger the town was. There were more shops, and three banks, rather than just the one that her father had run back then. It seemed somehow calmer than she remembered, despite there being more people everywhere. She walked slowly, taking note of the things she remembered and the memories they brought back. She'd played on these streets with her friends, enjoyed sweet treats on market day from the bakery with Mama, and visited her father in the bank to take him his lunch on the days that he forgot to take it with him. It had been a happier time, one she realized that she had let herself forget – as it was easier that way, because everything had changed overnight.

She found her father perched on the step of the postal office opposite the bank. She approached him cautiously. "Papa?"

"Imogen," he said, his tone clipped. He did not even turn his head to look her way, just kept staring at the bank.

"May I join you?"

"If you must."

Surprised that he had not just ignored her, Imogen sat down on the step beside him. "I think we need to talk, don't you?"

"Imogen, I am tired. I do not wish to hear you defend that man again."

"I am not here to defend him. He did an excellent job of that himself, if only you'd listened to a word of anyone's testimony but your own. And he has been handed down a punishment that is fair and has accepted it."

"So why are you here?"

"Because you are my father and I love you, and I cannot bear that there is so much ill-feeling between us."

"If you believe that sentence was just, I raised a fool," her father said angrily, turning to look at her for just a moment. His eyes were red-rimmed. He looked even more tired than usual. His skin looked gray and more wrinkled than she remembered.

"No, you did not. You raised me to be fair, to be reasonable. How can you not see that you are blinkered, no, blinded by your rage?"

"And do I not have a right to that rage?"

"Of course you do, but can you not see that it should be directed at those who were truly responsible, not towards a boy who was only trying to survive? Deadwood has never been an easy town to make a life in – of all people, you know that."

"He took his part in it. Many young men of the age he was are working, shouldering the same burdens as men. They are responsible, god-fearing boys. He chose a path that did not follow the law, knowingly. And that makes him responsible for all that happened that day."

"As responsible as the man who planned it? The men who executed it? The man who shot Marta Kelly?"

"He was a part of it," Papa said doggedly, though his voice seemed less certain than it had before. Or perhaps, that was just Imogen hearing what she needed to.

"No, he was charged as a lookout. He knew nothing of what happened in the bank. He was shocked when I told him of Marta."

"I find that hard to believe. Her death was reported in all the newspapers."

"And fifteen-year-old boys are well-known for reading newspapers, especially when they are running away from all they have ever known and don't wish to look back," Imogen remarked drily. "Papa, I know that day scarred you, that you can never forgive yourself for what happened to Marta, but you have to learn to forgive yourself – even if you cannot forgive Bart."

"I did nothing wrong."

"I know that. Mama knows that. Uncle Luther knows that – but do you? I mean truly?"

"Leave me be, Imogen. You're a child. You don't know what you are talking about – and I meant what I said. You chose him, and so you are no daughter of mine."

"I did not choose him, Papa," Imogen said with a heavy sigh as she got up and brushed down her skirts. "I simply applied your rules to his situation, that a man can change if given the chance to better himself. That youthful indiscretions should not be held against a man for the rest of his days. That you have chosen to forget that tells me that I have no father – at least not the one I thought I had."

CHAPTER 23

CHRISTMAS DAY, 1894, EAGLE CREEK, MONTANA

I t had been a strange relief to be returned to his quiet, warm cell in Eagle Creek after his brief sojourn in the more uncomfortable and unpleasant surroundings of the Deadwood jail. Bart knew he was lucky to have received so lenient a sentence, and though Nate had jokingly said he'd not tell a soul if Bart didn't see out his jail time, Bart had insisted that he take the punishment that the magistrate had handed down to him. It felt strangely good to finally be facing up to his past – and he could bear a few more weeks in the cell to gain true freedom at long last.

Nate was a kind jailer. He brought three good meals a day to his prisoner and let him have as many visitors as he liked. Imogen called daily, as did Mr. Hemsley who assured him regularly that he still had a position to return to, and that the hotel was managing without him – but only barely. But today was Christmas Day. Nate would be with his family, Mr. Hemsley and Joanna had told him about the plans for a big celebration at the hotel. Imogen had not mentioned it at all. He didn't know if she would return to her family, or if she feared she would not be welcome there. She would not talk to him about it.

So he was a little surprised when he heard voices in the sheriff's office, a little past eleven o'clock. Perhaps Nate had stopped by for something after church. After a few minutes the voices faded, and Nate's smiling face appeared as he unlocked the door of Bart's cell. "Well, Mr. Waters, it has been decided that you are to be released for one day into the capable hands of Mr. Hemsley, who is on a strict promise to call on me should you show any signs of ill behavior." He grinned and handed Bart some clean clothes. "You might want to take a bath before putting those on. We've got one ready in front of the stove for you."

Bart shook his head. "Well, this is a mighty fine surprise," he said happily.

"Be back here by ten o'clock tonight," Nate said.

"You don't think I'll try and run?"

"Given that you were the one who insisted on serving your time? No, Bart, I don't think I need to worry about that," Nate said with a chuckle. "They're expecting you up at the hotel. Have a wonderful Christmas, my friend."

"Thank you."

He left Bart alone in the office. The stove was warm and the galvanized tub in front of it was full of hot water. Nate had left a clean bath sheet, a small mirror, a razor and a bar of soap on his desk. Bart stripped off his dirty clothes and sank into the hot water. It was an unexpected luxury and one he would never take for granted again. He washed his hair and body thoroughly, then dunked his body under the water as best he could in the small tub. Once clean, he propped up the mirror on the top of the stove and lathered up the soap thickly and rubbed it over his neck and chin. Carefully, he shaved the beard and mustache that almost a month in jail had given him.

Feeling much more like himself, he got dressed and let himself out of the sheriff's office. A horse was hitched to a post outside with a note pinned to it. "Just for Today! From Jonas, Happy Christmas."

Bart smiled. It had surprised him just how many people in town cared for him. He rarely had a quiet moment, with people stopping by to tell him they were glad he was home and that they looked forward to when he regained his liberty and was back at work. It was something he had most certainly not expected. He had truly not realized how many friends he had here, but he was delighted to learn there were so many of them.

He rode up to the hotel slowly, enjoying the fresh mountain air and the space all around him. He'd always loved it here, but today everything seemed even more beautiful than ever. The Eyrie was blanketed with snow, nestling into the hillside with smoke coming from its many chimneys. It was so inviting, and he urged his mount to a canter.

With Jonas' Christmas gift stabled, he entered the hotel that he had helped to make such a success through the back door. But word seemed to spread quickly, because it seemed that the entire staff and all of their guests were waiting in the lobby to greet him with cheers. Mr. Hemsley shook his hand, then pulled him into a bear hug. "I'm glad to have you back where you belong, even if it is for just one day."

"It is good to be back," he agreed. "I've missed this place more than I ever thought it possible to miss anywhere."

"And you're barely a mile or two away."

"I know. It is strange how one place can be home, while another – even if right next door – is not."

"You think of this place as home?"

"I do," Bart admitted.

"So, you definitely aren't going to want to leave here? Not even for the new hotel?"

"Not even for that," Bart admitted. He'd had so much time to think about everything in recent weeks, and he knew that though a new hotel might give him a fresh start, he didn't want to make his life anywhere but here.

"Good, for I rather think that young Mr. Dobley might be ideal for the position there."

"I do, too," Bart admitted. "But who will be my chief clerk in his stead?"

"I was rather hoping that you might consider employing a woman," Imogen said, coming forward. "I've been helping out here, in your absence. I think I'm rather good at it, though you'd have to check with Eddie and Mr. Hemsley. I need a position. I have no money and no home. Working here would offer me both."

"It would, and it would mean I'd get to see you every day," Bart said. "I shall check your references and get back to you." He grinned at her. "It is so wonderful to see you."

"You see me every day," she said shyly as he took her hands in his.

"You know what I mean, away from that place."

"I do," she said, leaning over and kissing his cheek. "It is wonderful to see you, too."

They made their way through to the salon, where a number of regular guests greeted him warmly. Many had been sharing their gifts, piles of discarded wrappings sat nearby. Everyone seemed to be in fine spirits. An elderly couple sat at the piano. He played carols while she sang and encouraged everyone to join in. The mood was uplifting, and Bart felt truly content for the first time in his life.

He had spent so long looking back, always sure that someone would catch up to him, and would punish him for his misdeeds. His life had been lonely and full of fear, but he no longer had to worry about when he would be caught. It had happened, and he was blessed beyond all hope that his punishment had been so bearable. He had his friends to thank for that, and Imogen. He did not doubt that having the owner of the bank speaking up for him – no matter what it had cost her personally to get Mr. Fortescue to do so – had been what had swayed the magistrate towards leniency. Mr. Fortescue was a very wealthy man. His voice carried and was heard by those in the highest positions in the land. And he had been on Bart's side.

MR. HEMSLEY HAD SAVED them the sofas closest to the fire. Miss Hemsley stood up to greet him as they approached, but the biggest surprise was that Peter and Jane Algood had joined them, along with their infant daughter, Alison. Peter shook Bart's hand warmly. "Good to see you where you belong, my friend," he said.

"I am glad to see you both, and especially this little one," Bart said, leaning over and caressing the baby's cheek, before pressing a brotherly kiss to Jane's happy face. "She's growing so quickly."

"She eats constantly," Jane said. "I'm quite exhausted by it."

"You look radiant," Bart said as Alison caught his finger and held onto it tightly.

"I have an excellent nursemaid," she admitted, as Peter's

brother, Mark, and Peter's deaf-mute protégé, Wilbur, came in the French doors.

"Which of you is the nursemaid?" Bart asked, amused at the idea of either of the men being good with an infant.

"Wilbur," Mark said quickly. "I have no patience with her crying, though I am very proud to be an uncle. It helps that Wilbur can't hear her, I suppose."

Mark's frankness could sometimes be a little off-putting to many, but Bart found it rather refreshing. He well remembered Mark's first visit to Eagle Creek. It hadn't gone too well, but with familiarity, the somewhat awkward young man was coming to feel more at home here, and it seemed to do him good to get away from New York from time to time. He was much more relaxed now.

Wilbur, however, had been a delight from his very first visit. The lad didn't let his inability to speak or hear stop him in anything. He could scribble responses to people more quickly than many could speak them, and as long as he could see your lips, he had little trouble keeping up with even the trickiest conversations. Peter trusted him implicitly with all his business, and it was easy to see why. He was sharp and innovative, and adored his mentor.

She is a dote, Wilbur wrote on his pad quickly. *And though I can't hear her cry, I can feel it. She can be very loud when she wants something.* He grinned.

"I can imagine," Bart said.

One of the waiters brought through a tray of drinks as

people began to take their seats by the fire. "Dinner will be served at one o'clock," he informed them before he left.

"Thank you," Mr. Hemsley said.

"I am so grateful that I don't have to cook for everyone this year," Jane said with a grin. "I must confess that I was dreading it."

"But you love to cook!" Mark said, looking surprised.

"I do, very much," she admitted. "But cooking a Christmas lunch for all of you, with little Alison, well it would have been difficult to manage it all without at least one thing getting burned."

"I am glad we are here, then," Mark said solemnly. "I do not like burned food."

"I don't think anyone does," Peter said, giving his brother a friendly punch. "But I'm glad we're here, too. It is good to be amongst our friends, even though dear Cable was unable to join us this year. Important business at the hospital kept him from traveling in time."

He will be here to see in the New Year. Wilbur took Alison from her mother's arms and sat down on the floor with her. He seemed quite unbothered by the strange looks some of the other guests gave him, and continued to play with the little girl, pulling all manner of faces to make her gurgle with delight.

"I will be glad to see him again," Bart said, "though I'm not sure that Nate will let me out again so soon."

"I'll bring him to the jail," Peter assured him. "I know he'll want to visit with you very much."

"Thank you. You know, when I first handed myself in, I rather feared everyone's judgment. I didn't want any of you to see me there, behind bars. But you have all been so kind to me. I cannot tell you how grateful I am, and how lucky I feel to have you all in my life."

"We're lucky to have you," Mr. Hemsley said firmly. "And it is Christmas, so no more maudlin thoughts."

Dutifully, everyone did their best to tell jokes and share silly stories, but as the day wore on, Bart could see how much Imogen was forcing herself to appear happy. She seemed to be genuinely glad to be surrounded by so many of their friends, but it was clear to him that she was missing her family. After they had all eaten heartily, Bart invited her to join him for a short walk. She agreed and they bundled themselves up in thick fur coats and mittens to face the winter chill.

"You seem a thousand miles away at times," he said as she tucked her arm through his as they walked along the snow-covered paths outside the hotel.

"Just as far as Billings," she admitted sadly.

"I thought as much."

"It is the first Christmas I have ever spent away from them."

"That must be hard."

"Mama and I said we will write, but I feel the distance between us growing every day."

"I am so sorry, Imogen. All of this is my fault."

"No, it is Fitzgibbons' fault. I'll not have you take the blame for him, even if my father wishes I would."

"Fitzgibbons was hanged just two days ago," Bart said softly. "Nate told me. He said your father stayed in Dead-wood to see it, but that he didn't look happy at all."

"I always knew it wouldn't change anything for him. Even if he outlives you, he'll never let that day go. It formed him into who he is now. Without it, without his need for vengeance and retribution, I think he fears that there may be nothing left to keep fighting for."

"I am sorry for that, however small or large my part in making him that way was and is. I wish I could turn back the clock and change everything, but..."

"What's done is done?" Imogen said sadly.

"I suppose so. I should never have written to you. I have made everything in your life worse."

"No," she said firmly. "You have not. My friendship with you has been a joy to me. I would not change it or be without it – not for anything. Do not blame yourself for what has happened between me and my father. I think that we would have become estranged eventually anyway. He was too caught up in his own world, his own fear, his own pain to ever notice mine or Mama's. I think that in time, I would have come to despise him for that, for his weakness."

"He is not a weak man," Bart argued.

"No, he is weak. Other men have survived worse and gone on to lead healthy, happy lives. They don't dwell in the past, they do something about it. Like you. You ran away that day from all you knew, knowing it was wrong, determined to make something of yourself. And you did. You started afresh."

"And I ended up in jail," Bart said with a grin.

"You took responsibility for your part and have not once complained about your punishment. In truth, I feared you might beg the magistrate to keep you jailed for much longer."

"I think I was just too surprised that I wasn't going to swing, that I barely noticed how short a time I would be in that cell."

"I am glad for you. I don't think I could have ever forgiven my father if you had been hanged."

"You would have, you are the kindest person I've ever known," Bart assured her. "And though I do not deserve your friendship, I am grateful every single day that you think I am worthy of it."

"It is not just friendship," she said softly, turning to look him in the eyes. "You do know that, don't you?"

Bart felt his heart almost stop at her words. "I, I, I'm not sure that I do."

"I love you. I have loved you since that very first moment we met. You make me laugh, something there has been too little of in my life until I met you. You brought me my dear friend, Joanna, and you brought me here, to a place I already think of as home."

"You love me?" he asked, dumbfounded by what he'd just heard.

"I do," she said. "I do not expect you to love me back."

"Oh, but I do," he assured her, pulling her into his embrace and claiming her lips as his own.

CHAPTER 24

CHRISTMAS DAY, 1894, EAGLE CREEK, MONTANA

I mogen smiled up at him. In that moment everything felt perfect. He loved her, as she loved him. But they could not live in this moment forever, even if they wanted to. There were still so many barriers between them. How could they even try and pretend that they weren't there? She laid her head on his chest and tried to block out all of the thoughts in her head, and just be happy.

"Imogen," Bart said, as he pressed a kiss to the top of her head. "I want you to be my wife, but I will understand if you aren't ready for that."

She pulled out of his embrace. "I want it more than I have ever wanted anything in my life, but I want my mother and father to be there, for Papa to have given you his blessing to take my hand."

"I understand," he said. "I can wait."

"Can you?" she demanded. "I'm not sure I can. When I think of all I have already missed out on in my life because of my father, and now he will take this from me, too."

"Imogen, I know you don't mean that. We can be patient, he'll come around. He'll see how we feel about one another."

"That won't change his mind. He is prepared to say he has no daughter, simply because I argued your side of a matter that he will not see from any other perspective but his own. If I now go to him and tell him that I intend to marry that same man? No, he'll not even let me in the house, much less hear us out, Bart."

"So, what do we do?" he asked her. "Do we court one another until the end of time, simply because he will not acknowledge our love? Or do we wed anyway, despite him?"

"I don't know," Imogen said, tears pouring down her cheeks. She wanted to not care what her father thought. She wanted to be able to switch off the love she had for him and never look back. She wanted to tell Bart that she would gladly marry him the day he left Eagle Creek's jail. But she couldn't bring herself to say any of them – because none of them felt right to her.

"Give me some time to come to terms with things?" she

asked. "This has been the most peculiar time of my life, and I feel so very unsettled and unsure of everything but my love for you."

"From a girl who was uprooted as often as you, that is saying something," Bart teased, pulling her back into his arms. "I'll give you all the time in the world. Just don't shut me out. Talk to me."

"About what? How hopeless everything seems?"

"What happened after the trial? What did your parents actually say? You've never told me much, other than that your father disowned you."

"There wasn't much more to it than that. Mama promised to write to me, but I've written to her twice since we returned, and have heard nothing, not even her best wishes for Christmas. I feel so alone." She paused and shook her head. "Of course, she and Papa are still in Deadwood, she won't have even received them, yet. I must stop talking myself into despair. I will become as troubled as Papa."

"I know it isn't the same but remember that you have me. You hold my heart. And everyone here today loves you, Imogen. Believe me, I know what it is like to have no real family. But it gets easier to bear."

"Yours aren't still living barely an hour or two away on the train," Imogen reminded him, then wished immediately she hadn't said it. Of course, Bart must miss his family even if he had been so very young when he'd lost them – and he'd been alone for all that time since. He didn't moan and complain about it. "I'm sorry," she said. "That was thoughtless of me."

"No, in some ways you are right. It must be harder to have had family for as long as you have, no matter how troubled things may have been, and knowing they are alive and well – but won't see you. When someone dies, it is a clean break. You cannot bring them back and so it is in some ways easier to learn to live with the loss. I am so sorry that I brought about this loss for you."

"I will keep writing. I will not give up," Imogen said firmly. "I'll not lose them both – no matter how hard things get. I cannot lct that happen."

"Do you think your mother will write, eventually?"

"I can only hope so. She is probably having to be very careful around Papa right now. His moods can be dreadfully hard to bear. They take over the entire household, have us all walking on eggshells. I cannot imagine how he is feeling now. Will he finally be happy, because Fitzgibbons is dead? Or will he still be hankering after harsher punishment for you? Is he somehow hurting me, in order to punish you? And if that is the case, how could he be so cruel?"

"They are questions we cannot answer, and you would do best not to let them run through your head so freely," Bart said softly. "I know it is hard not to let our minds run free with such concerns, but we have to deal with what we know."

"Says the man who ran, and ran, and ran for eighteen years." She smiled wanly and he smiled back.

"Touché. But I am no longer running. I stopped and faced what had to be faced. And I did it, in part, for you – because I could not keep living my life that way, knowing that the ripples of what I had done all those years ago were still being felt so badly by those I didn't know and hadn't even thought about back then. I could not have confessed my love for you if I had not done so. It would have been selfish of me."

"Telling me you love me is not selfish. It is the most wonderful thing in the world to me," Imogen said.

"I'm glad you feel that way, for I intend to tell you every day," he murmured.

Imogen shivered a little as a cold wind gusted past them. "Perhaps we should go back inside," she suggested. "Even when dressed for the cold, it gets a little too much to bear when standing still for so long." He nodded and together they went inside.

Joanna handed Imogen a glass of punch as Bart went to speak with Peter and Wilbur. "So, did he ask you?"

"Did he ask me what?" Imogen asked, feigning ignorance.

"To marry him, of course."

"He said he wanted me to be his wife, but no, he did not actually ask me if I would care for that," Imogen said truthfully. Joanna's face fell. Imogen took her hands. "My dear, it simply isn't the right time for us. Too much has happened, and I am still reeling from it all. It would be wrong to take such a decision lightly, or in haste."

"I understand, but you make such a very lovely couple."

"He loves me, and I love him, and if we lived in a fairy tale, perhaps that might be enough. But in the real world, it is not that simple. If only it were."

"Mr. Algood's friend is rather handsome, isn't he," Joanna said changing the subject tactfully as she glanced over at Wilbur.

"He is, and very good with babies," Imogen said, grinning at her friend. "He would make an excellent husband to someone one day."

"They would have to go and live in New York, though," Joanna said sadly. "He seems very enamored with his work there."

"You seem to have learned a lot about him in my absence."

"He is very easy to talk to." They laughed a little at the absurdity of her statement, but it was also true. Wilbur, despite his difficulties, was an excellent conversationalist.

"More so than Mr. Tindall," Imogen said with a wink.

"Imogen, it is simply not the same," Joanna said. "I, well, I love Matthew. I get a little awkward around him because of it, as he does me. With Wilbur, it is not like that. We truly are just friends."

Imogen glanced over at Bart and smiled. "I'd say that

finding someone you can talk to easily might be a better choice."

"Not everyone can find a man like Bart."

"True, but just because you met Matthew first, does not mean you have to labor to find common ground when there is so little. Sometimes, you just have to take a chance on the one who you feel most comfortable with."

Joanna was saved from answering, though her blush told Imogen all she needed to know, as Mr. Hemsley joined them, beaming happily. "Joanna, dear, Mr. Dalton is asking if you might agree to accompany him and his wife to play some tunes so people can dance. She has her viola here, and I said I was sure that you would be delighted to join them. I fetched your violin and left it over by the piano for you."

"Do you have your flute?" Joanna asked Imogen.

"Sadly, I do not. It is still in Billings," Imogen replied.

"There is one in the stores, I don't know how good it is, but I could find it for you?" Mr. Hemsley said clapping his hands excitedly. "You do play so beautifully together. I am sure everyone would enjoy it very much."

"Then we shall find it and see," Imogen said, tucking her arm through his and following him to the storeroom, where they found the flute tucked away behind some spare linens.

She took it out and pursed her lips to the mouthpiece. It had a slightly dull sound, but as she began to play one of her favorite tunes, the flute and its tone grew warmer. "I think that will do nicely," she said.

When she returned, Joanna had found some sheet music, and the little quartet began to play. A few couples began to dance. Imogen let herself get lost in the music, enjoying the joy of making music with others, and having it be enjoyed by so many lovely people. After they had played four songs, Wilbur came and politely asked Joanna to dance. She blushed furiously. "Will you manage without me?" she asked her fellow musicians.

"Go," Imogen urged her.

It was a delight to watch them. For a man who heard nothing, Wilbur was an excellent dancer. He whirled Joanna around as Imogen and the Daltons played a lilting waltz. But what amused her the most, was watching Bart playing with baby Alison, whose parents were enjoying a brief moment for romance, staring into one another's eyes as they danced, oblivious to everyone else in the room. He was a natural with the child, who was getting a little fractious. She was probably overtired; she'd not napped all day. But Bart rocked her and sang a nonsense song along to the music until she drifted off into a peaceful sleep.

Wilbur relinquished Joanna to the quartet not long after Bart had settled Alison in a nest of blankets on one of the nearby sofas. They played a couple of lively reels, with Jane calling the dances. She was very good at it, especially as she continued to dance throughout. Bart laughed and joked with everyone, and when another waltz was called, just after the clock struck half past nine, he came and asked Imogen to dance with him. "It is my last chance, as I promised Nate that I would be back in my cell by ten o'clock," he said. "Let me go back with a song in my heart and the feeling of my girl in my arms?"

"Of course," she said, letting him lead her amongst the other couples already dancing. He took her in his arms, and she felt warm and safe. He would protect her from all harm, if he could. He wasn't as good a dancer as Wilbur, but he guided her round the floor with ease. It felt so right to be with him. How could it be wrong that they had found one another? Surely, all would turn out well in the end? It had to because things could not remain as they were. She simply couldn't bear the thought of being caught in this limbo of loving too many people and failing them all.

CHAPTER 25

JANUARY 9TH, 1895, EAGLE CREEK, MONTANA

The day of his release had come, and it was raining, turning the snow on the ground to a grayish-brown sludge. As he stepped onto the street, Bart still secretly felt that he had not received punishment sufficient for his crimes and knew all too well that few men enjoyed such a pleasant incarceration as he had. It almost felt like he'd not been punished at all, and that troubled him. He might be free now, but his soul was still troubled and felt as though he owed more than he had been asked to pay.

He chose to walk up the mountain to the hotel, to stretch his legs and refamiliarize himself with the outside world. Even in the terrible weather, with the gray sky overhead,

Eagle Creek had never looked lovelier to him. He took his time, stopping often to just stop and take a few deep breaths. He was surprised at how hard-going he found the walk, it had always been so easy in the past, but a month of sitting around had taken its toll on the muscles in his legs – and his chest it seemed. He struggled to draw breath as he tackled even the easiest parts of the climb.

His return to the hotel went almost unremarked, as if he had never been away, and for that he was grateful. Everyone knew what had happened to him, including all of the guests, yet nobody seemed to be concerned about it at all. It was most peculiar that there wasn't a single person in Eagle Creek who seemed to have any intention of holding it against him. He knew that such acceptance was extremely rare. Most men continued a life of crime simply because society closed its doors to them and gave them little chance to ever improve their lot in life. He was most certainly blessed in that regard.

He threw himself back into his work eagerly, catching himself up on all that had happened in his absence. Yet, his mind kept pondering the conundrum that faced him – one that had filled most of his waking hours while in jail, too – how he would ever get Mr. Potts to accept him as a suitable son-in-law. He understood entirely why Imogen was hesitant to marry him under the circumstances, but he could not bear the thought that she might never agree to be his wife. He had to do something to change Mr. Potts' mind. He had to get him to forgive Imogen, and to welcome her back into her home.

Not that Bart wanted her to leave the hotel. Between Eddie and Imogen, The Eyrie had been run smoothly and without incident in his absence. But Eddie would soon be leaving them, to go and run his own hotel for Mr. Hemsley, and The Eyrie would be his and Imogen's to run together. She had clearly won many hearts, not just his own. The guests absolutely loved her. He couldn't help but be proud of how well she had adapted to her change in situation. She truly was a remarkable woman.

"Bart, can you place more napkins on the linen order," she said as she came into the office. "I don't know where they go to, but we seem to lose at least fifty a month."

"Do you think the guests take them?"

"I would hate to suggest such a thing," she said with a smile. "But I can think of no other reason that so many disappear. That said, I did catch one of the waiters wiping up spills with one the other day, and fruits and sauces can be difficult stains to shift. Perhaps the laundresses simply don't put them back into circulation if they cannot get them clean enough?"

"I shall ask them," Bart said. "For if they are simply being set aside, we could reuse them as cleaning cloths, rather than have them go to waste."

"Perhaps they make use of them that way already," Imogen said with a wink, "just not here."

"You're probably right, and while I am happy for our staff to garner as many benefits to working here as we can afford to offer, we cannot afford to buy linens as often as we are now."

"How are you enjoying being back?" she said, perching on the edge of his desk and gently stroking his cheek.

"It is good to be busy again. I think the worst part of my time in jail was the boredom."

"Did we not bring you enough books?"

He smiled and took her hand and kissed her palm. "More than enough, but your thoughts wander a lot, it was hard to concentrate on them sometimes."

"That makes sense."

"Have you heard from your mother, yet?"

Imogen nodded. "It was only a short letter, but she wrote to let me know that they were safe home, and that my father is content that Fitzgibbons received the justice he deserved."

"Meaning he still thinks I did not?"

"I presume so. But we cannot worry about that now."

"No, we have a hotel to run and guests to make happy."

"And each other, we need to make ourselves happy, too."

"Just being near you every day brings me all the delight I could ever want," he said gallantly.

She gave him a sad smile. "It makes me happy, too, but it isn't enough, is it?"

"Not entirely," he admitted. "But it is what we have, and I never expected to even have that."

"Perhaps I should go to them again, try and reason with my father?"

"He won't be listening to reason, Imogen. Not for a while." He left unsaid that he feared that Mr. Potts would never listen to reason when it came to him.

"But he has to someday," she said hopefully. "He has to." She leaned over and kissed his cheek, then left his office, leaving Bart wishing there was more he could do to help her. Losing her family was too great a price to pay, and it was clear that she was terribly unhappy, even though she did all she could to assure him that she had all she needed and wanted.

With a heavy sigh, he made his way down to the laundry. The laundresses were busy, as always, scrubbing at stains, plunging the sheets into the vast copper vats on the fire, working the mangle and pressing the linens once they were dried. It was hot and humid down here, even though they had every window wide open – even though the temperature outside was below freezing.

"Is Mrs. Walcott in today?" he asked one of the girls working the mangle. She nodded and pointed towards the drying room.

Bart gave her a smile and crossed the laundry and went into the drying room. Racks filled with tablecloths, napkins and sheets hung from the high ceiling while a large stove kept the room warm. Mrs. Walcott was carefully draping sheets over one of the racks. She hoisted the rack as he approached her and tied it fast at the wall. "Mr. King, it is good to see you back where you belong," she said, wiping her hands on her apron before offering him a hand to shake.

"I am glad to be back," he said.

"We don't often see you down here," she said, leading him into her tiny office. It barely had room for an armchair by the fire, but she pulled out a stool from behind it and offered him her chair.

"No, I can take the stool," he said. "You sit down and enjoy a moment off your feet."

"I must confess that things are getting harder, the older I get. My joints creak something terrible," she admitted as she took the comfortable armchair.

"Is there anything I can do to help?" he asked. "Do you need more staff?"

"No, the girls I have are enough. What I need is a rich widower to come and sweep me off my feet so I never have to work again," she joked.

"I'm afraid I know few of those," Bart said with a grin. "But if any come by, I'll be sure to let you know."

"That'd be good of you, Sir. How may I help you today?"

"It's been noticed that we are losing a lot of napkins, bath sheets and other items, that we have to reorder linens more often than we should. I wondered what the practice was here if there are items too soiled to come back upstairs?"

"We cut them up and hem them for the chambermaids," Mrs. Walcott said without hesitation. "I don't like waste, but we don't lose many. Our Reba, she's a whizz at getting out stains, and Ellie can darn so neatly you'd never know that there'd been a tear."

Bart handed her the inventory list. "So, these numbers don't seem right to you, for what is being wasted or lost?"

"No, I'd say at most we lose one sheet a fortnight, perhaps a tablecloth a month and no more than ten napkins every quarter." Bart believed her. But that only left a mystery as to where all the other items were going. Could they all be accounted for by light-fingered guests? "Do you think we have a thief, Sir?" Mrs. Walcott asked. "Linens are terribly expensive. You'd be likely get a good price for them at the market in Billings, especially ones as fine as we have here."

"I think it is possible," he said. "But I hope not. I'd be grateful if you could keep your eyes open, though."

"Of course."

No closer to solving the mystery, Bart returned to his office. It didn't seem serious enough to bring to Nate's attention, but as he went over the lists that Imogen had brought him, he realized that the problem had been going on ever since the hotel had opened. Rather large sums of money had been spent to replace all that had been lost, and though one expected to have to buy new linens regularly in this business, it shouldn't be as often as The Eyrie was doing so. He wondered how he'd missed something so obvious, for all these years.

He pulled up the staff rosters from the past few months. Hotels often had quite a quick turnover of staff, but The Eyrie had kept most of its core team since the beginning. He looked over the names that had been here from when items started to go missing and drew up a list of those with access to the laundry and linen store, the dining room and bedchambers. It was a long list, but only four had regular access to all the places where linens could be taken from: himself, Mrs. Walcott, Jeffrey Haldane, and James Longworth.

He could not imagine that Mrs. Walcott would be involved in such a thing, though she had the most access, and he knew she had not done anything, so that only left the two men. Jeffrey Haldane brought all the deliveries from the station up to the hotel. He was responsible for checking everything that came into the hotel, and everything that went out. He was fastidious in his record keeping and a stickler for quality. His standards were high and his position at the hotel meant everything to him. Bart knew better than to assume that a man who seemed so honest and so proud couldn't be guilty, but he simply couldn't imagine Jeffery stealing so much as a single raisin from the larder, much less the amount of hotel linens that were missing.

James Longworth, the head waiter, seemed more likely. He was a little slapdash both professionally and personally, and a little profligate with his spending. He always had a ready smile and could be very charming, but often took advantage of his father's close friendship with Mr. Hemsley to avoid punishment when he was tardy, or a little less than hardworking. Bart had wanted to fire him – or at the very least demote him – ever since he'd arrived here. There were better waiters, and far better administrators among the wait staff than Longworth, but it was hard to do so when the man had been appointed by Mr. Hemsley himself.

But if Longworth had indeed been creaming a little extra from the hotel, on top of his already generous wages, Bart would have reason to finally be rid of him. He tried not to get his hopes up, for many an innocent man has been treated as guilty with no proof. He had no desire to ruin any man's reputation, at least not without solid evidence that it was him. His own run-in with the law could have ruined his life. He was blessed that it had not, but he knew many men were not so lucky.

He called for one of the bellboys and asked him to bring Longworth to his office. The lad nodded and hurried off to find him. Bart knew that asking outright would not work, but he had an idea about how to catch his thief. Longworth sauntered into his office almost thirty minutes later. "Sorry for the delay, we were laying the tables ready for tonight," he said, almost launching himself into the chair opposite Bart's without waiting to be asked to do so.

"No matter," Bart said, though the man's casual disregard for his authority irked him. "You've been here for many years, Jeffrey, and I noticed that you've not taken much time off, other than your allotted day and a half each week."

"No, I like to be busy," Jeffrey said, giving Bart a wink. Both men knew that to be a lie.

"Well, I think it is important that all our staff take some time, every year, to rest and recuperate. Our work is hard, with long hours and little thanks. So, I am going to start insisting that people take their permitted allowances for leave each year. You are owed more than a month, and I'd like you to take it now, before things get busy again in spring."

Longworth looked stunned, and just a little bit annoyed – or was it afraid? Bart wasn't entirely sure. "I'm quite well," he insisted. "I don't need any time off. Perhaps one of my boys can take some time instead?"

"I think it best if I start with those who run each of the areas of the hotel. Seeing your manager do something sets an example to those below, so they might be more likely to do the same."

"But what will I do for an entire month? And I presume there'd be no pay if I'm not working?"

"Of course, you'll be paid," Bart said. "You have a contractual obligation to this time. Most men would be delighted when their employers insist that they take time off."

"Oh," Jeffrey said, but he didn't look entirely relieved by the news. "I'll be off, then." He got up to go.

"And I'd like you to hand over your keys," Bart said before Longworth reached the door. Jeffrey's face was a picture. He took the keys from his pocket and stared at them, he almost looked as if he might cry.

"But you've your own," he said a little stupidly.

"But whoever I ask to step up in your absence does not," Bart said. "We only have so many sets of keys, Jeffrey. Leave them on the shelf there, if you will?" he nodded towards the bookshelf to Longworth's right. "Thank you. Enjoy your time off. I look forward to hearing all about it upon your return."

CHAPTER 26

Imogen couldn't help but smile as she took inventory. For four weeks running, the linen store showed a reasonable amount of wastage, rather than the excessive numbers of missing items she'd noticed before. She finished her lists and took them up to Bart's office. He took them and skimmed over them, only pausing to look at the linen sheets more closely. He grinned. "We found our man," he said.

"You found him. I'd not have thought of Jeffrey in a month of Sundays. He always seemed so nice."

"That is because you are pretty and lovely, and he thought he could pull the wool over your eyes," Bart said.

"Which was rather silly of him, because you are one of the cleverest people at The Eyrie."

"I'm not sure about that," Imogen said, feeling her cheeks flush hot at his compliment. "I would never have thought how to whittle down the list of suspects to one, and then find a way to be sure it was him without ever even mentioning a word about it to him."

"Once a thief, always a thief, I suppose," Bart said. "As Mr. Hemsley said on the day of my trial, if you want to find one, it is best to ask another thief how he'd do it. I tried to think who had sufficient access to things, then who had motive to do so. Jeffrey likes to live the highlife, or at least what passes for it in these parts. He buys fancy suits and likes to show off – a lot, and I know we don't pay him that well. It struck me that he had to be doing something else to make the extra money, or else he'd be in a lot of debt."

"He must have looked a little scared when you told him he'd be taking so long off work."

"He really didn't look happy about it. I'd been hoping I was wrong until I saw that. But these figures prove it. Not a single unaccounted loss since he's been gone. I don't look forward to it, but I am going to have to let him go, though I have my concerns about what Mr. Hemsley will say about it."

"Mr. Hemsley will understand," Imogen assured him. "He'd not want a thief in his employ."

"Well, we shall find out soon enough, for he arrives tonight with Joanna," Bart said.

"He does? They did not tell me," Imogen said, delighted at the news.

"I received a telegram just this morning," Bart said. "But his timing could not be better, so I can speak to him before Longworth's return to work."

"That is indeed serendipitous," Imogen agreed. "Oh, I shall so enjoy seeing Joanna. I have missed her."

"I know," Bart said softly. "But you are making good friends here now, aren't you?"

"I am," Imogen admitted. "But it isn't the same. Joanna understands me. She knows all about, well, everything."

Bart nodded. "I'm sorry," he said, for the umpteenth time.

"It isn't your fault," she assured him, and wondered how many times they would both say these words to one another. "But perhaps I should go and see my father soon. I know he may not have had time enough to calm himself or to examine his irrational hatred of you, but I'm not sure that I can continue seeing you every day and not being able to call you my husband."

"You still wish to be my wife?" Bart asked her, pulling her onto his lap and kissing her lips tenderly.

"I've never stopped wanting it," she admitted as she brushed his hair back off his face. "I love you."

"And what happens if he still won't listen? If he continues to disavow you?"

"Then I have to learn to accept that he will not change his mind and find a way to let go my hopes of him giving his blessing and walking me down the aisle."

"And you'll marry me?"

She laughed. "If you ask me properly, I may have to seriously consider it."

He held her tightly against him. "It has only been a month, I can wait," he assured her. "Because you are worth waiting for."

"I'm not sure about that, but I am glad you said that. However, I am not prepared to wait. I feel we have already lost too much time. I want to be your wife. I want us to start a family and to build a life together."

"I do, too. But not at the cost of the life you lived before you met me. I know that your father is a difficult man, that he made your life harder than it needed to be, but he is still your father and I know that you love him."

"I do. But I don't think that he has ever thought about me, or Mama, in all these years. Not once." Imogen frowned. "Everything has been about his happiness, his peace of mind, his pride. He's not once thought about all Mama has to do, always following him everywhere. Not once has he thought about whether I was ever able to make friends anywhere and how it would feel for me to leave them behind each time we moved on. He couldn't even think of my happiness, his pride and his vengeance were so much more important to him. I want to forgive him for that, but I'm not entirely sure that I can."

"You don't sound like you're ready, either," Bart said softly. He caressed her cheek.

"He has already disowned me," Imogen said. "How much worse can it be? Perhaps I need to see him, to know that it is perfectly understandable for me to disavow him, too?"

"Perhaps you do, but don't rush. Talk to Joanna about it first, see what she thinks. She may have word from your mother. We have time, my darling. I'm not going anywhere. I can promise you that. You hold my heart, and you always will."

Reluctantly, Imogen left his embrace and went upstairs to ensure that the master suite was cleaned and ready for when Mr. Hemsley and Joanna arrived. She had come to very much enjoy her work at The Eyrie. It was varied and kept her busy enough that she didn't spend all of her day thinking about her estrangement from her father. Sometimes she truly believed that confronting him would bring some kind of resolution for her, but most of the time she knew that neither of them were ready to talk everything through calmly. And if they could not do that, then there could be little hope of reconciliation.

Mama wrote sporadically, but she rarely said anything about Papa. It worried Imogen, making her fearful that Papa was perhaps having one of his turns and that Mama was trying to protect Imogen from it. But Imogen had long ago accepted that her father's episodes were nothing to do with her and everything to do with him. If he could not let the past go, if he could not forgive Bart or himself for whatever reason, then Imogen was sure that he would continue to have times when he simply was not himself. And if he could not let go of his fears and learn to be more at ease with the world, then he would never be happy. And that meant that she and Mama would forever be walking on eggshells around him. Well, not her, not anymore. She was done with trying to please him, done with catering to his nerves and the visions in his head – and she wanted to tell him that.

When Joanna and Mr. Hemsley arrived, Imogen hurried out to greet them, hugging her friend tightly and receiving a fatherly kiss from Mr. Hemsley. "I swear you are lovelier with each passing day, Miss Potts," he said as they went inside.

"You are too kind, and really should call me Imogen," she insisted.

"I shall be honored," he said as Bart joined them in the lobby.

The two men closeted themselves away in Bart's office and Imogen took Joanna up to the suite. "You do look well," Joanna said as they collapsed onto the sofa together.

"I think it is the mountain air, and being with Bart every day," Imogen admitted.

"You aren't having nightmares about your father anymore then?"

"No, now I just dream of giving him a piece of my mind."

Joanna laughed a little awkwardly. "I saw them, your mother and father, just last week, getting into a carriage outside your house."

"How did they look?"

Joanna paused, as if trying to find the right words. "Your mother looks tired. She's aged ten years since we saw them at the trial."

"And Papa?"

"I hesitate to say it," Joanna said biting her lip. "But he did not look well, Imogen. I think all of this is affecting him very badly."

"I spoke to Bart earlier, about going to visit with them, but he thinks I should wait, to give Papa more time. What do you think?"

"Honestly? I think you should go to them. I'm not sure how much time your father might have, and I know it would haunt you if you do not try and reconcile with him."

"You fear he is that unwell? That he might die?"

"I am not a doctor, and I did not speak with your parents, though your Mama waved to me, but I have seen those close to death and I fear that your Papa has that look about him,"

Joanna said honestly. "If you wish, I could come with you. I know that it will not be an easy thing for you to do."

"You are the sweetest of friends to me," Imogen said. "But I fear that if I do decide to go, that it will be something that I need to do alone. I would welcome a place to stay, though, somewhere I can come back to afterwards where I know I will be welcome."

"You are always welcome in our home, Imogen. I only wish there was more I could do to help you through this."

"Just listening to me and offering your counsel is more than I have ever hoped for. I can count on less than one hand the true friends that I have made in my life. You are the best of all of them. And to think, I'd not know you if it weren't for Bart, too. I have so much to thank him for. He is such a good man, yet I doubt that my father will ever see that."

"He is a good man, and he loves you very much."

"How can I be so blessed and so cursed, all at once?" Imogen said, only half joking.

"I do not know," Joanna said with a sad smile. "Perhaps things will work out in time."

"I do hope so."

Imogen called down for some tea for them both, then sat back down beside her friend. "Now we have talked about all the misery in my life, I wish to hear something wonderful. Tell me, have you heard from Wilbur? Don't think that I did not notice that the two of you danced together almost all night on New Year's Eve."

Joanna blushed a little. "What point would there be? His life is in New York. Mine is wherever my father takes me."

"You would like there to be something though, I can tell."

"He is very charming, very good looking, and an excellent dancer. I'm afraid I can tell you nothing more than that," Joanna said a little coquettishly.

"You could write to him, get to know one another better, as Bart and I did," Imogen said seriously. "At least then you would know if there was more to it than just a few dances at Christmas."

"It is best that I don't get my hopes up that way," Joanna said firmly. "I am sure he has countless ladies in New York who would be flattered to gain his attentions."

"I'm sure he does, but that doesn't mean that he wants any of them."

"Imogen, please. I could not ever live there. And Papa intends us to go and spend months setting up his new hotel."

"Do you not wish to go?"

"Not really. I will be too far away from you, but he won't let me stay in Billings alone."

"Then why not stay here, with us?" Imogen said excitedly. She could think of nothing better than to be reunited with her dearest friend. "We have plenty of rooms, after all we are a hotel."

"Oh, how I would love that," Joanna sighed. "But Papa will not agree. He likes to have me always with him."

"He will have to let you go one day, when some young man does ask you to be his wife."

"I think I am already a little too old to hope for that," Joanna said sadly.

"You are not. You must not give up hope. And I still think that you should consider placing an advertisement, or at least looking through them to see if there is someone you might consider writing to."

"Then you must ask Papa at dinner tonight. I shall not do it. I have begged him too often for such things and he always says no."

"He'll not say no to me," Imogen promised her. "Now, I shall let you rest, and in an hour will send up the maids with a bath for you."

"Thank you."

Imogen closed the door behind her and walked slowly along the corridor to the back stairway. Joanna's words about Papa worried her. If he really was sick, why was he out in a carriage? Was Mama taking him to an institution somewhere, where he might rest and recoup his health? And why had Mama looked so aged? Was she trying to carry the entire burden of her husband's mania in Imogen's absence? Why had she not told Imogen about it in her letters if things were so bad?

She climbed the stairs up to her own room under the eaves. Bart had almost managed to talk her out of going back to Billings just this morning, but now she was even more determined than ever that she had to face her father. She could not let him think she did not love him, that she did not forgive him – even if he could not forgive her and no longer wanted her as his daughter. And she would not let her mother carry the burden of his care alone.

CHAPTER 27

I mogen stood on the corner and stared at the house that had so recently been her home. It looked empty and silent, the drapes still pulled despite it being past midday. Mama never left the drapes closed beyond eight o'clock, even if it was still dark outside. It worried Imogen to see it. Slowly, she approached the house and knocked loudly on the door. She craned her neck to listen for noises behind it, but there was nothing. Where was everyone? Even if Mama and Papa had gone away, surely the servants would still be there.

She knocked again, wishing and praying that someone would answer the door and tell her what was going on, but nobody did. Wearily, she climbed down the stone steps to the street, turned back and stared up at the house. Of all the places they had lived, it had been her favorite and now it stood empty and silent. It did not seem right. She turned away, trying to hold back tears, and started to walk briskly down the street. She had barely gone ten yards before a voice called out to her from behind.

She turned back to see their neighbor, Mrs. Tinsley, hurrying towards her. "Oh, Miss Potts, I've been so worried," she said breathlessly. "I've not heard a word from your dear mama since they went, and she promised me that she would let me know how your father was. Have you heard from them?"

"I'm sorry, Mrs. Tinsley, but I'm afraid I don't know what you're talking about." She paused, unsure whether it would be wise to tell the elderly lady about her family's estrangement. Mrs. Tinsley was a terrible gossip, and their business would be all over town before nightfall. But if she knew anything about where Mama and Papa had gone, Imogen needed to know it. "My parents and I had a small falling out. I didn't even know that they had gone away. Do you know where they went?"

Mrs. Tinsley's jaw dropped, and her eyes widened. "Oh, my dear, I didn't know about that. They didn't tell me exactly, just that they were going to go somewhere for Mr. Potts' health. He's been terribly peaky of late."

"He has been unwell?"

"Oh, for quite some time, my dear. Your mother tried to

hide it, but when a man as conscientious as your father isn't at work, people talk. And when we saw him in church, he looked so pale and so thin."

"Since before Christmas?"

"I'd say so," Mrs. Tinsley said thoughtfully.

"He didn't get better after I left," Imogen said softly to herself. "He was still unwell when I tried to reason with him, and when he went to Deadwood."

"What's that, dear?"

"Nothing, Mrs. Tinsley. Did Mama leave a forwarding address with you?"

"No, but she may have told young Mr. Waters more, at the bank."

"Thank you," Imogen said, clasping the elderly lady's hands and leaning to press a kiss to her powdered cheek. "Take care of yourself, Mrs. Tinsley. If I learn anything, I shall write and let you know."

"I'd be glad of that. I've grown ever so fond of your mother. When she said they were closing the house and didn't know when they'd return, I was very upset. And all your servants, they were out on the street with barely a day's notice. It's not right, Imogen."

"No, it's not."

Imogen bade Mrs. Tinsley farewell and walked away slowly, her heart full of fear. In all their moves her parents had never just upped and left without giving the staff suitable notice, and there had always been somewhere particular they were moving on to. That they had moved out so swiftly, without explanation, could only mean that Papa's delicate mind had broken irreparably, and Mama had been forced to have him taken away from all he knew. But where would they have gone? Why had Mama gone, too? Surely an institution would have insisted that she stay away for a time, too? They had last time, though Mama had begged to be able to visit with her husband.

As Imogen walked along the street towards the bank, she prayed that Mr. Waters, her father's head clerk, would know more, but she was beginning to suspect that he may know as little about what had happened here as Mrs. Tinsley did. The bank was on the main thoroughfare, an imposing building with fancy columns and elegantly carved images on the façade. It had always reminded Imogen of the pictures of Roman and Greek temples that she'd seen in books of the ancient world. She climbed up the steps and entered the lobby.

A liveried young man hurried towards her, smiling warmly. His pants and cuffs were too short for his gangly limbs and he hunched just a little to hide how tall he really was. "How may I be of help, Miss Potts?" he asked her.

"I'm here to see Mr. Waters, Bert," Imogen told the boy. "How are you? You've grown another half a foot since I saw you last."

Bert grinned. "My Ma says she fears I'll never stop growing."

"I fear she may be right," Imogen said with a smile.

"I'll take you through," Bert said and led her through into the main foyer of the bank. They passed the tellers kiosks on either side of the aisle and entered a narrow corridor at the rear of the building. Bert stopped outside one of the doors and knocked on it politely. "Just a moment, Miss. I'll announce you."

Imogen knew that the door led to her father's office, but the brass plate on the door announced it as belonging to Mr. Waters now, along with the title of manager. So, Papa no longer worked here. Her parents truly had left everything behind. Bert appeared a moment later and indicated with his head that she should go in.

Nathanial Waters hurried towards her from behind his desk and took her hands in his. "My dear Miss Potts, how lovely to see you today."

His words were welcoming, but his tone was strained. "I'm not sure it is so lovely," she said. "And I'm rather hoping you may be able to explain, at least something, as to why everything here is so different now."

He bit his lip and nodded. "Come, sit down. I'll send for some tea, and we can talk," he said, showing her towards a couple of comfortable chairs by the fireplace.

She sat down and waited for him to call out of the door to his secretary, her father's old secretary. He took the seat opposite her and frowned slightly. "Where are they, Nathanial? Why is your name on my father's door?"

"I'm not sure how much I should say," he said softly. "Your mother swore me to secrecy."

"I am their daughter. I deserve to know where they are at least, even if you cannot tell me why they have left everything here behind without a word to me, and barely any notice to anyone else."

"You're quite right," he said. "You do deserve an explanation."

"So, what is going on?"

"You are aware of your father's peculiarities, I know," Nathanial began cautiously.

"Of course."

"I'm not sure if you had already gone away, but in the middle of December last, your mother sent word that he was unwell and would be taking a few weeks off. Well, we thought little of it, and assumed that he would return in the New Year. Well, I had heard nothing by the seventh, so I sent a messenger to the house. The maid simply told him that Mr. Potts was still unwell and would be taking a little more time off. Obviously, I contacted Mr. Fortescue to ask him what to do. I don't know what happened, whether he contacted your father and mother or not, but three days later he sent me a telegram appointing me as manager. He said nothing else."

"Oh," Imogen said. She had hoped that Nathanial would be able to tell her so much more than this. "So, you don't know where they have gone?"

"Where they have gone? I'm sorry, I don't understand."

"The house is closed up," Imogen told him. "They've gone somewhere, and nobody seems to know where."

"If anyone at the bank might know, perhaps Mr. Fortescue does, but I'm afraid I know no more than I've told you."

Frustrated, Imogen left his office. It seemed that she would have to pay her Uncle Luther another visit. And if he knew what was going on, why had he not already sent word to her? Why was everyone keeping secrets from her? Father's episodes were usually relatively short-lived. Some rest, and the promise of a new place to go were usually enough to snap him out of his doldrums in a few weeks at most. Nothing made sense to her. And why had Mama not said a word? Her letters had been short, but she had insisted that they were both well. Why would she lie?

Feeling more concerned than she had ever been, she made her way to the train station. She sat in the waiting room for a few minutes but felt too restless to just sit patiently and wait for her train. She stood up, smoothed her skirts and headed out onto the platform where she paced up and down the full length of it. The movement did little to ease her mind, but it helped her to use up the nervous energy her thoughts seemed to be creating inside her.

It felt like the train back to Eagle Creek took a lifetime. She had never been more glad to see anyone than she was to see Bart waiting for her on the platform. "You don't look well," he said, taking her chin and looking into her face. "And you've been crying, haven't you? It didn't go well?"

"No, it did not go well. My parents have gone one step further in their ability to move on when times are tough. They've left everything behind, except a forwarding address."

"Everything?"

"Yes, Papa's job is no longer his. The house is closed up and nobody knows where they are."

Bart took her out to the carriage and helped her inside it. He tucked a blanket around her knees and pulled her into his arms. "Imogen, I'm so sorry. What can I do to help?"

"I have to go to Buffalo again, to talk to my uncle. If anyone knows where they are it will be him."

"I'll come with you."

"No, Bart. It will be better if I go alone. And one of us needs to be at the hotel to run it, now that Eddie has gone."

He cursed under his breath. "You're right, of course. At least take Joanna with you. I need to know that someone is by your side."

"Is she still here? Did Mr. Hemsley finally relent and let her stay?"

"She is, and he did," Bart said with a gentle smile.

"Oh, I am so glad. I don't think I have ever needed a friend more."

"Am I not enough for you?"

"Of course," she assured him. "But there are some things that you cannot help me with, and Joanna can."

"That is code for saying that you feel you cannot burden me with everything to do with your parents, because so much of the trouble is caused by me being in your life, am I right?"

"No, and yes," Imogen said kissing his cheek. "Some of it is that I just like to talk about you."

He kissed her lips and grinned. "Let us get you home," he said, then climbed out of the carriage and up onto the driver's perch.

Imogen took off her glove and let her fingers play over her lips where his had touched them. She still marveled that such chaste caresses could leave her feeling almost giddy. It had certainly never been like that when anyone else had kissed her. She leaned out of the window and let the cold mountain air bring the color back to her cheeks. Winter wasn't quite done with Eagle Creek yet, but there were signs that spring was not far away. Tiny buds were appearing on the trees, and the green leaves of some of the early flowering plants were beginning to peek through the drifts of old snow. Of course, all could disappear in a moment, if another heavy snowfall occurred, and there was a risk of that for some time to come yet.

She wished that her parents could see this place. The air and the beauty here would help to heal her father, she was sure of it. But while Bart was here, she didn't doubt that her mother and father would never set foot in the little town. She tried not to dwell on it, but she couldn't help wondering if she had perhaps broken her father irreparably by siding with Bart. She had never wanted to choose between her family and the man she loved, but she could not have let Bart hang for a boyhood mistake. Why could her father, who had brought her up to respect justice and decency, and the right of men to make mistakes and start afresh, not see that Bart deserved those things as much as any other man?

CHAPTER 28

FEBRUARY 9TH, 1895, EAGLE CREEK, MONTANA

The waiting staff had gathered in the dining room. Bart smiled as he saw them lined up neatly, every one of them dressed as they should be, without so much as a hair out of place. Longworth was gone, though Mr. Hemsley had requested that Bart at least send him away with a good character reference so he might find work elsewhere. It had been one of the hardest things that Bart had ever had to do, trying to find the words to praise a man who had been so much trouble. But he had not wished to lie, either, for hc feared that if he did so it could rebound on The Eyrie and lower the hotel's standing in the trade.

"Good morning," Bart said smiling at them. "You are all aware that Mr. Longworth has left us, and that his departure leaves a position to be filled. I would very much like that position to be filled within the family. All of you, however, are equally valued and equally adept in your work, so it is an incredibly difficult choice to make."

He glanced up and down the line, trying to gauge each of the waiters' response to his words. Most glanced a little nervously at one another, some had a tiny glint in their eyes and others just continued to look steadily at Bart. "I feel that, as a team, you know one another best," he continued. "And as that is the case, we are going to decide this as democratically as we can. I suggest that you each write down the name of who you think would represent you best and who can rise to the challenge of running this team. You may not nominate yourself. We will eliminate the candidate with the least votes after each round of voting."

His suggestion was greeted with a sudden rush of whispers. Bart grinned. He and Imogen, along with Joanna, had discussed what to do until late the night before. Imogen had been sure that Eli Goldman was the best man for the job, while Joanna favored Clint Carter. Bart could not decide if he preferred Hamish Mactaggart, or Willie Jones. None of them could decide who would be best, and so Joanna had suggested that they put it to a vote amongst the staff themselves as to who they thought would be best suited to lead them. Both Imogen and Bart had agreed that it was unorthodox, but about as fair a way to decide as could be.

He tapped the box he'd brought for them to place their

votes in. "I'll be back in fifteen minutes to collect this and make the count for the first round."

He left them alone and made his way back into the hotel lobby where he caught a glimpse of Imogen rushing from the breakfast room into the staff corridor. She had insisted on working today, despite all her woes, though he had been adamant that they could manage. She wanted to keep working so her mind had less time to think of terrible things, she had said. But Bart knew that she wanted to set out to visit with her uncle as soon as possible. He'd suggested she send him a telegram, but she was certain that she needed to see him in person, to be sure that he wasn't lying to her. He hated that he was responsible for causing her to doubt her loved ones, and for the rift that meant she had no clue as to where her father and mother even were.

He dealt with some paperwork then went back into the dining room. The wait staff were busy polishing the silverware ready for the evening meal. He could see their surreptitious looks as he unlocked the ballot box and took out the papers within. He began sorting them into piles as the team began to gather around him. He smiled up at them. "Well, I'm afraid to say that nobody voted for you, Dylan," he said to the youngest and newest member of the team.

"Phew," Dylan said. "I was worried someone might think I'm ready, and I'm really not." Everyone smiled. He had only just turned seventeen, and while he was a hard

worker and well-liked, he wasn't ready for such a responsible position.

"I'm sure that nobody is surprised that Eli, Clint, Hamish
and Willie are in the lead with the most votes. Do those of
you who voted for someone else wish we continue through
every elimination round, or are you happy for me to say that
the four of them are the ones to go through to the next lot of
voting?" A few looks passed between people, but within just
a few minutes they all seemed to be agreed that the four be
the ones to go through.

Bart left them with the ballot box once more and went to
his office. A pile of mail was sitting on his desk, including a
letter for Imogen. He recognized the handwriting at once as
belonging to her mother. He grabbed it and hurried to find
her, almost knocking over one of the bellboys in his haste to
cross the lobby. He ran down the back stairs and looked in
each room along the service corridor for Imogen. He found
her in the kitchen, sitting at the large pine table eating a slice
of cake. She looked so lovely, with stray strands of her hair
coming down from her usually neat chignon, framing her
face as if she were in a painting. "You call this hard work?"
he teased as he took a seat beside her.

"I didn't have time for breakfast today," she said, then
frowned. "No, I simply didn't feel like eating breakfast
today. I just wanted to be busy, but I felt myself starting to
get a little queasy as I helped with the laundry, so thought it
best to eat something. The cooks wouldn't let me make

myself some eggs, they shooed me out of their way and insisted I eat something already cooked. The cake was all there was."

"I'll believe you," he said with a smile, then remembered why he'd hurried to find her. "A letter came for you, it's from your mother and it has a postal mark on it from Great Falls."

"Great Falls? Whyever would they be there?" Imogen asked as she took it from him and stared at the postal mark. She took a knife from the jar on the table and sliced it open and began to read it.

Dear Imogen,

I am sorry I have not written to you as often as perhaps we would both have liked, but things have been somewhat difficult at home.

You saw what your father was like, before you left for Eagle Creek in December, and again in Deadwood at the trial. I prayed that once the trials were both done with, that his mania would subside, that he would finally get some rest and find some peace. But I am sad to say that it has only gotten worse.

I should have told you sooner, but I did not want you to worry, or to blame yourself for what has occurred, but I know that you would want to know. I truly feared that I might lose him completely, and so was forced to act swiftly.

I have taken your father to an institution recommended by Dr. Barnard. I am not sure how much they are helping him. They have him taking medications that make him so sleepy and confused. I sometimes wonder if he was better off tormented by his demons, at least then I knew he was still there. Sometimes I look at him now, his vacant stare and I wonder if my dear husband is still in there at all.

I am sorry I did not confide in you earlier, but your father forbade me to do so. But I must confess that seeing him as he is now, I need your counsel and support. I cannot do this alone. I know that we have wronged you, and you would be justified in ignoring my plea for help, but I beg you to come and join me here.

With all my love,

Your loving and most apologetic, Mama

"I WAS NOT EXPECTING THAT," Bart said, shaking his head as Imogen finished reading the letter aloud. "What will you do?"

"I will go to Mama, and I will see for myself what is happening. If I can, I will try and convince her to bring Papa here. Strikes The Iron once spoke of how she would be glad to help him, and I am growing ever more convinced that The Crow may be the only people who can bring my father back to me."

"I will come with you," he insisted. She placed a hand over his and gave him a sad smile.

"No, Joanna will. If my father is as unwell as Mama

says, I fear you will only make things worse. If I am to stand any hope of convincing Mama to move him again, you cannot accompany me."

"I want to be by your side," Bart said, though he understood. "It is so infuriating that I cannot be there for you when you need me the most."

"But you will be with me," Imogen assured him. "I carry you in my heart everywhere, and I know that you hold me in yours."

"I most definitely do," he said, pulling her into his arms. "I shall miss you, for who knows how long you may be gone."

"I shall write every day," she promised him. "Great Falls is not so far away so you'll receive them quickly enough. And you must tell me how everything is here."

"I shall," he promised her. "When will you leave?"

"As soon as we can. I shall send one of the boys down to find out when the next train to Great Falls comes through."

Bart nodded and kissed the top of her head. "Stay safe, my darling."

Imogen pulled out of his embrace reluctantly, picked her letter up, kissed his lips tenderly, then hurried up to her rooms to pack. Bart frowned. He had caused her and her family so much pain and yet she still loved him. He did not deserve her love, though he was grateful every day that she loved him. He felt so useless, though, unable to help her or her father. All he had to offer was his prayers, and he hoped that would be enough.

He went out to the stable yard where Fred was grooming the carriage horses. "Can you go to the station and check the timetable for trains to Great Falls?" he asked the lad.

Fred nodded. "But I don't need to go down there to do that. Mr. Cowper gave me a copy of the timetable, so I didn't have to keep checking it all the time for when the guests arrived," he said laying down his brushes and beckoning Bart to follow him into the yard's tiny office space.

Pinned on the wall was a neatly printed timetable of all the regular trains in and out of Eagle Creek. Bart skimmed down it and noticed that there would be a train in the early evening. "Can you have the carriage ready for five o'clock?" he asked Fred.

"Of course," Fred said. "For a guest is it?"

"No, for Miss Potts and Miss Hemsley, so make sure the carriage is spotless and the horses shining," he winked at the lad, who grinned back.

"Will do," he said.

Suddenly, Bart remembered the ballot for the new head of waiting staff, Imogen's news had made it completely slip his mind. He hurried back up to the dining room and opened the ballot box. This time all but two votes were for one man, Eli Goldman. He held up the pile of ballots in one hand and waved them. "This is the winner." In the other hand he held up the three votes for the others. "These are all for different people. Are you happy to say that you have voted for Mr. Goldman?"

A cheer went up, though Bart noticed that Eli did not look entirely happy about the decision. "What's wrong?" he asked.

"I rather hoped that Hamish would get it," Eli said frankly. "I think he is better suited to the role than I."

"It seems that the others did not agree," Bart said. "Though one voter would have preferred it to be Willie, though the handwriting on that ballot is surprisingly similar to Willie's own."

Willie flushed bright red. "You caught me," he admitted. "I was sure Eli would get it and will be glad to work under him."

"I should hope so," Bart said. He turned back to Eli. "Will you accept the post?"

"I will," Eli said, "though I will need a lot of help."

"I am sure that we can ensure you get all the assistance that you need. Congratulations, Eli. I know Miss Potts will be delighted when I tell her. She was sure you were the man for the job from the start."

"I am honored to know that, Mr. King," Eli said.

"Now, you'd best get back to work all of you, there's still tonight's meal to prepare for," Bart said.

He could still hear the waiters celebrating Eli's promotion as he chatted with some of the guests on the other side of the lobby. It had been a most peculiar day, one of genuine happiness for Eli, and gut-wrenching sadness for Imogen. He sent up a silent prayer to the heavens, that Imogen would be able to convince Mrs. Potts to bring her husband to Eagle Creek, to the Crow Village, where Strikes The Iron and the other elders of the tribe skilled in healing might be able to truly help Mr. Potts to regain his health. He wasn't sure if any of it was possible, but all he could do was pray for a miracle.

CHAPTER 29

FEBRUARY 15TH, 1895, GREAT FALLS, MONTANA

Upon leaving the station, Joanna hurried to a row of hansom cabs while Imogen rummaged in her bag to find the name and address of the boarding house her mother was staying in. By the time she caught up with Joanna, the driver of one of the cabs had loaded their luggage and was back up on his perch. She handed him the address and he nodded. "I'll have you there in no time," he promised.

They climbed inside and got themselves settled, then Joanna slapped the side to let the driver know it was safe to drive on. "You must be terribly nervous," she said taking Imogen's hand and giving it a supportive squeeze.

"A little," Imogen admitted. "My father has been

admitted for treatment before, but I fear it did more harm than good. Mama must have felt truly desperate to do this again, she always swore she would not ever let him go through that again."

"Do you think you'll be able to convince her to try something else?"

"I hope so. It will depend very much on how well, or badly, Papa is being treated here. I know nothing of this institution, and I doubt she did until she brought him. Doctors have a tendency to send you to their friends rather than the places best suited to the patient, often with little idea of the methods used in such facilities. I often think they would be shocked to learn how cruel some of the treatments for those with such issues are, they tend to see their friends as curious, compassionate and clever – the young man they knew at medical school. They don't think that a person's cleverness, or curiosity can lead to questionable methods of treatment, in the name of scientific research."

"I am so glad that I have never had to learn these things until now," Joanna said. "And I am beyond sorry that you had to learn them so young."

They held hands for the remainder of the journey across town. The hansom drew to a halt outside a neat-looking house, with a white fence and rose bushes in the front yard. Of course, there were no blooms, it was far too early for that, but Imogen could imagine how pretty it must look in just a few months' time, when the flowers began to emerge. "At least Mama seems to have found suitable lodgings," Imogen said as she took in how pretty it was. "I should probably have sent word that we were coming, so she could arrange somewhere for us to stay as well."

"It looks lovely, perhaps they will have room for us, too," Joanna said optimistically.

"We shall soon find out – though I'd not like to make Mama feel uncomfortable by staying here if she does not want us to."

"I am sure her landlady will know somewhere we can go."

Imogen nodded and got out of the cab. She handed the driver some money from her purse, and waited while he unloaded their baggage. She stared at the pretty little house while the butterflies in her belly began to swarm and flutter. How would Mama receive them? Would she be glad to see her? She had written that she wanted Imogen's help, but had she truly meant it?

Summoning up every ounce of courage she possessed, Imogen picked up her bag, let herself in through the gate and marched up onto the porch. She knocked on the door three times, then stepped back. She could hear the sound of slippers dragging slightly across the floor inside the house, and after what felt like an eternity the door opened to reveal an elderly lady, with perfectly pinned white hair and a kindly smile. She had roses in her cheeks and the sweetest dimples that Imogen had ever seen. "May I help you dear?" the old lady asked, in an unexpected southern drawl.

"Good day to you, I hope so. My mother, Mrs. Potts, is staying with you, I believe?"

"Oh, come in, come in. You must be Miss Imogen," the lady said. "I'm Mrs. Dupree. She'll be glad to know you came. She's talked of little but you since she arrived."

"She has?" Imogen asked, surprised.

"And your poor Papa, of course."

"How is he, has she said?"

"She fears he is getting worse, not better."

Imogen sighed. She had so hoped that history would not be repeating itself. "Is she here now?"

"Yes, she's been helping me in the kitchens. Leave your bags and follow me," Mrs. Dupree said. "She likes to keep busy, and I enjoy the company."

Joanna came in through the door, carrying the rest of their luggage. "This is my friend, Joanna Hemsley, Mrs. Dupree," Imogen said.

"A pleasure to meet you both. Now, close the door. You must be hungry and tired. I'll send my girl up to prepare some rooms for you while I get you something to eat and drink, and you catch up with your mama. You're lucky, we're quiet at the moment." She started to shuffle along the corridor and beckoned to them to follow.

"Oh, we didn't expect you to…"

"Oh, it is no trouble at all. Your mother will want you close by."

"It may be best to confirm that with her first," Imogen said awkwardly. "We've not been…"

"I know all about it," Mrs. Dupree said with a wink. "But from what I understand, your problem was with your Papa, not dear Clarissa."

"You are right, but I would not want her to feel disloyal to him."

Mama appeared from a door to their right. She was wearing a floral apron over her dress and her hair was only loosely pinned. "I would not feel disloyal to him," she assured Imogen as she pulled her into a hug. "Though I fear I have been disloyal to you. I allowed myself to get caught up in his madness, and for that I am sorry. I should have seen some time ago just how bad off he was. Perhaps I should have insisted he seek proper help before you even left in December."

"Mama, how could you know? We have seen him snap out of his funks in just a day or two at times. It is so hard to know whether an attack will be short-lived or drag out as this one has."

"I do know I shouldn't have sent you away," she said, finally releasing Imogen and nodding politely to Joanna. "And I should have told him that I would not let him push you away from me, even if he wished to do so for himself."

"That was his madness, Mama."

"I have tried to convince myself of that, too, darling," Mama said. "I only hope you are right. For I am not sure how I will bear it if he remains adamant that you are no longer his daughter."

"First, we must get him well. We can worry about everything else later."

They sat down at the large kitchen table and Mrs. Dupree made them a cup of coffee with chicory in it and urged them all to take a slice of apple cake. The coffee was unusual, but strangely delicious. Imogen had never much liked coffee before, she found it too bitter, but with the addition of the chicory it seemed somehow mellower, and she even asked for another cup. Joanna did not seem so enamored with it, but she sipped at hers politely.

"How is he? Will I be permitted to see him, or do you think it will make things worse?" Imogen asked.

Mama frowned. "I am not even allowed to visit with him," she said. "It worries me, for the reports the doctor sends me each day do not sound as if he is improving, though Dr. Firmin assures me that his methods are working, though they may take some time."

"And how do you feel about Dr. Firmin? Is he a man that inspires your trust?"

Mama shook her head. "I must confess that I do not share Dr. Barnard's faith in him. He seems altogether too delighted about having another patient to try his methods out on, rather than showing any compassion for your poor father, or his past. He's asked me so very little about anything and is always just a little bit too charming when I have called on him."

"Then we need to take him out of there," Imogen said firmly. "I will not leave Papa in the hands of someone who has no genuine care for him."

"But where can we take him? I cannot care for him as he is, Imogen, though I wish I could. He is too agitated."

Imogen knew what that meant. He had been violent towards her again. No wonder she had felt she had nowhere else to turn. "Mama, I know this might seem unusual, but there is a woman I know. She is a good friend and a very wise lady, an elder of her tribe."

"An Indian?" Mama asked, aghast.

"Strikes The Iron and The Crow are not like the Indians around Deadwood, or that you read about in the newspapers, Mama," Imogen assured her. "They are kind and generous, and their Chief, Plenty Coups – Strikes The Iron's husband – saw long ago that they would need to cooperate with our kind. They trade in Eagle Creek, and many of them work there, though they live in their own village on the other side of the mountain."

Her mother did not look convinced. But Imogen knew that she had to push ahead. She was certain that her father needed time and care to recover, not endless treatments of dubious efficacy. "Mama, they believe in balance, of mind, body, heart, and spirit. Strikes The Iron explained to me that when madness ensues, it is because at least one of those is not in balance, and that because Papa is always looking backwards, that he cannot find himself anymore. She said they can help, and I truly believe her. She is very well-respected as a healer."

"Clarissa, I know it is not my place to intrude," Mrs. Dupree interjected, "but I know of this woman. She is well known throughout Montana for her skills and wisdom. And I know of people who were sick, unto death, that The Crow medicine men and women have healed. They have skills we have lost. And what harm could it do to try?"

"Mrs. Potts, it is certainly not my place to tell you how to do anything," Joanna added. "But the doctors in Eagle Creek often call on The Crow for their help. They truly are gifted people."

Imogen watched her mother's face as she listened and thought about all that had been said. There were so many more lines around her eyes and mouth now, it was as if these past months had aged her ten years or more. She looked so tired, so unhappy. Her eyes were red-rimmed from all the tears she no doubt shed when she was alone in her room, and she had lost weight. Imogen had already noted that she had barely taken more than a mouthful of the delicious apple cake in front of her.

"I shall go to the hospital," she announced, standing up and removing her apron. "I shall insist on seeing your father and will see for myself how he fares. If he is no better, or worse than when I brought him here, I will sign the release papers and we will take him to your healer. But if he is improving, I have to trust that Dr. Firmin's methods are working, no matter how odious I might find him."

"Would you like me to come with you?" Imogen said. "Even if I don't come inside, I could wait in a hansom outside for you, so you are not alone."

"I would like that, and I may need the courage of your convictions if I feel I have to remove your father from Dr. Firmin's care," Mama said softly. "I am all out of fight."

"I have enough in me for us both," Imogen assured her. "Let us do our best for Papa, whatever that turns out to be."

CHAPTER 30

FEBRUARY 15TH, 1895, GREAT FALLS, MONTANA

D r. Firmin's hospital was a large, gray, stone building. It had an air of foreboding about it, as if the building itself had taken on the troubles of those inside. Imogen shuddered as she looked up at it as she got out of the hansom cab. She turned to help her mother. "Please tell me it looks more welcoming inside?" she asked.

"Not really," Mama said. "Other than the entrance hall and Dr. Firmin's office, the little I was permitted to see is very sparsely furnished, and plainly decorated. Dr. Firmin explained that fewer external distractions mean that the patients are less likely to get overwhelmed."

"I would imagine that some home comforts would be more soothing," Imogen said with a shake of her head.

She turned to the cab driver. "Would you mind waiting for us? I doubt we will be much longer than an hour."

"Happy to, Miss," he said cheerfully. "I'll see if there's anywhere I can get my old nag a drink."

Imogen smiled at him then took her mother's arm as they climbed the twenty stone steps up to the vast, ornately carved double doors, that did nothing to make her feel more welcome here.

"I must confess that I would have thought so, too. But he is a learned man. I have to have faith that he knows what he is doing."

"Dr. Kilgarry was a learned man," Imogen reminded her. "Look what he did to Papa. Dosed him up with laudanum so he could barely move or speak and left him to lie in his own excrement."

"Most doctors are not like Dr. Kilgarry," Mama said, but her voice wavered, telling Imogen that her mother shared her fears.

The entrance hall was cold, but beautifully decorated. No expense seemed to have been spared on making it seem attractive, probably to reassure the families of the patients that their loved ones were in excellent hands and would receive the very best care. Imogen was not impressed by it. Mama led her towards a wide corridor that led off to the right. It was brightly lit, with some fine artwork on the walls. The heavy oak doors on either side of the corridor had brass nameplates on them, and fancy titles and specialties detailed on them. To an unsuspecting person it would seem that everyone here was highly qualified, which should inspire confidence, but Imogen was not reassured by it at all.

The last door, at the very end of the corridor, belonged to Dr. Firmin. Mama straightened her spine and took a deep breath before knocking. There was no answer. "He must be on his rounds," she said.

"Then perhaps we should try to find him?" Imogen suggested.

"I'm not sure, he has always insisted that people don't wander the corridors, that it might be upsetting for his patients to see strangers staring at them."

"We would not be staring at anyone. We simply wish to speak with Papa's doctor. You may wait here if you prefer, but I intend to find him."

"You will not leave me here alone," Mama said, her eyes wide.

"This place is rather scary, isn't it?" Imogen said. "Come with me, Mama. Perhaps we'll find Papa, too."

Imogen tucked her arm through her mother's and together they made their way back along the corridor to the grand entrance hall and took the corridor to the left that led to the wards. Almost as soon as they were out of sight of the hallway, the décor changed. Plain white walls glared at them on each side. Occasionally they spied a patient wandering the corridors alone, muttering to themselves. One continually slapped his own head, and another kept hitching up his nightgown to show his buttocks. But the worst thing was the moans and screams they heard coming from behind some of the closed doors.

It surprised Imogen that there were no guards, or even nurses patrolling the corridors to usher the strays back to their rooms. She had even begun to wonder if they had such things at all, when they found Papa. He was clutching at his hair with one hand, so tightly that Imogen feared he might pull it all out, and clutching at his groin with the other, as if he was tormented by a need to pass urine. His nightgown was soiled, with great brown stains at the back and yellowing ones at the front. He had clearly soiled himself. Imogen wanted to cry, but she forced herself to be strong for her mother's sake.

Mama hurried towards him. "Ansell my love, are you quite well?" she asked, tears flooding silently down her cheeks as she put an arm around him and trying to push his hand away from his groin.

He stared blankly at her. Clearly Dr. Firmin believed strongly in medication for the mentally unstable. Papa clearly did not recognize either of them. In truth, he looked scared of them. He stuttered as he tried to call out for some-one. But nobody came. Imogen stared at him, stunned at the differences in him since she had last seen him in Deadwood. That man had been mad, but he still had some control over himself. This man was broken, in every sense of the word.

"Mama, we cannot leave him here," she said urgently.

"There is nobody here caring for these people at all. We've not seen a single nurse or doctor, for all those fancy plaques on the doors back there."

"You're right. But we can't just go without telling anyone," Mama said.

"We can write to them later," Imogen suggested. "I have no desire to wander around this place any longer than I have to."

Her mother nodded and tried to urge her father to come with them. At first, he wouldn't budge, stubbornly forcing the two women to push him along the corridor. He wailed a little, but still nobody came. It took them some time, but eventually they stood outside the hospital. The hansom driver had waited for them, and he looked shocked by Papa's appearance. "I'd heard things about this place," he said shaking his head and hurrying forward with a blanket to keep Papa warm. "I didn't like to believe them."

"Please just get us back to the boarding house," Imogen asked him as he helped them settle Papa into his hansom. "I don't even want to think about this place ever again."

Mrs. Dupree and Joanna were waiting for them in the front parlor. As soon as she saw Papa, her jolly face grew sad. "Fetch the bath and plenty of hot water," she called to the maid as Imogen and her mother helped her father inside. "Whatever have they done to him?"

"I do not know, and I do not think that we will ever wish to know," Mama said. She had barely stopped crying since they'd found Papa and Imogen could hardly blame her. It was painful to see her father this way. Even throughout all his troubled times, he had never been like this. It was as if he were only barely alive, dead in all the ways that mattered, only his body still continued to function as it always had.

"What will you do now?" Joanna asked.

Mama glanced over at Imogen. "I think we have no choice but to see what your Crow friend can do for him. I will never trust another doctor near him again."

"I truly believe that it will be for the best," Imogen said nodding. "We should leave as soon as possible."

"I'll send Harriet out to purchase your train tickets," Mrs. Dupree said. "On the very first train to Eagle Creek."

"Please, let it be the first train in the morning," Imogen said. "I am so tired I can barely stand."

Mrs. Dupree nodded, and once her maid had set up the bath she sent her out with some money to purchase the tickets. Mrs. Dupree and Joanna politely retreated to the kitchen and left the Potts' alone in front of the fire. Imogen helped her mother to strip off her father's soiled nightgown. Mama threw it straight into the fire and stared at it for a moment as it caught light. Papa shivered, his teeth clattering loudly. Imogen encouraged him to climb into the bath. He seemed content to do so, which was a welcome change after his stubbornness getting him here.

Mama tenderly washed his hair and scrubbed him clean. Papa sat like a small child, just letting her do what she wished, wincing occasionally when she scrubbed too hard. Mrs. Dupree knocked on the door. Imogen opened it only a crack to preserve her father's modesty. "I thought you might like some clean clothes for him. These were my husband's. I think that the two of them are close enough in size that they'll fit your father." She handed Imogen a clean night-gown and a smart suit in a thick woolen fabric that would feel soft against Papa's skin and keep him warm as they trav-elled the next day.

"Thank you, you have been so very kind," Imogen told her. "We will see that they are returned to you as soon as we can."

"There's no need. Poor Elliot is no longer here to wear them. He'd be glad to know they were doing someone a good turn."

Imogen helped her father to stand and climb out of the tub and waited as her mother dried his skin gently, then eased the clean nightgown over his head. They led him up the stairs to Mama's room and settled him in the bed, where he curled up on his side and fell fast asleep. "I wonder what medicines they have been giving him?" Imogen said, as they stood in the doorway and watched him rest. "He is barely there at all."

"It is certainly something more than laudanum," Mama said. "I think we will need to be prepared for him to be out of sorts as the effects wear off. He was the very devil when he came off laudanum."

"I remember it all too clearly," Imogen agreed. "But thankfully it is not far to Eagle Creek. Hopefully we will get him settled in Strikes The Iron's care before he gets too bad. She may have something she can give him to ease the transition."

"We can only hope so, for his sake, hers, and ours."

When they went back downstairs, the bath had already been tidied away and Joanna and Mrs. Dupree were waiting for them with hot chocolate and more cake. "I can fetch you some stew or soup if you'd rather," the elderly lady said. "But I always want sweet things when I have had a hard day."

"This is perfect, Imogen said sipping the rich and creamy chocolate drink. "It is soothing. I don't think I could manage a real meal; my belly is still turning somersaults."

"No child should have to do all you do for your father," Mama said sadly. "You have always been so brave."

"No braver than you," Imogen said, reaching out and taking her mother's hand. "We have done what we can together. And whatever happens with father once he is well, you can always be sure that I will be there when you need me."

"I do not deserve you, and he most certainly does not after the way he spoke to you."

"It is not a question of that, is it? When you love someone, you do what you can, no matter what," Joanna said sagely.

They all smiled a little sadly. Imogen finished her cake and surprised herself by asking for another slice. She was clearly hungrier than she had thought. Mrs. Dupree was happy to oblige, but when Mama almost fell asleep with a forkful between plate and mouth, Joanna insisted that they all go up to bed. Imogen was glad to rest her weary body, but her racing thoughts seemed disinclined to let her sleep. She stared at the ceiling and prayed fervently that Strikes The Iron would be able to bring her father back, and that when she did, that he might forgive her.

CHAPTER 31

FEBRUARY 16TH, 1895, EAGLE CREEK, MONTANA

The hotel had been running smoothly in Imogen's absence, but Bart missed her terribly. He could hardly wait for her return and was delighted when he received a telegram saying that she was on her way back. He prepared a room for her mother in the hotel and rode out to the Crow Village to speak with Strikes The Iron. He set out early in the morning, wanting to be back in time to meet the Potts' at the station later that afternoon.

Chief Plenty Coups was sitting outside the home he shared with his wife, whittling a piece of wood into a spoon by a roaring fire. "Mr. King, we don't often see you here," he said with a warm smile. "Come, sit down with me and share some tea."

"I actually came to call on your lovely wife," Bart said with a smile. "Is she home?"

"I'm afraid you have just missed her. You have to get up very early to catch my wife before she sets about her morning calls and chores," Plenty Coups said. "Sit, drink tea. She will be back soon."

"Thank you."

Bart took a seat by the fire and warmed his hands by the flames and Plenty Coups poured him some raspberry leaf tea. "How are things on your side of the mountain?" the chief asked.

"The town prospers, I think most people are well. It has been a good winter, we've not lost too many."

"Here, too," Plenty Coups said. "The old ones often don't do too well in the cold."

"No. Do you think we are likely to have another cold spell? It seems to be warming earlier this year to me."

"It is hard to be sure, but I do not think winter has any intention of leaving us yet."

"I feared you might say that," Bart said with a grin. He took a sip of his tea. It was warming and soothing, though he'd never quite gotten used to the taste of raspberry leaf tea.

Moments later Strikes The Iron appeared. She smiled at Bart. "Mr. King, what a pleasant surprise."

"I am afraid it may not be so pleasant," Bart said cautiously. "Do you remember my friend, Miss Potts? She bought many baskets and other things from you."

"I do, she is a lovely young lady. Have you asked her to marry you, yet?"

Bart grinned. "Not yet, and in part the reason I have not is why I am here."

"Tell me, if you wish to," the older woman said as she took a seat beside her husband and he handed her a cup of tea, too.

"Do you remember her speaking of her father?"

"I do, she feared for him greatly."

"She is bringing him here. Well, to Eagle Creek. She hopes you will agree to treat him. I fear he is very unwell indeed, even more so than she feared."

"Of course, she must bring him here. We will bring him back to himself."

"You are sure it will not be an imposition?"

"I like your Miss Potts. She has an old spirit, but she is too sad for a girl her age – no doubt thanks to the troubles she has been through in her short life. If I can help to bring her joy, I will be glad to do so."

"Thank you. They will be in Eagle Creek later today, should I bring them straight here?"

"Yes. I shall prepare a place for him."

Bart left the camp and returned to the hotel, his heart a little lighter. Strikes The Iron's certainty that The Crow could help Mr. Potts was very reassuring. He hoped it would have a similar effect on Imogen. Her heart was so heavy with worry. He hated that there was so little he could do to help, he longed to bring her the happiness she deserved, but he knew it was not in his gift. Perhaps it was in Strikes The Iron's, but mostly it lay in the hands of Mr. Potts.

When it was time to go to the station, Bart took the largest carriage into Eagle Creek to fetch them all. He listened for the whistle then hurried inside the station and out onto the platform. The train arrived in a cloud of smoke that made him cough a little, but he thought nothing of it and moved to the edge of the platform to catch a glimpse of Imogen as the train came to a halt. He ran alongside the train until he saw Joanna peering out of one of the windows. He reached for the handle and opened the carriage door. Joanna smiled at him, but he only had eyes for Imogen.

She looked so tired but was cheerfully trying to coax her father to his feet. Mr. Potts looked utterly bewildered, and got a little cross with her as she took one arm and Mrs. Potts took the other and together they hauled him onto his feet. Bart gave Imogen an encouraging look. "Strikes The Iron is ready for him. I thought we could take him there straight away, though we can only take the carriage up as far as The Eyrie. We'll have to take the cart from there, so one of you will need to stay behind as there won't be room."

"Mama should go with him. He'll probably settle more easily with her there."

"If The Crow would not mind, I would be glad to stay somewhere in their village so I might be near to him," Mrs. Potts said, glancing up at Bart.

"I am sure they will be glad to accommodate you, though you would be more comfortable, I think, at the hotel."

"It is hard to be comfortable in any surroundings when someone you love is so unwell," Mrs. Potts told him. "I'll be happy even if I have to sleep on the floor next to him."

Imogen gave Bart a look that told him quite clearly that arguing with her mother would be futile. He smiled at them both. "Shall we go?"

They nodded and followed him out to the carriage. Mrs. Potts' eyes widened as they left the station, a look of wonder crossing over her troubled features. "Oh, my," she said looking all around them. "I can see why you love it here so very much."

"Eagle Creek is not large, but it most certainly has its charms," Bart said with a smile.

"You wait until you see the view from The Eyrie, Mama," Imogen added. "It makes this seem quite everyday. And you really should see it in the fall as the colors change, and I am told that in spring as the flowers and trees come into bloom that it is quite spectacular. It is still a little sorry for itself at the moment, though the signs are there."

"How does anyone get any work done at all, when you have such beauty all around you?" Mrs. Potts marveled. "Look, Ansell, at how lovely it all is?" Mr. Potts barely acknowledged that she'd spoken. He certainly didn't look around him. He seemed trapped inside himself, caught in a world of misery. Bart had never seen anything so sad. He truly wished that Strikes The Iron would be able to help him, to help the entire Potts family, as they had all suffered so much, and no matter how many times Imogen, or Peter, or anyone else told him that it was not his fault, he couldn't help feeling guilty about it.

Once everyone was settled, Bart climbed up onto the driver's perch and clicked to the horses to walk on. Around every bend he could hear Mrs. Potts sighs of delight, and her attempts to interest her husband in the landscape around him. Bart admired how hard she was trying to coax her husband back to her, but having seen Mr. Potts, he was unsure if The Crow would be able to help him. How did you bring a man back to reality who is so far gone from it?

When they reached The Eyrie, Fred hurried forward to help him unpack the bags from the carriage. Imogen told him which ones were to go into the cart, to go onwards over the mountain. She embraced her mother tightly, kissed her father's cheek. He swiped at his face, as if it had been a fly rather than his daughter's kiss. Imogen's forced smile faltered just a little. "Get well, Papa," she told him and turned away for a moment while she pulled herself back together, so nobody would see how much it had hurt.

Bart kissed her tenderly on the forehead. "It will all be fine," he assured her. "I'll get them there safely and will call on you the moment I return."

"Thank you," she said softly. "I am so grateful. You

could have said no. I wouldn't have blamed you, considering all my father said about you at the trial."

"I know that he is unwell. But it is not just that. He is your father. I never wished you to have to choose between us, and I never will."

The drive to the Crow Village was along a narrow track. Fred had harnessed their most sure-footed pony in the shafts of the cart and Bart mostly let him pick his own way along the tricky paths. Mrs. Potts clung tightly to the side of the cart, her face a little pale, but she did not complain once. Mr. Potts continued to say nothing. He didn't even react when the cart rumbled over a particularly prominent stone in the track, unbalancing it a little bit and throwing them all to the right.

"I'm glad I did not have to undertake that journey in the dark," Mrs. Potts said when Bart helped her down outside Strikes The Irons home. She looked around at the mixture of structures around them, the traditional bark shelters and more permanent lodges, and of course tipis that the more traditional members of the tribe continued to use. "I'm not sure what I was expecting, but those lodges look almost like many of the houses in Eagle Creek."

"The Crow still hold to many of their ancestral traditions," Bart explained, "but many see the benefits of a home without too many draughts in the winter."

He began to unload the baggage from the cart and was about to help Mr. Potts down when Strikes The Iron and

Chief Plenty Coups came out of their home to welcome them. Bart made the introductions quickly. "We have a place in our healing lodge for your husband," Strikes The Iron explained to Mrs. Potts.

"Will I be permitted to stay with him?"

"It might be best for you to stay with us, if you would like to stay near your husband. You will need to rest and regain your strength, too," Strikes The Iron said gently.

"That would be most kind of you. I could not impose on you. Heaven only knows how long it might take."

"You may stay as long as you need to."

"If you are sure it would not be an imposition," Mrs. Potts insisted.

"Plenty Coups will take your bags into our home, while Bart can bring the cart and your husband with me to the healing lodge. Will you come with us, and help me to settle him in?"

"I would be glad to."

Strikes The Iron led the way, pointing out all the places that Mrs. Potts would need to know about as they made their way through the village. Bart walked at the pony's head behind them, occasionally glancing back to check that Mr. Potts was content. He seemed oddly fascinated by Runs With Horses' dogs as they passed by The Eyrie's stable manager's lodge. They tilted their heads to one side and barked loudly, and Mr. Potts tilted his head in a mirror image of them and smiled. It was the most Bart had seen him move since his arrival. Perhaps being here might be the answer after all.

The healing lodge was a large, warm building with perhaps a dozen beds inside it. Each one was covered in furs and colorful woven blankets. The walls were adorned with similar woven artworks, making it seem a bright and happy place to be. "Oh my!" Mrs. Potts said as Bart and Strikes The Iron helped Mr. Potts to sit down on one of the beds. "This is lovely. The hospital in Great Falls was so stark and miserable. This is so welcoming."

"We believe that healing is not just about healing the body," Strikes The Iron explained. "We are more than just our physical selves. We are our minds, our hearts, and our spirits. The balance between these and our physical bodies is crucial, and easily upset. Surrounding those who are unwell in whatever aspect of these elements with love, beauty, and joy is vital to restore them."

"Do you truly think you can bring him back?" Mrs. Potts asked, her eyes so full of hope that it almost broke Bart's heart.

"We will do all we can," Strikes The Iron said, not making any promises that she felt she might not be able to keep. "Though he will have to want to come back and do some of the work himself."

Mrs. Potts nodded and sat down next to her husband on the bed. She took his hands in hers. "I have to leave you, my darling," she told him. "But I will visit every day.

Please do all that they ask of you. Come back to us. I need you."

"You are satisfied he will be well cared for?" Strikes The Iron asked as Mrs. Potts stood up again and pressed a kiss to her husband's cheek.

"I am. And you are right that I need to rest, too. I don't think I had realized just how much until seeing him here, in this beautiful place, hearing you speak, offering him such dignity and kindness."

"Then we shall get you settled into our home, and Mr. King may return to The Eyrie and reassure your daughter that you are both in good hands," Strikes The Iron said.

CHAPTER 32

APRIL 2ND, 1895, EAGLE CREEK, MONTANA

Imogen grabbed some warm blankets and made her way out onto the terrace. Mama sat at one of the tables, looking out over the mountains. She beamed when she saw her daughter. Imogen kissed her cheek and handed her a blanket. "If you insist on enjoying the view, we should at least be warm," she said as she sat down opposite her mother.

"It is so hard to ever go inside now," Mama admitted. "I am quite enamored with everything about this place. I cannot seem to get enough of it."

"I feel the same way, but it is a little cold still to sit out all the time for me."

"Perhaps living with The Crow for so long is rubbing off

on me. So much of their lives are spent outside. I cannot say that I blame them, when their ancestral lands are so full of majesty."

They watched as an eagle surfed the air currents overhead, neither saying a word. Imogen could see many changes in her mother. The lines on her forehead, around her eyes and mouth seemed to have softened, as if someone had ironed them away. Her eyes were brighter, and she no longer hunched as though her back was giving her pain. It was as if someone had taken a heavy load from her shoulders and offered her joy to take its place.

"How is Papa?" Imogen asked, after one of the waiters had brought them out a pot of tea and some cake.

"He is very well. He wants to see you."

"Is he well enough for that? Does Strikes The Iron think it is a good idea? I do not wish to set him back again."

"Strikes The Iron believes that it is up to your father to dictate how he needs to recover. In the beginning of course, it was about doing what was necessary to make him as physically strong as possible, but as he regained his strength, she encouraged him to speak about whatever he wished. He must have told her his entire life story over these past weeks. She says that letting someone talk helps them to see the patterns in their minds, to notice the gaps in their spirit. I did not understand it at first, but it seems to have made a big difference."

"I am so glad that he is healing," Imogen said.

"You will find him a changed man," Mama said. "You will come back with me, today, won't you?"

"Of course," Imogen said hurriedly, but she couldn't help feeling nervous about it. The last time she had actually spoken with her father had been so full of anger and acrimony. She did not wish to go through the pain of him pushing her away again. But she also longed to reassure herself that he truly was making progress with his recovery. Whatever had passed between them in the past, she wanted both her parents to be able to lead happy, healthy lives.

After they had finished their tea, Imogen went inside and found Bart. He was sitting in the lobby, talking animatedly with Peter. They both stood up as she approached. Peter kissed her hand. "How are you, Imogen?" he asked politely.

"As well as can be expected," she said. "Would you mind if I borrow Bart for a moment?"

"Take him away," Peter said with a grin. "Or rather, I shall take this moment to take my leave. If we don't stop talking, I'll never get all my chores done, and then I will be in terrible trouble at home. I shall see you both soon, I hope." He reached for his hat, shook Bart's hand and kissed Imogen's cheek and went on his way.

"Is everything alright?" Bart asked her, his face full of concern.

"I hope so," she said a little nervously, "but Papa wants to see me, today," she said.

"That is good, isn't it?"

"I hope so, but I have no real idea if it is, or it isn't. Mama says he is doing well, that he is a different man, but will that man want me to be his daughter?"

Bart hugged her tightly. "If your mother is sure of him, I think you may be, too. She would not wish to bring you any more pain. I've seen you together, she is so much happier now and she loves you. I doubt she'd want to take you to him if she thought it would cause either of you pain."

"I wish you could come with me," she admitted. "But I think that may be a step too far for Papa at this time."

"Perhaps you should ask Joanna to go with you, if you want someone to be there for you," he suggested. "I'd certainly feel much happier knowing she is with you, especially if it is difficult for you, so you have someone to comfort you on your way home."

"That is a good idea," Imogen agreed. "I know that Mama will be there, but she'll stay in the Crow Village. Having someone there on my way home – to drive me if I am too upset by it all, would be wise. Do you know where I'll find her?"

"I think that she is currently overseeing the chambermaids." He shook his head and smiled. "She is such a fine housekeeper. I know her father does not like the idea of her working, but it seems to me that she loves the work, and I would very much like her to stay on. Good housekeepers have proven hard to find since I've been here. I've had four already."

"I'm sure if you spoke to her about it, she'd find a way to talk her father around," Imogen assured him. "He only wants her to be happy – and he does not have a son, so perhaps knowing his daughter is following in his footsteps and will continue his hard work when he no longer can, well, that might appeal to him," Imogen said with a smile. "And you are right, she does love the work. She's never been happier."

"I will talk with her later then," Bart said leaning over to kiss her lips.

"Do you think you can spare both of us this afternoon?" she asked him. "Mama wants me to return with her now."

"I think so," he said. "And stay as long as you need to."

Imogen hurried upstairs to find Joanna, who was showing one of the new chambermaids how to make the beds. "Fold the corner like this," she said, patiently showing the girl again how to keep the sheets tight to the mattress.

"Miss Hemsley, a moment of your time, if I may," Imogen said.

Joanna nodded as she followed Imogen out of the room. "You can do this," she said turning back to the young girl. "You did it perfectly earlier, remember?"

Joanna closed the door behind her. "What is it?"

"Bart has given me permission to take you away from it all this afternoon, Joanna," Imogen said with an extravagant wave.

"Oh, I must say I'd be glad of a rest. My feet hurt more

than I ever thought it possible for anything to hurt," Joanna said with a groan.

"I'm not sure how restful it will be, but you may at least get to put your feet up for a while," Imogen said wryly. "Mama is here, and she says that my father wishes to see me. Bart is sure that she would not encourage me to go if he wasn't ready, but I must confess that even if he is, I'm not sure that I am."

"I can understand that. Your last conversation was hardly pleasant for you," Joanna said. "If you can wait just fifteen minutes, so I can help Loulou remember how to do the corners, I can come."

"I am sure Mama won't object to watching the eagles for another fifteen minutes," Imogen said. "Thank you. You are the most wonderful friend."

When she rejoined her mother, Imogen could see Fred was already waiting outside the hotel entrance with the cart for them. "You don't mind if I bring Joanna, do you?" she asked her mother. "She's not seen the Crow Village yet and would very much like to."

"And you would like to have a friend to support you," Mama said perceptively. "I understand, my darling – and I am glad you have such a loyal one. I wish I'd had someone like her in my life all these years. I fear I put far too much responsibility for both my wellbeing and your father's onto your shoulders instead."

"I would not have had it any other way," Imogen assured her.

"Did Bart not wish to come?"

"He said he would have gladly offered but knows that his presence might not yet be welcomed. He was the one that suggested I ask Joanna instead. He did not want me to feel alone."

"I should hope you do not feel alone, my darling. I know your father has always been my priority, but after him it is always you and your happiness," Mama said, looking upset.

"Mama, he meant on the way home. If it is difficult for me, he wanted me to have someone with me, so I did not have to come back alone."

"Oh," Mama said, only a little mollified by her explanation. "I hope it will not be difficult for you. I am sure that your father wishes to apologize, to make up for all he did to hurt you."

"After all this time, that may be as difficult to hear as anything else," Imogen admitted sadly. "And there is Bart, too. I cannot accept an apology that does not acknowledge that Bart is a part of my life. Even if Papa can never bring himself to like him or condone what he did – and Bart himself most certainly does not condone anything he did in those years – he has to live by the words he taught me to live by, to give people a second chance."

"I understand, darling. At least, I want to." Imogen kissed her mother's cheek and gave her a gentle squeeze.

"That you like Bart helps a lot, Mama. Because you do, don't you?"

"I do. He is a very kind man. He has been most generous, and he clearly adores you. I could wish for no better son-in-law, and I do sincerely hope that Ansell will come to see Bart for who he is now, not who he was in the past."

Joanna drove them to the Crow Village. She had soft hands and a light touch, and because of it the horses in the stables at The Eyrie all worked well for her. Imogen couldn't help admiring how much her friend had grown and blossomed in these past months. She had so much more confidence in who she was, and no longer deferred to anyone else's opinion but her own. Imogen wondered how long she would stay that way once Mr. Hemsley returned in late May, though she hoped that Joanna would be strong enough to stand up to him more often than she once had.

Strikes The Iron welcomed them warmly when they reached the healing lodge. "He is very bright today and has been eager for your visit, Miss Imogen," she said as she showed them inside.

"Thank you for all you have done for him. Mama tells me that he has been making great progress."

"He has, but he knows he has more work to do. But he sees the purpose of doing so, and that is half the battle, don't you think?"

"I do," Mama said fervently. "Shall we go in too, or do

you think it would be for the best for you to see him alone, Imogen?"

"Perhaps I should go in alone," she said, though she longed to beg all three of them to join her.

After her mother and Joanna had given her a hug of encouragement, Strikes The Iron showed her through to a small garden at the back of the lodge. Her father was weeding the ground, something she'd never seen him do before. As she approached, he looked up from his work and beamed. Imogen's heart caught, and she felt tears sting her eyes. He had not been seeing anything but the inside of his own thoughts the last time she'd seen him, he certainly hadn't recognized her, and now he was smiling at her as he used to when she was a tiny child – before everything had changed.

He looked well. He had lost his pallor and had a touch of pink in his cheeks. He was obviously eating better as his slight frame had filled out a little. And he was engaged with the world around him. He looked settled here, in a way she couldn't remember him being anywhere else. Strikes The Iron had clearly worked a miracle in him.

"Imogen," he said getting up off his knees and hurrying towards her. He brushed the dirt off his hands and tried to wipe them clean with his handkerchief. She didn't mind about the dirt as he clasped her hands in his. "You came."

"Of course," she said. "Why would you think that I wouldn't?"

"I feared I had said too much, gone too far, but you are here." He looked so surprised by that. Tears welled up in his eyes.

"Papa, whatever you said to me I know that it was not you but the demons in your head talking – at least, I very much hope that it was."

"Oh, my darling girl, it was," he assured her. "You are the very light of my life. You always have been. From the moment your mother told me you were coming into our lives, I loved you with all my heart."

"You do not know how glad I am to hear that."

"Imogen, I am so very sorry for everything I said. I wish that I could take it all back, to start over, to get the help I needed from the very start rather than waiting all this time."

"It would have helped if we had known Strikes The Iron all those years ago," Imogen joked weakly, emotion filling her heart and making her voice husky. "She is a very wise, and very skilled lady."

"It most certainly would have," Papa agreed. "You have to know that you will always be my daughter, and I will always love you, no matter what."

"No matter what?" Imogen queried. "Even if I were to marry Mr. King? Would you still love me and accept me then?"

"If he is your choice, I must respect that," Papa said, but his lips tightened and his voice seemed strained as he said it.

"Papa, you want me to give you a second chance, do you not?"

"Is it simply a second chance? I have done so many things to ruin both your life and your mother's over all these years," Papa admitted.

"You hope that I can find it in my heart to forgive you for all those times when you scared me half to death, when Mama was worn ragged looking after you, for denying me and telling me I was no longer your daughter, simply because I love a man who has a past. Can you not see how that might seem to me? That you hope for something that you are not able to give to Bart? Can you not give him a second chance, too? Especially after all he has done to help me, Mama – and you. Without him you would not be here now, for I would never have come to Eagle Creek if I had not met him. You cannot expect me to forgive you for your past if you cannot forgive him for his."

CHAPTER 33

APRIL 3RD, 1895, EAGLE CREEK, MONTANA

At times it had felt like the days had passed too slowly for Imogen since her mother and father had come to Eagle Creek, and at others as if they had flown by as swiftly as an eagle diving to snatch its prey. Waking up on this sunny spring morning and gazing out at the blossoms on the trees, she was torn. She couldn't help feeling hopeful that the improvement she had seen in her father the day before might, at last, be permanent. In so many ways he had seemed lighter than she could ever remember him being, as if he was finally starting to let go of the past. But he was also still clinging on tightly to his hatred of Bart and could not seem to see that what he was asking of her was all she was asking of him.

She tried to remember that Strikes The Iron had said that he still had a lot of work to do before he was truly healed, but she feared that all she'd said might set him back. She knew that she had needed to say those things, and that he had needed to hear them, for she would not lie to him. Strikes The Iron had also said that lying to him, not being truly honest with him would not serve him, that he needed to know what he had to work on, and that while Imogen and her mother had done what they could, pandering to his troubles to try and ease them, that it was time to stop doing so. It had been hard saying those words, but she knew that he had to hear how much he had hurt them all, how much damage he had done.

And so, she had been glad that Joanna had been there to comfort her and bring her back to the hotel afterwards. It had been a difficult afternoon. Mama had been upset that it hadn't gone as well as she had hoped, and Imogen had been saddened that Papa still could not see that he had to forgive, too. She and Mama could not be the ones to always forgive him. He had to forgive Bart and accept that he was the man that Imogen loved. And he had to forgive himself, too.

She set about her day and soon lost herself in her tasks. There was always something that needed doing, and today she helped the chambermaids to clean all the silver and brass throughout the hotel. It was hard work, but it was a job she actually enjoyed because it seemed to keep her mind busy and help her to work off any angst she was feeling. But even rubbing until her arms, wrists, and elbows were sore didn't seem to get rid of the restlessness inside her today. She hated that she had left her father with things no more resolved than they had been before. She wanted him in her life. But she wanted Bart, too. She hated to admit it, but she was coming to fear that she may actually have to choose which was most important to her and say goodbye forever to the other.

Joanna found her working on the fire irons in the dining room just before midday. "You will rub so hard there will be nothing left," she teased.

Imogen looked up, then back at the shine she'd put onto the poker. "Well, it certainly isn't dirty anymore, is it?" She set it back onto the rack and stood up. "Did you need anything?"

Joanna bit her lip and raised her eyebrows briefly. "Your father is here, in the lobby."

"Papa? Here? But he's not ready to leave the healing lodge, Strikes The Iron said he still has much to do before he is well."

"I don't know if he asked permission, but he's here and he wants to see you and Bart."

"And Bart?" Imogen untied her apron and threw it to the ground. "I'll not let him hurt him too. Bart already feels enough guilt for all that has happened to me, to Mama – and to Papa, too."

"I don't think he's here to point fingers, Imogen. He

seemed a little scared, but very determined. I think he may be here to forgive Bart."

"My father is the most stubborn man I know, there is no possibility that he is here to forgive Bart just a day after I told him that was what he needed to do. And if he is, then how can we be sure that he is genuine? It is too soon."

"Hear him out," Joanna urged. "He is your father, and I of all people know how much you miss him."

"Oh, Joanna, of course I miss him. But if I am honest, I don't know which one I actually miss. The generous, open, funny man who was there before Deadwood, or the some-what neurotic one after. I know I don't miss having to deal with his demons when they got to be too much."

"He's in Bart's office, and I need to go and find Bart. So stop trying to guess what he is here for and go and find out."

"I liked you better when you didn't tell me what to do," Imogen said with a grin.

"It is your fault. You're the one who taught me to stand up for what I want," Joanna joked back.

Imogen tidied away her things and made her way across the lobby to Bart's office. She hovered outside for a moment, unsure what she should say or do in this particular situation. Nothing she had ever learned prepared a young lady for such a moment. She was about to open the door when Bart arrived. "Are you as nervous as I am?" he asked, taking her hand in his.

"I don't know. My butterflies are very busy again. How are your snakes?"

"Wiggling uncomfortably," he said with a nervous smile. "Shall we go in?"

"I suppose we should."

"He is just a man, a kind man who loves you. You do not have to fear him, Imogen," Bart said softly.

"I do not fear him. I fear for you, for me, for our future. For if it does not contain my family, it will never be quite whole."

"Are you saying that whatever happens in there," he nodded towards the door, "that you will become my wife?"

She nodded. "If you ask me nicely enough."

"I think that something can be arranged," he said softly.

Together they opened the office door. Papa was hovering by the fireplace, tapping his fingers together and muttering to himself. For a moment, Imogen feared that he was unwell again, that her outburst had somehow sent him back into himself, but he stopped immediately when he heard the door creak open. He took a deep breath, stood up straight and turned to face them as they entered the room.

"I'm so glad you agreed to come, both of you," he said, his words too fast. "I have done so much talking and thinking, thinking and talking, and Imogen, my darling, you were right to say what you did. Absolutely right. I needed to hear that. I needed to be told that I am expecting more of others than I am offering. That isn't right, it isn't fair. And I want to change. I have to change. Because I cannot lose you, or your mother. I just cannot do that. And I trust you both, and you both love this man, here. You both think he is a good man, one who has learned from his past. I need to follow his example. I need to learn from mine. I do. I need to learn the lessons I somehow taught you so well, my darling girl."

When he finally stopped speaking, he was a little breathless. Imogen stepped forward, took his arm and encouraged him to take a seat. "Papa, slowly," she said sitting down beside him on the small sofa. "I'm not entirely sure what it is that you are trying to say to us."

He nodded and looked at her with wide eyes. "I'm sorry." He glanced up at Bart, who was still hovering a little nervously by the door. "And I am especially sorry for what I said at your trial."

"You had good reason," Bart said simply. "I can assure you that I am not the foolish boy I was all those years ago."

"So I am told," Papa said with a wry smile. "Half the Crow tell me often what a good man you are, that you are honest to a fault and that they would rather do business with you than any other man."

"I am blessed to have many friends in their village and in Eagle Creek," Bart said. "Though I don't think I realized just how many until my trial."

"I couldn't let myself hear any of them then," Papa admitted. "I wasn't ready. I don't think I was even me. My mind feels so very different now from the way it did then."

"I am glad that you are starting to find some peace, Sir," Bart said.

"Have you found peace, Mr. King?"

Imogen was surprised by the question, and it seemed that so was Bart. He cocked his head to one side a little as he pondered how to answer. "I think I may be drawing closer to it," he admitted finally. "In great part, thanks to your daughter."

"I do not know how I raised such an angel," Papa said, taking Imogen's hand and patting it fondly. "Everything good that her mother and I tried to teach her seemed to come naturally to her. She was never any trouble, not even the tiniest bit. And she is so brave and so strong. She most certainly gets that from her mother, and not from me."

"Papa, I am no angel," Imogen insisted. "I make mistakes. I say things I don't mean."

"Oh, no. You definitely meant all you said yesterday, I know that because your mouth purses just so and your eyes have a particular set to them when you are telling the truth. You have never been able to hide that," Papa said fondly. "And every word you said was true. It would be hypocritical of me to expect you to give me a second chance if I cannot consider doing the same thing – though I must have already had second, third, and many more chances over the years. That you, and your mother, have been so patient with me is more than I deserved."

"You taught me that nobody is beyond redemption, Papa."

"I did, and now I must show that I can hold to my own teachings."

"We know that it will not be easy, under the circumstances," Imogen said softly.

"There should be no circumstances where a man cannot forgive – for our Lord would do so, no matter how heinously we have sinned," Papa said.

"I am truly sorry for my part in that dreadful day, and those that went before it," Bart said solemnly as he drew closer and took a seat opposite them. "You have to know that. I have done all I can ever since to be a better man."

"And my daughter sees that good man in you. And so, I am going to trust her, and trust my wife, until I can convince the voices in my head of that."

"Are the voices still so very loud, Papa?"

"No, my darling," he said with a smile. "They are much quieter now, but they have not yet been banished for good. I am hopeful that they will be gone one day, though, and I never believed that could be possible until you brought me here. I will always thank both of you most sincerely for that."

"It is a place that feeds the soul," Imogen said. "And it brings you back to yourself. I am a different person than the one I was when I came here, as are you, Papa."

"I am, too," Bart admitted.

They sat quietly for a moment, each of them thinking about the person they had been before they came to Eagle Creek. It was not uncomfortable. It almost seemed as though they had reached some unspoken accord. Imogen did not dare to speak, in case the moment passed and everything returned to the way it had been before. She so longed for her father to see the man she loved the way that she did. She dreamed of him offering them his blessing and walking her down the aisle of the church in Eagle Creek, giving her hand to Bart without any qualms or hesitation.

"Mr. King, I understand that you wish to marry my daughter but would not do so without my blessing," Papa said suddenly. "I want you to know that I give you that blessing. I cannot promise that I will never get caught up in our shared past again, that the demons in my head will not start shouting at me that I cannot trust you, but I want you to know that I do trust you to love her and care for her as she deserves."

"Do you truly mean that, Papa?" Imogen said, amazed. "Just yesterday, you refused to consider that he could change."

"Just yesterday, you had not pointed out how unreasonable I was being, how hypocritical it was of me to ask for your forgiveness if I could not forgive Mr. King. It alerted me to an area of my healing that I still need to work on – and though the demons in my head are still telling me that I should never forgive, I am able to drown out their voices when I hear reason now. I will continue to work on it, because I have to – not just for your sake, or your mother's, Imogen, but for my own. I cannot let my life be run by voices not my own."

Imogen flung her arms around her father and hugged him tightly. "We will do all we can to help you, Papa. And you will see that Bart is the very best of men."

"I think I already do," Papa said hugging her back. "Because you see it."

CHAPTER 34

APRIL 30TH, 1895, EAGLE CREEK, MONTANA

The door of the master suite was flung open, and Joanna appeared, almost hidden by a large vase of flowers. She set it down on the dresser and grinned at Bart. "I can't believe how romantic all this is," she sighed.

"She said I had to ask her nicely," he said simply. "I want it to be the most special night. She deserves that. She has gone through so much and has had to settle for second-best or worse so often."

"I'm sure she doesn't need all of this," Joanna reminded him. "But I know it will mean the world to her."

"As long as she says yes," Bart said.

"Oh, she'll say yes."

Bart polished the silver and laid the small dining table in the window, while Joanna came back and forth with more flowers. She arranged the displays carefully around the suite. They brought color and life to the space as well as a light, fresh fragrance. Imogen loved flowers, wildflowers especially. He had often seen her wandering outside the hotel gathering them to put in the rooms she shared with Joanna.

When he was sure that everything was perfect, he went to his own room where he bathed and dressed, combing his hair carefully so not a single strand was out of place. He opened the drawer in his bedside table and took out the tiny velvet-covered box that held a ring he'd purchased in Billings many months ago. At times, he'd taken it from the drawer and stared at it, wondering if there would ever be a time when he would get to put it on Imogen's finger. He'd been patient, and finally, he would be able to make her his wife.

He tucked it into his pocket and left the room. He strode along the corridor where all the staff who lived in had their rooms and knocked on the door of the double room at the end, where Imogen and Joanna had moved to after Mr. Hemsley left. He'd been insistent that they should stay in their suite in the main part of the hotel, but neither of the young women had wished to be seen as any different than anyone else working there.

"One moment," Imogen called out from behind the door.

Bart waited, tapping his foot on the ground, then leaning

against the wall, then taking a few steps left and right of the door. Finally, Imogen opened it. "You look terribly fancy," she said, her eyes lighting up as she saw him. "Is there an event in the hotel tonight that I didn't know about? Should I have done something for it? I do hope I didn't forget and let you down, I've been so caught up with everything with my father."

"There is nothing you needed to remember, and nothing you had to do," he assured her with a smile. She was dressed in a plain gray gown, as she always was when she worked in the hotel. On many, it might have seemed drab but on Imogen it looked wonderful. But he wanted her to feel more special for this. He smiled. "You might wish to get changed, though," he suggested with a smile. "And perhaps you might agree to meet me in the library in, shall we say, half an hour?"

"Whatever are you up to?" she asked him, giving him a quizzical look.

"You will find out later," he said. "Now, hurry and get changed."

He turned away and began to walk back along the corridor. He glanced back over his shoulder as he reached the staircase. She was still standing in her doorway, shaking her head and looking puzzled. He grinned, patted his pocket and almost skipped down the stairs. He checked on the suite, the string quartet had arrived and had set themselves up in the corner of the room, then hurried down to the kitchens to check that Cook, the formidable and wonderful cook at the Denny house, who occasionally graced his kitchens to impart her knowledge to his own team of chefs, was ready. She beamed as he approached. "I'm so eager to find out if she says yes," she told him in her deep, southern drawl. Her voice was as rich and smooth as her caramel.

"I am, too. Is everything ready? You've made all her favorite things?"

"I have, chile. Don't you be worryin' 'bout that. My food will not be what ruins things tonight. Just you worry about your part in the proceedin's."

"I'm trying not to worry," Bart admitted. "But she did assure me that if I asked nicely that she'd say yes, so I'm rather hoping my plans are sufficient to be considered nice."

"I've seen that room you've had prepared for tonight. I'd be delighted if my man proposed to me this way," Cook assured him. "And she loves you, is as plain as the nose on my face."

"Thank you, Cook. And thank you for coming up here tonight to help me."

"Oh, I'd not have missed it for all the world," she said returning to her stove and stirring something on top of it that smelled delicious.

He glanced at the big clock on the kitchen wall. "I'd better hurry, or she'll be waiting before I am."

"Good luck, chile, not that you need it!"

He stopped by the wine cellar and took out a bottle of

champagne from the racks and two glasses, which he carried into the library, where he opened the bottle. It popped loudly, just as Imogen appeared. The plain gray gown was gone. In its place was a red velvet, with a bodice embroidered in black thread. Her creamy skin seemed luminous, her neck endless above the sweeping neckline that exposed most of her shoulders and décolletage. Her cheeks were flushed, her eyes bright. Bart always thought that she was beautiful, but every now and again she completely stole his breath. Tonight, she stopped his heart, too. She was simply perfect.

"Are we celebrating something?" she asked him as he pulled himself together, poured the champagne and handed her a glass.

"Possibly," he said a little enigmatically. "Your father is getting better each day, after all."

"He is," she admitted. "And I am glad that you have been able to find a little time to spend with him, he needs to get to know you for himself – not just trust mine and Mama's word that you are a good man."

"I hope I am managing to make him like me a little, at least, and I pray that he will one day be completely free of the worries he has carried so long. Though I am sure that will be very hard for him. I know that it has always been impossible for me to do. I don't think I'll ever stop feeling guilty for what I put all of you through."

"Perhaps we should send you to Strikes The Iron, too," Imogen teased as they both took a sip of the cold, sparkling wine. Bart felt the bubbles tickle at his skin as he tried to negotiate the flute around his rather long, straight nose.

"Perhaps we should, though you have done a fine job in helping me to see the error of living my life always looking backwards. I think I am much better at looking forwards now, and for being here where we are, in this moment, too."

"I am glad to hear that, but what is this moment all about?" Imogen asked again, gesturing at the elegantly decorated rooms.

"We've not had time to spend any time together in so long," he said simply. "I thought it might be nice to spend an evening together. Everyone is on the strictest orders not to disturb us."

"Well that certainly sounds delightful," Imogen said. "But I fear we may be a little easy to find if we stay in here."

"Perhaps we should retire to one of the guest rooms?" Bart said, trying to seem nonchalant about it – then realized his words might be easily misconstrued. "Obviously, so they cannot find us, not because I have any untoward intentions towards you. I respect you and honor you completely."

She grinned. "Knowing that you are a complete gentleman, I would never think you had any other intentions. Though, perhaps I should ask Joanna to chaperone us, just in case?"

Bart started to panic, then looked into her face and saw her raised eyebrow and look of merriment, and realized that she was teasing him. "I believe she is busy tonight," he said softly.

"Let's go then," Imogen said with a giggle, "before anyone finds us." Bart took her hand with his left and grabbed the bottle of champagne in his right. She took both their glasses, and they ran up the grand staircase to the guest bedrooms.

"I think the only free room is the master," he said as they made their way along the corridor and stopped outside the double doors of the very best suite in the hotel. He pulled his keys from his pocket and let them inside.

Imogen gasped. She raised her hands to her cheeks and looked around. Bart grinned. "Oh, my," she said, over and over. "However did you do this without me knowing?"

"Joanna was a great help," he admitted, slipping an arm around her waist. She leaned her head on his shoulder.

"It is beautiful, and the loveliest surprise I think I have ever had."

"I am glad," he said, walking her to the table by the window and pulling out her chair so she might sit. He quickly rang the bell to summon Joanna and the first course of their meal then poured them both another glass of champagne. Imogen stood briefly, to pull the filmy inner curtains back so they could look out over the mountains as the sun set.

Joanna appeared, dressed in the uniform of one of the waiters from the dining room. Imogen laughed to see her friend attired that way, but Bart rather thought it suited her. "Thank you," Imogen said, as Joanna set down bowls of Cook's famous spring soup. Joanna nodded politely, but didn't say a word, she simply retreated out of sight. Bart wasn't sure how she could keep a straight face.

Bart dipped his spoon into the flavorful soup. The crisp spring vegetables and the tender chicken were perfect, as always. Imogen sighed as she took her first sip. "I do not know how Cook makes this, it is so utterly perfect every time. It is Cook down there in the kitchen, isn't it?" She grinned at him.

"Nothing but the best for you," he assured her. "The woman is a sorceress in the kitchen. I so wish I could convince her to work here all the time. We'd be the most esteemed hotel in the entire Northwest in no time at all."

"She'll never leave Marianne," Imogen said. "Especially with all those children for her to coo over and spoil at the Denny house, and more at Jane's across the street."

"They are an unlikely trio, but they have a stronger bond than most families."

"I envy them that," Imogen admitted.

"But you have me, and Joanna. Our bond is strong, isn't it?" he said, teasing only a tiny bit.

"It is, and I am glad of you both. And I'm sure that once Papa is truly well, that things will be better with him too. I only hope that they don't move too far away when the time comes. I rather like having them here."

"I would like that for you."

"But what about you? Who do you have, other than me and Joanna, of course? "

"There's Peter, I suppose. My relationship with him is strong – and if my short stay in jail taught me anything, it is that I am more well-cared for here than I could have ever imagined."

"We are blessed, in our own ways," she said, looking out of the window. As she did so, Bart could see her shoulders relax and her expression soften. She so loved this place, even more than he did. It brought him so much joy to see her this way. "And of course, there are always the eagles," she added, pointing as one lazily circled on the wind currents overhead.

"There are most certainly, the eagles," he agreed.

As they finished their soup, Bart decided that he could wait no longer. He knelt down beside her and pulled out the tiny box. He opened it and held it out to her. "Imogen Potts, I do not know what I ever did that was so very right, that you should have been sent into my life. I didn't think I deserved to ever find love and would most certainly not have expected to find it in the heart of someone I did so much wrong to once upon a time. I do not deserve your forgiveness or your love, but I am grateful every single day that I have them both. And so, hoping that this proposal has been done nicely enough for you, I pray that you will say yes. Please, darling Imogen, will you marry me?"

She cupped his face with her palms and giggled. "Oh, my darling Bart, what took you so long?" She pressed a passionate kiss to his lips, then took the ring and placed it upon her finger. "Of course I will marry you. I'd do so tomorrow if it weren't for the fact that we really should get married here at the hotel, and that I'd rather like to be a June bride." He shook his head, laughed, then claimed her lips as his own.

CHAPTER 35

The door to the master suite opened. Bart reluctantly let Imogen go as Joanna entered the room to clear their plates. She took one look at them both, then grinned. "You were supposed to wait until after dessert," she chided Bart.

"I couldn't wait," he admitted.

Imogen shook her head. "I cannot believe that you have both been hiding all of this behind my back."

"Bart wanted to surprise you, to give you a truly special night," Joanna explained.

"And I couldn't do it alone, because I know nothing about buying jewelry or arranging flowers," Bart said. "And

I wanted everything to be perfect, because you deserve the very best, always."

"He's had that ring for months," Joanna confided as she inspected it on Imogen's finger. "He's just been biding his time. He wanted your family to be reconciled before he asked you."

"I wanted your father's blessing, too. Not just his acceptance of our courtship, or him saying he would trust your judgment or your mother's. I wanted him to be sure. I know how much your family means to you, and how much it hurt you to be estranged," Bart said.

Imogen smiled at them both. "I'm not sure I'll ever be able to trust any of you again."

"But it was a good surprise, wasn't it?" Joanna said, looking a little concerned.

"The very best," Imogen agreed. Joanna beamed. She hugged them both in turn, then picked up the plates and hurried from the room.

"You spoke to my father about this yesterday, when you went over there to see Runs With Horses, didn't you?" she asked.

He nodded. "I did. He was the one that brought it up, in truth. He wondered why I'd not asked you yet."

"And he is sure? Truly sure of you?"

"He admitted that he may never truly trust anyone ever again, but that he trusted me as much as he thought possible, to look after your heart."

"Oh, I am so glad. He's been doing so well. He and Mama are considering moving into town for a while at least, to see how he gets on away from the Crow Village. I think Mama fears he may retreat into his old ways if he leaves, but he seems very eager to begin his life again."

"At least if they stay nearby, Strikes The Iron won't be far away to bring him back to himself. And you'll get to see them every day still."

"I want them to stay forever. Papa is so much happier here. Mr. Macomber actually spoke to me about offering Papa a job, if he wanted one. It seems that my father's reputation for safety and security has even reached this far."

"Do you think he'd consider it?"

"I don't know. I know that my godfather would like him back, but is too afraid to suggest it, in case it makes Papa worse again."

"So, despite everything, he is still in demand."

"As are you," Imogen said with a grin, pulling out a letter from the pocket in her skirts. "I opened it accidentally, it got left in the pile of bills for the accounts by accident, I think."

Bart took the letter from her. Imogen bit at her lip and held her breath, wondering how he would react to the offer of a position in a grand New York hotel. She was almost entirely certain that he would dismiss it out of hand. He loved Eagle Creek as much as she did. But they were

offering a lot of money, and it would be an important oppor-
tunity for his career.

He read the letter and threw it down on the table.
"Edward Dalrymple has been trying to convince me to leave
Mr. Hemsley and work for him for some time," he said with
a frown. "I thought I'd ensured there would be no more of
these letters after my time in jail. I know that the hotel world
is a small one, and even news from a place as far-flung as
this finds its way into peoples' ears soon enough."

"Why would you not take a position? Even I know of
Mr. Dalrymple – and I've barely been in the hotel trade for
more than a few months."

"Because, despite the offer he has made me, he is known
for not paying his staff wages they can actually live on, and
that he treats them terribly," Bart said simply. "Also, why
would any man in his right senses want to leave all of this,"
he gestured out of the window, "to live in dirty, smelly New
York?"

"I must confess I am glad you said that. I'm not sure I
would want to live in New York, and I very much doubt that
a big city hotel would let me work as I do. If they let me
work at all, it might perhaps be as a chambermaid or in the
kitchens, but I enjoy my work and I am good at it. I'd hate to
have to give it up."

"I owe Mr. Hemsley much more than to leave him when
the first man offering me a raise comes knocking," Bart said.
"He has stood by me. He didn't have to. And he is the finest

employer, as he lets me run this place as I wish to. Dalrymple would be peering over my shoulder at all times, no doubt, and criticizing everything."

"So, we are to stay here?"

"Most certainly," Bart assured her. "What would we do without the eagles?"

"Be most unhappy," Imogen said. "I am so glad. As soon as I read it, I was sure you would say this, but I think I understand more and more what Papa says about his demons, there is always a voice in the back of your head somewhere, trying to convince you that you're wrong."

"Well, I will pray that your voices never try and talk you out of marrying me," Bart said. "Because I don't think that I could live without you."

"I'm certain I could live without you," Imogen said and grinned when Bart looked shocked. "But I am so very glad that I don't have to choose whether or not to do so."

MAY 1ST, 1895, THE CROW VILLAGE, MONTANA

"Are you sure that your father will be glad to see me?" Mr. Macomber asked. Imogen turned to look at him and grinned at the sight of the town's bank manager, struggling to hang onto the sides of the rickety cart.

"He will be delighted that someone wishes him to be

gainfully employed again, I am sure of it," she assured him. "And I cannot tell you how much it means to me that you do."

"Your father is most highly respected, Miss Potts. I'd be lucky to have him, if he'll agree to it."

"I know that, but his reputation has been a little tarnished lately, and you do not seem to mind that one bit."

"He is still the foremost authority on bank security in the entire Northwest, perhaps even the entirety of these United States," Mr. Macomber said with a smile. "No, it will be me that owes you gratitude for this introduction if things go well."

Bart brought the cart to a halt outside the village, and they walked to the healing lodge together. Papa sat on a log by the fire, wearing a smart suit and tie, his hair trimmed and brushed, and his chin shaved. He looked more like the man she remembered him to be when she was a little girl, before everything had gone so wrong, even down to the twinkle in his eye. He hugged her tightly. "Papa, this is Mr. Byron Macomber. He runs the bank here, and he asked if he might come and talk with you."

"I know of you, of course," Papa said, shaking Mr. Macomber's hand. "You have had a distinguished career, in New York if I remember rightly, before you came here?"

"Indeed," Mr. Macomber said. "And I know of you, too. I doubt there is a bank manager in the entire country who has not."

Imogen stood back and tucked her arm into Bart's. They both watched a little nervously. Imogen wondered if her father was truly ready for this, though both Strikes The Iron and her mother were sure that Papa would benefit from having an occupation once more. But would he want to return to a bank? Would that be too much to ask of him?

"How may I help you?" Papa asked and indicated that he and Mr. Macomber should sit down by the fire together.

Mama came out of the lodge with cups of coffee for the two men. Once delivered, she joined Imogen and Bart. "How is it going?" she whispered.

"They've barely been introduced," Imogen said as she tried to stifle a giggle. "But I think they have established that they both know of one another, which seems to be a good start."

"Perhaps we should leave them to it?" Bart suggested. "We could take a walk."

Mama glanced over her shoulder at Papa nervously, then nodded. "I think we have to show that we trust him to make sensible choices for himself."

Together they walked through the village and out into the nearby woodland. Bart led them along a narrow path that led towards a babbling stream. "Oh, this is lovely," Imogen said as they emerged from the trees, out into the small, grassy clearing where the stream passed through. The spring sunshine bathed the grass and made the rippling water glisten.

"How did you know about this place?" Mama asked.

"Runs With Horses brought me here one day. It isn't as dramatic as many places in these parts, but it is one of my favorite spots to sit and think."

"The sound of the water, and the birds, it's all so peaceful," Imogen agreed, as she sat down on a rather conveniently situated rock and listened intently. Mama sat beside her while Bart rolled up his pants, took off his boots and socks.

"You aren't intending to wade? The water must be freezing," Mama said, aghast.

"I find it refreshing," he said with a smile. "There's a lovely pool up the mountain, and I often swim in it, even this early in the year."

"You are quite mad," Mama decided. She turned to Imogen. "You haven't taken to doing such foolish things, I hope?"

"No, I prefer to stay as warm as I can, no matter the time of year," she laughed.

"Do you think Mr. Macomber has asked him yet?" Mama asked.

"Probably," Bart said.

"Should we go back? He might want to talk it over with us before he makes a decision."

"Mama, you were the one who said that it must be left up to Papa to choose. You cannot go back on that now."

"I know, I know. But I am so afraid for him, all the time. I can hardly remember a time when I didn't need to be."

"Perhaps if we talk of something else, that will help. We could make plans for our wedding," Imogen suggested.

Mama smiled at that. "I am so happy for you both. It is about time."

"We're thinking June, at the church in Eagle Creek, and a big party at the hotel," Imogen said.

"That sounds lovely. Perhaps you should write to Emily. I'm sure she'd like to know how you are, she might even wish to come. You were such good friends with her, given how short a time we stayed in Sheridan."

"I might, but she is in Texas now, married to William Hansen, I doubt they'd be able to come."

"To the young Hansen boy, but wasn't he an absolute dolt? And lovely though Emily is, I can't imagine Mr. Hansen welcoming that match," Mama said with a frown.

"Well, for once he showed a little gumption," Imogen said. "He disobeyed his father to marry her. Mr. Hansen disowned him, as he'd promised to do, and they fled Wyoming. But the old man soon welcomed him back into the fold once William found silver under the land he bought to farm there."

"William Hansen has a silver mine?" Mama said, her eyes wide. "My goodness, as if that family didn't have enough wealth already."

Bart pulled out his pocket watch and looked at the time.

"We've been gone for a little over an hour," he said. "I think that would be long enough, don't you?"

Mama nodded eagerly. Imogen was almost as eager to know whether her father had agreed to Mr. Macomber's proposal or not. They started to walk slowly back through the woods. When they reached the healing lodge, the two men were no longer seated around the fire outside. Mama went inside. She was gone just a few moments. "He's not here," she said when she emerged. "Where could they be?"

They were about to start searching when a young boy ran through the lodges and came to a breathless halt in front of them. "Mr. Potts said to tell you he's gone to Eagle Creek, to see Mr. Macomber's bank."

"Well, that sounds hopeful," Mama said. "Very hopeful indeed."

CHAPTER 36

JUNE 8TH, 1895, EAGLE CREEK, MONTANA

Bart woke up very early. The hotel was peculiarly quiet at this hour, with nobody around. He made himself a cup of coffee and took it out onto the terrace to watch the sun come up. The day had finally come. Today, he and Imogen would speak their vows to one another, and she would become his wife. He was so excited that he'd barely slept a wink. In under an hour, the hotel would start making the preparations for the biggest party it had ever thrown. The entire village was invited, along with many of The Crow.

Imogen had insisted that without their help this day would never have come, and so their presence, and their influence over the celebrations had been important to her.

Strikes The Iron and Mrs. Potts had become the very best of friends during the Potts' stay in The Village, and together the two women had helped Imogen to plan every detail of the day's revelries. Bart cared little about any of the trappings. The only part of today that mattered to him would be over before everything else began. He just wanted the world to know that he loved Imogen, and that he pledged himself fully to her.

As he finished his coffee, he saw four horses coming along the path that led over the mountain. He set his cup down on the table and got up to greet Strikes The Iron, Walks With Horses, Many Birds and Walks With The Sun. "Good morning."

"And to you," Many Birds said with a smile. "I hear that you may need some help today. Is there anything I can do?"

"I'm sure that Walks With Horses and Fred would be grateful for your assistance in getting all the carriages and other vehicles ready to bring guests to and from the hotel," Bart said, shaking the man's hand gratefully. He didn't know Many Birds that well, so it was particularly kind of him to come along so early.

"I should go, but I do hope all goes well for you and Miss Potts," Walks With The Sun said. "She is a very pretty lady. You are a lucky man."

"I think so," Bart said, amused by the young man's way of wishing him good fortune. "Will you be working in the forge all day? I do hope you'll be able to stop by on your way home, perhaps."

"Jonas has said we'll finish by midday because of your wedding. I hope to be able to come to the church, too."

"He's a good man," Bart said. "I shall see you later."

They all watched as the boy continued on along the path down to Eagle Creek, then the Crow dismounted. Strikes The Iron handed the halter rope of her horse to Walks With Horses, who led her mount and his own towards the stables, followed by Many Birds and his. Strikes The Iron walked into the hotel with Bart. "Imogen is happy?" she asked him.

"I certainly hope so," he said. "Her father seems settled, and is doing well at the bank, I think any fears she had are slowly dissipating."

"Mr. Potts is a new man," she said with a smile. "I am glad for him, and for the women who love him. I think he will be safe from himself now."

"I know that we all hope for that," Bart said. "And we are indebted to you and the Crows for all you have done to heal and restore him."

"Mrs. Potts has given me a list to follow," Strikes The Iron said, pulling it from her tunic. "My first task was to ensure you are up, so at least we have managed that."

Bart took it from her and grinned. "I am to be bathed, have my hair cut and have a close shave. Do I have any choice in the matter?"

"None at all," she said. "And here is the man I need now,

to make sure you do all of these things – and stay out of my way."

Bart turned to see Peter coming through the lobby, a suit draped over one arm. "Good morning, good morning," he said happily. "Reporting for duty." He offered Strikes The Iron a smart salute. She frowned at him and shooed both men away.

"Get away from here. Do not come back down until he is clean, tidy and ready to leave."

Peter didn't wait to be told twice. He herded Bart up the stairs. "She is almost as frightening as Mrs. Potts," he said shaking his head and glancing back over his shoulder at Strikes The Iron, who had already started to order the staff around.

"Mrs. Potts is not frightening," Bart said.

"She is when she knocks on the door before dawn to ensure I got up here," Peter said with a chuckle. "She just wants Imogen's day to be perfect, though."

"They can all be as scary as they like, if that is what they want."

"My lovely wife's sentiments entirely," Peter said. "I am so happy for you, my friend. Imogen has changed you, but it has most certainly been for the better."

"In what way?"

"You let people in now, and you're truly here, in Eagle Creek, with us. You're not looking onwards anymore. I'm glad of that, for I'd not like to have to say goodbye to you."

"I'm not going anywhere, unless she wants me to go," Bart assured him. "And I don't think that she wants to be anywhere but here."

"Then I get to keep my friend," Peter said happily. "And I am grateful indeed to her for that."

HER MOTHER and father had taken a house just off Main Street. It was small but had everything they needed. Imogen pulled back the drapes and smiled as she saw the sunshine. She felt a fizzing feeling in her belly, not butterflies. She wasn't nervous. This was pure excitement. She could hardly wait until midday, when she would walk down the aisle to become Mrs. Bartholomew King. Mama knocked on the door. "Come in," Imogen called out.

Mama entered with a tray in her hands. She set it down on the dresser by the bed. "I made hot chocolate, and though I know that you should have a good breakfast, but if your stomach feels anything like mine did on the day I married your father, you'll not manage anything substantial until it is all over. So, we have cake."

Imogen laughed. "Any excuse to indulge your own sweet tooth."

"Are you telling me that your belly is not feeling peculiar? If it is not, then perhaps you're making a terrible mistake."

"Don't fret, Mama," Imogen said. "It is bubbling away quite merrily. You're quite right, I doubt I could manage anything much to eat. But the hot chocolate will be a delicious treat. I've not had any in such a long time."

"Your dress has been delivered, perfectly pressed. Mrs. Algood really is a wonder, isn't she?"

"One of the finest seamstresses that I think I've ever come across, though you have seen many more than me, Mama."

"She has a real talent, and an excellent eye. You will be the most beautiful bride."

"As long as I am a beloved one, I don't mind about anything else."

"Oh, you are most certainly that," Papa said as he entered the room. "Beloved by your young man, and by us both. You are the most precious jewel we possess."

Imogen felt her eyes welling up. Her father was such a changed man. "Just don't lock me up in one of your vaults," she said.

"I should, the world is not safe, but you have most certainly learned how to manage it far better than I did."

"But you are doing so now," Mama said softly. "Better than ever."

"I like it here. Working for Byron is actually fun. I don't feel the stresses and strains that I used to. And I get to leave the bank and walk in the most beautiful scenery and be with my wife and daughter."

"Do you think you will stay then? For good, I mean," Imogen asked hopefully.

"We've already spoken with the town carpenter and asked him to build us a house, something a little further up the mountain, so we're closer to you and the eagles," Papa said with a smile.

Imogen flung her arms around his neck and hugged him tightly. "Oh, I am so glad. This is the best wedding gift you could possibly have given to us."

"That's as well as may be," Mama said, pulling them apart and shooing her husband back out of the door. "But you are getting married today, and I'll not send Bart a slovenly bride."

The rest of the morning seemed to fly by. A hot bath and hair wash, followed by Mama brushing it out until there was not a single tangle, then plaiting and pinning it carefully. As a finishing touch, she placed tiny pearl pins and flowers in the elaborate knot at the back of Imogen's head. She smiled at her creation in the mirror and hugged Imogen carefully. "My girl, you have always had to be so grown up, but you have become such a remarkable young woman," she said, not managing to hold back tears.

Imogen turned and embraced her properly. "Mama, you raised me. I didn't manage to grow up alone."

"Oh, but you did, I know that my darling. My attention was always for your father, there never seemed to be enough left for you. Yet you blossomed despite that."

"I'd not swap either of you for an easier childhood," Imogen said softly. "I love you both, very much, and I am so very glad you've decided to stay here."

"Your father is so much happier here," Mama said, pulling away and wiping her eyes and nose with a handkerchief.

"So are you, admit it," Imogen said with a smile. "You have a true friend in Strikes The Iron, and I know you've been getting closer to Mrs. Merryweather, too."

"She is a very welcoming lady. And I do love it here, mostly because you are here, though."

They embraced again before Mama helped Imogen into her gown. It was a soft ivory silk, with intricate embroidery on the bodice and hem of the dress. Seed pearls, like the ones in her hair, brought light and attention to the most exquisite stitching. Imogen felt like a princess as her mother fiddled with the tiny pearl buttons. "Perfect," Mama said with a sigh as she stood back and admired Imogen. "Just perfect."

They went down the stairs to where Papa was waiting for them with Joanna. After many hugs and lots of compliments, the small wedding party walked slowly towards the church. Some of the townsfolk, who weren't already at the church waiting, followed behind them, cheering and clapping. Imogen felt a well of emotion deep inside. She had never known a real home, a place she belonged to, until she'd come to Eagle Creek, and it made her very happy that the town had welcomed her so warmly.

Mama led her neighbors inside after kissing Imogen one last time. Papa took her arm and Joanna fussed over her gown, then opened the door to the church. "It is time," she said, with tears in her eyes.

Imogen glanced at her father and saw that he, too, had tears in his eyes. "Today is supposed to be a happy day," she pointed out to them both.

"We are happy," they both insisted.

"Then we should go in, don't you think?" Imogen said.

"Yes, we should," Papa said. "Your Bart will be waiting."

As she and her father followed Joanna down the aisle, all Imogen could see was Bart. He looked so handsome in his suit, with his hair neatly trimmed. As her father placed her hand into Bart's, Imogen finally felt as though she had come home. Bart was her home, and even if they ever left Eagle Creek, and she prayed that they never would, she would never feel lost or alone again, as long as he continued to look at her with love, as he did now.

EPILOGUE

11TH APRIL, 1900, DEADWOOD, SOUTH DAKOTA

art stood outside the bank, on the corner where
he'd stood twenty-five years ago, on the day that
his life had changed forever. His father-in-law
stood across the street, on the steps of the bank he'd once
been the manager of. He seemed lost in his own memories of
the place, and that day. Bart worried that the decision to
come here might somehow trigger Ansell's madness again,
but he seemed calm enough for now.

Bart had never thought that he would come back here, to
this place. It had been hard enough returning to face trial
here. But as he glanced down at his young son, James and
his daughter, Lily, standing just a few feet away holding
tightly to their grandmother's hand, and then over at his

389

wife, he knew that without this place, and that fateful day that he'd never have found the happiness he had now.

"Is it as you remember it?" Imogen asked him. "My memories of this place are fuzzy, but I was so young when we lived here. I remember thinking it was bigger, when we came for your trial, but it never seems to change that much, does it?"

"Maybe we can't see past the Deadwood of our past?" Bart said. "I felt that way when Nate drove me through here, for the trial. And I felt like I was that scared boy, all over again."

"Why did you want to come here, Papa?" Imogen asked her father. "It's been twenty-five years. And I thought you were happy letting the past lie?"

"Oh, I am. It was something Strikes The Iron said to me, just before she passed in the fall. That you never know if you can truly let the past remain buried unless you revisit it one last time."

"And is it still buried?" his mother in law asked.

He turned and faced them all. "I think so. Two of the worst events of my life happened here, in Deadwood. The robbery, and the day I almost sent my daughter out of my life for good. I am so glad that neither of those days and the hatred and anger within them has remained with us."

"I am, too," Imogen said. "But it is strange to think that had those days not happened, that none of us would be here together now. It is as if we were destined to find Bart.

Perhaps if we'd found him before the robbery, he'd never have been a part of it, but had he not, then he'd not have kept moving, and then I'd not have met him when I went searching for a place to call home."

"And had I not answered your advertisement," Bart said, "I'd still be moving from place to place, never free of my past, always waiting for it to catch up to me."

"And I'd still be making your lives a misery, your's and your mother's," Ansell said, as he took his daughter's hand. "I'd still be living a half-life, not sure if the thoughts in my head were my own, or those of my madness, my obsession with that one, terrible day."

"I'm still sorry for being a part of all that, Sir," Bart said to him.

"And I am glad to say that I forgive you. And thanks to the patience of my wife and daughter and the kindness of dear Strikes The Iron, I can honestly say that I have learned to forgive myself for what happened that day."

"You've more than made up for it since, with the measures you've helped banks to put in place," Clarissa reminded him. "As have you, Bart. You've made so many people happy over the years."

"Especially me," Imogen said.

"And me," said James.

"And me," said Lily.

Everyone laughed. "So, what do we do now?" Bart asked.

"We go and have dinner, and tomorrow we go home," Ansell said. "The demons are silent at last."

Later in the hotel, after they had put the children to bed, Imogen joined Bart out on the porch for a quiet glass of wine before they turned in. "Are your demons silent, too, my love?" she asked him as she took the rocking chair next to his. "I know they've never been quite like Papa's, but they were still there, weren't they?"

"Oh, most certainly," he admitted, leaning forward in his seat and taking her hand in his. "I had so much more reason for them to linger, too. Your father did all he could to save his staff and his customers. I was the one that put all of them at risk."

"Not the only one, and not even the one truly responsible," Imogen reminded him, then kissed the back of his hand.

"But I knew of the plans and did nothing to stop them. It wasn't the first bank we robbed, though it was the first time anyone was killed. I knew how ruthless Fitzgibbons could be, and if I'd had any courage at all, I should have gone to the sheriff long before I did."

"How many times do I need to remind you that you were only a boy and could hardly be held responsible for the actions of grown men around you?" she asked softly.

He smiled. "Until I met you, I never told a soul of my past. I couldn't run the risk of people turning away from me. I would have lost my job and been as penniless and alone as

I had been twenty-five years ago, when I ran away from Fitzgibbons." He paused for a moment and took a deep breath. "I was a coward. But it is easy to be a coward when the only person you have to protect is yourself. Things changed when suddenly there was this beautiful, kind woman who was somehow able to forgive me – despite all I had done to ruin her life."

"My life wasn't ruined," she insisted.

"It certainly wasn't as it should have been," he reminded her. "You should not have had to become an adult so young, taking care of your father as you had to, supporting your mother as she needed you to. You should have been carefree, enjoying your life, as every child should."

"I did sneak a little fun into my life where I could, you know," she said, her eyes twinkling in the darkness as she got up from her rocking chair and sat down in his lap.

"Imogen, you will never know how much it means to me that you could forgive me, as you did. That you could love me and continue to love me."

"Oh, I can tell you a million reasons why I continue to love you, and at least a hundred why I was able to love you from the start," she assured him. "But I'll not bother, because you'd never believe me." She giggled. Bart kissed her lips. She melted into his body, fitting perfectly against him, kissing him back with fervent passion, her fingers twining in the hair at his nape.

"You are perfect," he whispered against her lips.

"Oh, I do hope not," she said. "Where would the fun be in that? I'd have nothing left to work on."

"In my eyes, there is nothing more you need to be, or do," he said, brushing a strand of hair back from her cheek and tucking it behind her ear.

"Well, I do wish I could say the same for you," she teased. "You have so much to learn about how to do the dishes, and you still haven't learned to do the voices properly when you read to the children, and you'll never remember to turn out the lamps when you come up to bed after me, but I love you despite your imperfections."

"I am glad of that," he said chuckling. "And I promise I shall work on all those things, especially the lamps."

"Bart, you never had to be anything more than the man I met. Greg Waters died on this day, twenty-five years ago. You left him so far behind you that he may as well have been buried in a grave. You changed. All alone. You didn't wait for someone to tell you that you were doing wrong, that you should try and be a better man. You chose to do that."

"And just kept on running."

"But would you have learned all you could about the hotel business if you had not moved around so many of them when you were younger?" she asked him seriously. "I know that many men would do exactly as you did, in order to gain experience. You, unwittingly perhaps, managed to build a career because you were willing to move when it was needed."

"I never thought of it that way, but you are right that the only way to learn is to travel in our industry."

"And now you are a partner in a thriving hotel chain, because of the knowledge and experience you gleaned from your nomadic past. It worked in your favor."

"I'm not sure of that," Bart said.

Imogen stared at him for a moment, as if she were either utterly infuriated with him, or simply trying to find the words she wanted. Sometimes, even after all this time, he wasn't always sure. "When you agreed to come here, for Papa, did you hope to find something here, too?" she asked him eventually. "For you know that we would all have understood if you didn't wish to come with us."

He thought about it for a few moments. He hadn't really wished to come at all but had done so because he hadn't wanted Imogen to have to support her mother and father alone. But had that been the only reason? He couldn't be sure. Deadwood represented the very worst times in his life, but it had also brought about the greatest changes in his life, the things that had made him the man he was today.

"I suppose that I wanted to find redemption," he said finally. "I wanted to know that young Greg had truly escaped the life he had here."

"And did you find it?"

"I think I may have found it in Eagle Creek, when I saw your advertisement," he said softly. "But perhaps I only see that now we're here. You have stood by me, even against your own family, despite knowing everything, despite the pain I caused you and your family. You're right, Greg Waters did not deserve that. But it is time to bury him here, like you said. Because Bartholomew King is a man so blessed, that I must also be a man redeemed."

Imogen smiled and kissed him again. "You are a good man, Bart King. A wonderful father. A loving son-in-law, an average husband." She giggled. He tickled her.

"Take that back," he demanded with a grin.

"I give in," she squealed. "You are the very best husband. And I love you with all my heart."

OTHER SERIES BY KARLA

Sun River Brides

Ruby Springs Brides

Silver River Brides

Eagle Creek Brides

Iron Creek Brides

Faith Creek Brides

CONNECT WITH KARLA GRACEY

Visit my website at www.karlagracey.com to sign up to my newsletter and get free books and be notified as to when my new releases are available.

Printed in Great Britain
by Amazon

34244172R00231